R.L.

IVY & BONE

WILLOW
HAVEN
PRESS

IVY & BONE

Published by Willow Haven Press 2022

United States of America

Cover Art by Blue Raven Book Covers

ISBN: 978-1-955035-17-0

www.rlperez.com

Askir Mountains
Faido
Thanassian Empire
Voiceless Jungle
Sodara
Ruins
Rhe
Realm of Gaia

Emdale Mountains

Murane

Voula City

Salwaki Islands

Krenia

anos Ocean

CONTENTS

For my Tuesday Tribe. Thanks for listening to me rant.

And for my family. I love you. You are my rock.
But please never read this book. Trust me when I say it's
way too steamy for you.

". . . A CHASM OPENED IN THE EARTH AND OUT OF IT COAL-BLACK HORSES SPRANG, DRAWING A CHARIOT AND DRIVEN BY ONE WHO HAD A LOOK OF DARK SPLENDOR, MAJESTIC AND BEAUTIFUL AND TERRIBLE. HE CAUGHT HER TO HIM AND HELD HER CLOSE. THE NEXT MOMENT SHE WAS BEING BORNE AWAY FROM THE RADIANCE OF EARTH IN SPRINGTIME TO THE WORLD OF THE DEAD BY THE KING WHO RULES IT."

EDITH HAMILTON, *MYTHOLOGY*

MUTINY

CYRUS

WITH A BRUSH OF HIS POWER, Cyrus felt the air change.

It wasn't alarming or explosive; in fact, if he'd been otherwise preoccupied, he might have missed the subtle shift of the wind, the whispers that lingered as Cyrus walked past the rivers of the Underworld.

Something was growing. Waiting. Watching.

Though his magic made no outward appearance, it still burned in his bones, an ever-present entity that fed him information and heightened his senses.

Cyrus kept his head held high, the crown of bones settled comfortably atop his silver hair marking him as the ruler of this domain. The cool babble of the river Styx soothed him, reminding him of all he possessed. He peered into its silver depths, finding the wispy souls floating from within. An echo of their sorrow nagged at his mind, tugging at something deep inside that he'd tried to squash for so long.

Loneliness.

Yes, he was powerful. But he was also utterly and completely alone.

This was a necessity, though. He couldn't afford to trust anyone. Trust led to vulnerability and betrayal. But that didn't mean he had to like his isolated lifestyle. Constantly monitoring his brothers, overseeing the rivers, trusting nothing and no one but himself and his own magic. . . The burden weighed heavily on him, and sometimes a tiny part of his mind wished there was someone else to help him carry it.

Cyrus continued patrolling the rivers, ensuring all the assigned guardians were in place. His older brother, Romanos, surveyed the river Styx, nodding grimly to Cyrus as he passed. Romanos learned long ago not to test Cyrus, and he was one of the few princes who quickly adapted. As such, Cyrus had no reason to torment him like he did the others.

Romanos was obedient. He followed orders.

The others were not so wise.

Even though Cyrus was the youngest of six princes of Hell, he possessed enough power to rule over the realm and force his older brothers—and his father—into submission.

But his power came with a price. He was bound to the mortal realm. He thought of the enchanted grimoire that bound him, and he ground his teeth. That book served as a gate between the Underworld and mortal realm, hidden somewhere in the land of the living. His one weakness.

It was a fair trade, Cyrus thought. Yes, he was connected to that wretched world of humans, but if it meant more power? He would've made the trade all over again.

Even if it meant spending an eternity alone. Yes, it was worth it.

But as often as Cyrus thought the words, he believed it less and less. *Is it worth it? Truly?*

Cyrus pushed aside these feelings of unease, along with the warning in his magic, because he presumed that it was just that miserable mortal realm calling to him as it always did. He could ignore it once more. The incessant beckoning, the whispers in his mind, the way his thoughts often turned to that tiny village he'd sheltered in so long ago. . . He was accustomed to shoving those promptings aside.

But it felt different this time. It wasn't just the thoughts and memories nagging at his mind. This strange new feeling was something else. Something colder. Like a swell of ice in his chest that made it difficult to breathe.

As Cyrus continued past the gaping abyss of Tartarus, he reached the edge of the dead forest that lined Acheron. The foul stench of sorrow and suffering stung his nostrils. Despite the bleak surroundings, he smiled. Every time he set foot in Acheron, his former domain, he was reminded of the humiliating and grueling life he'd left behind.

Now, his older brother, Leonidas, was tasked with overseeing the river of pain and torment.

When Cyrus reached the riverbank, he frowned. Instead of finding his brother, haggard and worn from his time surrounded by devastation and pain, he found his father, Aidoneus. The once mighty god of the Underworld stood facing the river, wielding his hands together to summon tendrils of black flame that speared into the water's depths. With each stroke, the already murky stream darkened until it resembled liquid ash.

Cyrus halted, his magic swelling inside him with alarm and distrust. "What are you doing here?"

Aidoneus didn't answer at first. He continued summoning magic as if he hadn't heard his son.

Anger boiled within Cyrus, and he raised his hand, prepared to conjure his own dark flames, even if it meant wounding his father. It wouldn't have been the first time.

Before he could, Aidoneus turned to face him. Something about his father's face struck a bolt of uncertainty through Cyrus's chest. There was a calm assuredness in Aidoneus's expression that unsettled him. His father had always regarded him with wary apprehension and veiled disgust. It was clear Cyrus's immense power frightened his father.

But today, something was different. And it made Cyrus's already restless magic churn uncontrollably.

The air is wrong today, Cyrus thought. *My magic can feel it.*

And, judging by the look on his face, Aidoneus knew it, too.

"You know, don't you?" Aidoneus asked.

"Know what?" Cyrus's eyebrows lifted, and he raised his hands in exasperation. "Where Leonidas is? No. Please enlighten me. If he's abandoned his post again, he'll be soundly punished for it."

Aidoneus smirked as if he could see right through Cyrus's bravado. "Leonidas is with Marcellus and Vasileios. The three of them felt it, too."

Marcellus and Vasileios. The former was a warrior that Cyrus had humiliated upon gaining his power. The latter was the previous heir to the throne, whose crown Cyrus had taken by force.

If the three brothers who loathed Cyrus the most were convening, that couldn't be good.

"Your magic is hiding the truth from you." Aidoneus's eyes turned serious. "Be careful of that."

"Like I would believe anything you say," Cyrus sneered. "When did you ever give a damn about me and my magic?"

Sorrow stirred in Aidoneus's gaze, and for a moment,

Cyrus caught a glimpse of regret. But it was gone in an instant.

"Consider this a warning." Aidoneus drew closer. He still dwarfed Cyrus, but the feeble amount of power emanating from his father made him seem pathetic and small. How had this pitiful god ever possessed enough power to rule?

"Mutiny is upon you, my son," Aidoneus murmured, his eyes flashing. "And you best be ready for it when it arrives. Your brothers have been waiting for the perfect opportunity to usurp you."

"And that's now?" Cyrus asked coldly, his eyes narrowing. Even *if* his brothers were uniting against him, there was no way they could match his power. They had tried before—and failed.

In the Underworld, Cyrus was the only being with enough magic to wound another god. None other had such power.

He could kill them all. And they knew it. For so long, that threat had kept order in the Underworld.

"Seek the answers you need from your magic," Aidoneus said. "You are still bound to the mortal realm, Cyrus. And things are changing up there."

"How do *you* know this?" A surge of fear welled up inside Cyrus. What if his father spoke the truth?

"I did not make the same fatal bargain you did. I still have a leash on my magic. But you—you gave up your soul for more power. That comes with a price. *You* are the one on a leash. Have a care before it pulls you in a direction you do not want to go."

Cyrus's nostrils flared. "Don't you dare lecture me as if you have some great wisdom to impart on me, Aidoneus. You were never a father to me. And you never will be."

That same strange sorrow flickered in Aidoneus's eyes once more. "I know."

Cyrus blinked. He hadn't expected that response. He clenched his teeth, his gaze dropping to the foggy contents of the river. "What are you doing to Acheron?"

Aidoneus smiled, but it lacked warmth. It was a sharp curve of his mouth and a mischievous glint in his eyes. "This will always be your domain, my son. Even if you have claimed the throne of Styx, your essence is tethered to this river because it is your origin. Your connection here is the only thing keeping you in the Underworld. Otherwise, that cursed book would yank you to the land of the living, trapping you there permanently."

Cyrus's brows lowered. "That doesn't answer my question."

Aidoneus looked positively smug now. "I am poisoning it."

Anger and alarm burned in Cyrus's chest until he couldn't breathe. In an explosion of flames, Cyrus struck his father down. Aidoneus raised his hands to deflect the blow, but Cyrus's magic was stronger. *Far* stronger.

Aidoneus groaned and sank to one knee, his wispy black smoke pitiful compared to Cyrus's all-consuming fire.

Cyrus pushed harder, prepared to shove his father into the poisoned river just to see how he fared. But he faltered when he realized Aidoneus was *laughing*.

"You're too late," Aidoneus said hoarsely. Sweat poured down his face, and his arms quivered from the effort of holding Cyrus's power at bay. Even so, amusement danced in his eyes, and it only infuriated Cyrus further.

"Why?" Cyrus bit out, baring his teeth.

"When the poison takes effect," Aidoneus said, "This river will dry up. The souls will be destroyed. And the anchor binding you to the Underworld will deteriorate. You'll have nowhere left to go except the mortal realm."

Cyrus gritted his teeth so tightly his head throbbed. With a swift movement, he slashed his hands through the air, cutting off his flames. Aidoneus crumpled, clutching at the gash Cyrus had carved in his gut. Silver blood oozed, pooling onto the grass and mingling with the souls in the river.

"You're lying," Cyrus growled.

"I'm not. And you know it." Despite his labored breathing, Aidoneus's mouth stretched into a lethal grin. "This realm will descend into chaos. And you won't be here to maintain control."

Cyrus drew closer to his father, shaking with fury. "You think you can get rid of me so easily?"

"The Book of Eyes has been opened," Aidoneus hissed. "That grimoire that's bound to your soul? It's in the hands of *witches*. And they own you now. You're bound for the mortal realm, boy. It's only a matter of time before they summon you, and when they do . . . you won't have a home to come back to."

HAUNTED

PRUE

"YOU'RE SULKING AGAIN," Mona whispered.

Prue crossed her arms, facing the rippling waves of the ocean as she tried to drown out her sister's taunting voice.

"Isn't there something more productive you could be doing?" Mona went on. "Something less . . . broody?"

Prue rolled her eyes. "I am *not* brooding."

"Really? Then tell me why you're out here, completely alone, with that grumpy look on your face."

"I am . . . going over the plan in my head," Prue said softly. "I need to be alone so the others in the coven won't be suspicious." Her mother, Polina, could always read her like an open book. And, as the Maiden of their coven, Prue was constantly called upon to use her magic to strengthen the village. It was exhausting. Every time

Prue was summoned for it, she had to bite back a snarl of anger and resentment.

She didn't want this. She'd *never* wanted this.

Mona was always supposed to be the Maiden. It should have been her.

If Prue didn't come out here to glare at the horizon on a regular basis, she would probably end up cursing the entire coven into oblivion.

"So, the plan is in motion then?" Mona asked.

Prue nodded, keeping her gaze fixed on the slowly setting sun. *Not long now,* she thought. Today was Samhain, marking the end of the harvest season and the start of winter. This was when the veil between worlds was the thinnest.

This was the only night Prue could break open the gates of the Underworld. She had waited for this for more than six months. If she failed, she would have to wait another year.

She couldn't. She just couldn't. She would rather die than spend another year in the service of her coven, when Mona . . .

"It'll work," Mona reassured her. "You're strong, Prue. You've studied this for months now. You *will* succeed."

Prue finally turned to face her sister. She didn't often look Mona in the eye because she knew what she would see.

An apparition. A transparent fog. A whisper

compared to who Mona had been when she was alive. The ghostly form resembled Mona in so many ways—the same dark wavy hair that was much smoother and less wild than Prue's; the proud chin, delicate nose, and full lips that Prue shared; and even the darker skin tone, making her ghost appear smoky gray instead of pearly white.

But the spirit lacked Mona's vibrancy, the luminescent glow of her sea-foam-colored eyes, the laughter gleaming in her gaze. This spirit was only a shadow. A constant reminder that Prue had already failed once before. She had failed to keep her sister alive.

She would *not* fail again.

"And you will play your part?" Prue asked, eyebrows raised.

Mona smiled, but it lacked the energy and spark that Prue knew so well. Her sister had been bright and cunning, always eager to find new avenues to use her magic. This smile was feeble by comparison. It was a mockery.

"Of course," Mona said. "I've saved myself for this moment. For when it will matter most."

Prue nodded again, though uncertainty bubbled within her. Her curls billowed around her with the fierce ocean breeze, and she impatiently tucked the loose strands behind her ear. Prue had a feeling *she* was the only one who could see Mona. None of the other villagers mentioned seeing Mona's ghost, and the apparition always vanished when others approached.

But it made perfect sense. Prue deserved this. Mona had sacrificed herself to save the village—to save Prue—from unholy destruction at the hands of the undead souls of the Underworld. Prue had been prepared to pay the price, but Mona had stepped in first.

This was Prue's punishment: to always be haunted by her sister's ghost. It was so fitting that Prue doubted whether Mona *could* play her part. What if no one else in the coven could see her? They hadn't seen her yet, so why would that change now?

"The veil is thin tonight," Mona said. "Even those who refuse to see will have no other choice. I will be the first one through. I promise."

Prue had been attending Samhain ceremonies since she was a toddler. She knew what to expect. Once the spell was cast and the spirits were summoned, the coven would wait to see who wished to commune with them, to impart the wisdom of the dead to the land of the living.

If Mona was insistent enough, she would get through. If anything, it would catch Polina's attention. She had been grieving just as much as Prue, though in a different way. While Polina sought comfort from others, like her lover Sybil, Prue had withdrawn completely from everyone. This was her burden to bear, and hers alone.

It was her problem to fix. And she would do just that. Or die trying.

But Mona didn't need to know that. She didn't need to know just how far Prue was willing to go to get her back.

"It's almost time now," Mona said. "You should go prepare."

Prue took one last long look at the rippling ocean waves, trying not to imagine this as her last time gazing at the sea. If this plan didn't work, Prue would die.

And if it *did* work, she would be bound to the Underworld. She would likely never see her home again.

But it would be worth it. For Mona.

Tears clouded Prue's eyes as she finally turned away from the ocean to gaze at her sister. "I miss you."

Mona's eyes turned soft. "I miss you, too. But don't worry. We'll see each other soon."

Prue swallowed hard. Emotion clogged her throat, suffocating her. "Mona . . ."

Mona stared at her, waiting.

"I'm sorry." Prue choked on the words that had been slicing through her ever since Mona had died. She had never been brave enough to say them, but she had to now. Just in case this didn't work. "I'm sorry for not saving you."

Mona's form trembled slightly, and for one terrifying moment, Prue worried her sister would vanish right then and there. But gradually, the shimmering glow of her figure solidified, and Mona stretched out her hand. It passed right through Prue, making her shiver.

"I've already forgiven you," Mona whispered. "I would do it all over again for you, Prue."

Tears streamed down Prue's face, her expression crumpling as the grief consumed her. Goddess, she missed her twin. So much that it tore through her, opening up a gaping wound in her chest that would never heal. It only festered and throbbed, burning more intensely each day.

"Good luck," Mona said. She flashed a sad smile that was so familiar, so like Mona to reassure Prue even when all was lost. Then, she turned and faded into the trees. The palm fronds swayed in the breeze as the ghostly apparition dissolved from view.

Prue sank to her knees and wept, unable to hold it in any longer. She knew she needed to get to work, that she was running out of time. But she had held in her regret and anguish for so long that she had to unleash it, just a little bit. Otherwise, it would drown her.

When her sobs finally subsided and her shoulders stopped shaking, Prue wiped her eyes and rose to her feet. With a few deep breaths, her calm demeanor returned, and she squared her shoulders.

"This is it," she told herself. "No turning back now. After today, Mona will be here and all will be right with the world again."

With this comforting reminder, resolve coursed

through her, and she strode down the path toward her house.

THANKFULLY, most of the coven was already in the town square preparing for the ceremony. This left Prue uninterrupted time to scour her mother's cupboards for the proper spell ingredients.

It was just as well. She certainly didn't want anyone witnessing her stealing her mother's hemlock or nightshade. Such deadly ingredients would definitely warrant a few questions, and Prue didn't have time to concoct a lie. She was nervous enough.

Unfortunately, as Prue was grabbing the last ingredient—fresh pomegranates from the garden—she heard a startled voice cry, "There you are!"

Shit. Prue forced a pleasant expression on her face and looked up, spotting her mother, Polina, approaching from the other side of the garden. Prue quickly shoved her sack of ingredients behind her, out of view of her mother, and used her forearm to wipe the sweat from her brow.

Polina's blue eyes were wide and wild, her hair a frayed mass of brown around her face. "What are you doing here? We need you in the square!"

"I, uh . . ." *Think, think, think!* But all of Prue's

mental strength was channeled toward her task at hand. She had no room left for elaborate lies or excuses. It already took all her energies to bolster her courage to go through with this. Anything else, and she might explode from the pressure.

Prue inhaled shakily, suddenly finding it hard to breathe.

"Oh, my sweet child," said another deeper voice.

Prue blinked and glanced up to find Sybil, Polina's lover, joining them in the garden. Her soft eyes were sad as she took in Prue, who was kneeling in the flowers, the hem of her skirt stained with dirt.

"What?" Polina snapped, glancing between them as if she'd missed something.

Sybil laid a hand on Polina's shoulder. "Stop and pay attention, love." She gestured to the rosebushes next to Prue.

Oh. *Oh.* Roses had been Mona's favorite flower. When she'd been alive, her grace, or magical specialty, had been conjuring roses. For years Prue had been desperate to mimic this gift. But she hadn't succeeded . . . until Mona had died, her magic funneling into Prue.

Prue would've given up *all* her magic if it meant Mona could still be here. No amount of power in the world would change that.

Seizing her opportunity, Prue sniffed and cast her gaze downward. "I'm sorry." She pitched her voice a bit higher than normal as if she'd been crying. "I just—I keep thinking I might see her tonight. This is the first Samhain since . . ."

Polina drew in a sharp breath, her eyes shuddering.

Sybil squeezed Polina's shoulder. "I know, sweet. It's hard for us, too."

Prue didn't doubt this. Sybil had been like a second mother to her and Mona. Though the twin sisters weren't technically her flesh and blood, it had still been as painful as losing her own child. Watching Sybil and Polina grieve together had been proof enough for Prue to realize how much this hurt them, too.

All the more reason for me to go through with this plan, she thought firmly. *Bringing Mona back will help* everyone.

Sybil glanced at Polina. "Surely, the elders can wait? We've asked so much of her this week."

Damn right, Prue thought bitterly, but she bit her tongue. It would be just like her to start an argument with Polina when she was trying to win her over. Instead, Prue blinked rapidly as if warding off incoming tears. She stuck out her lower lip until it trembled slightly.

Polina deflated, her frame sagging visibly as if she had no more strength left to keep up appearances. Prue knew that feeling well. "All right." Grief and frustration mingled in Polina's eyes, and Prue could tell her mother was torn between mourning her lost child and attending to her duties as Mother of the coven.

"I'm sorry," Prue said, and she meant it. The last thing she wanted to do was put more stress on her mother. They had never been particularly close—it always seemed Polina disapproved of everything Prue did—but they'd suffered the same loss. Prue felt a kinship with her mother because of that alone.

"Don't be sorry, Prudence," Polina said softly, her eyes distant, as if she, too, were reflecting on her broken family.

Prue flinched at her given name. Polina was the only person in the damned village who insisted on calling her that.

Polina smoothed her hands along her skirts and huffed a sigh. "I will hold them off, but they are growing impatient. We'll need your magic to begin the ceremony, so . . . so try not to take too long." Her eyes glistened as she nodded stiffly and turned away, no doubt to hide her imminent tears.

That was one of the many, many ways Polina differed from Prue. The Mother pressed on with her duties because she felt it was her responsibility, despite her emotions. But Prue didn't give a damn. She didn't care who saw her grief because the pain was hers and hers alone. No one else mattered, and she processed her feelings her own way.

"Thank you," Prue said, and the tremor in her voice

was genuine. If this didn't work, this might be the last time she'd ever see her mother again. "Mama?"

Polina halted but didn't turn around. Her shoulders were squared, and Prue knew without a doubt her mother was crying.

"You are strong," Prue said. "Don't let yourself think otherwise."

Polina's shoulders shook, and a rattled gasp echoed around them. But Prue's mother said nothing as she left the gardens.

Sybil lingered a moment longer, her gentle gaze fixed on Prue. Sybil never cried, but she bore all her emotions for the world to see. Prue respected her for that. Right now, for instance, Sybil's eyes shone with a raw devastation so potent that Prue couldn't meet her gaze. If she did, it would break her.

"You're strong, too, Prue." Sybil's voice was nothing more than a whisper. She pressed two fingers to her lips, which was a symbol for love in their coven.

A hard lump formed in Prue's throat as she watched the other woman leave. Goddess, it was so hard lying to the people she loved.

This is the last time, she promised herself. *Everything will change after today.*

Without delay, she grabbed a fresh pomegranate, shoved it in her bag, and rushed out of the garden, eager to proceed with the plan and finally get her sister back.

PLEA

CYRUS

AFTER RECEIVING his father's warning—or rather, his threat—Cyrus had snapped into action, knowing his time was limited. Every year in the mortal realm was a mere blink in the Underworld, and if the Book of Eyes had indeed been apprehended by witches, then Cyrus perhaps had seconds left until he would be snatched up by their realm.

As much as he wanted to, he couldn't deny the truth: the mortal realm called to him. Ever since he'd been marked by the Book of Eyes and imparted his soul to that grimoire, he'd felt the pull of the mortal realm calling him back. He'd always shoved it aside, relying instead on the power flowing through him—the reason he bound himself to the Book of Eyes in the first place. It had all been worth it.

But now, he was questioning everything. *Had* it been

worth it, if this one weakness of his would be the very thing that dragged him away from his home?

Cyrus strengthened the enchantments surrounding his throne in the caves of Styx, and then, after a moment's hesitation, removed his crown of bones and placed it atop the throne. He enveloped the crown in his black flames, whispering a curse upon anyone who dared touch it before his return. He smirked, imagining Vasileios and the look of horror on his face as his flesh melted away from his bones.

Next, he visited Acheron. His father was no longer there, but it didn't matter. The waters within were still and silent, nothing more than a murky gray pool with lifeless depths. No screams. No souls. Nothing.

A hard lump formed in Cyrus's throat as he stared at the motionless river. Were the souls gone? Had Aidoneus's poison already taken effect? Cyrus didn't feel any different, but perhaps he wouldn't notice the change until he was yanked from the Underworld.

That sobering thought sent a fresh wave of urgency pulsing through him. He hurried downhill, staying close to the riverbank as he headed south. Gradually, Acheron forked, and he followed the left branch, which became Cocytus. Evander's realm.

Cyrus didn't realize how tense he'd become until he found these waters clear and churning, the babbling brook a welcome relief to his ears. So, the poison in Acheron hadn't spread to Cocytus. Yet.

Cyrus found Evander crouched in front of the river, head bent as he peered into its depths. He didn't look up at his brother's approach.

"To what do I owe the honor, Your Majesty?" Evander's voice sounded bored.

"Help me," Cyrus pleaded. Evander was the only one of his brothers he could turn to. He had no other options. "I don't have long now, brother. I need you."

Evander turned to look at him with guarded eyes, the same expression he always wore around Cyrus these days. Once, long ago, Evander had shared secrets and laughter with him. But now, Cyrus was something to fear.

"You don't need me," Evander said quietly. "Or anyone. Not anymore."

Cyrus blinked. A whirlwind of emotions rose up inside him. Indignation. Anger. Grief. Regret. He had cast Evander aside as soon as he'd gained his power. But he'd justified it as a blessing; he was doing Evander a favor by ignoring him. It was better than the utter torment he inflicted on his other brothers, the ones who deserved it.

Cyrus squashed his impatience and urgency with difficulty. "Father has made a move against me. He's poisoned Acheron."

Alarm flared in Evander's silver eyes. "What?"

"The Book of Eyes has been taken, and it's only a matter of time before I'm summoned to the mortal realm," Cyrus went on, hoping he could get through to the only brother he could rely on. Even if he didn't deserve it. "This realm will be in utter chaos. Even if you don't wish me to rule, I know you don't want that."

Evander's eyes darkened. "You don't know what I want."

"At one point, I did," Cyrus argued. "You wanted a realm of peace and cooperation. Or has that changed? Have *you* changed, just as I have?"

Evander shot him a scathing look. "Not at all. I would never."

The disgust on his face made Cyrus's chest roar, whether in fury or anguish, he couldn't tell. The two feelings were so similar. "Evander, we were once close. You were the only one to treat me with a modicum of respect. I know I do not deserve your help, but I am begging you for help now. Please. Watch over Acheron in my absence and do what you can to keep Father and the others at bay. At least until I return."

Evander arched an eyebrow. "And then? What happens when you return? Will things go back to what they were? Will you resume your persecution of our brothers and father?"

Cyrus sighed, closing his eyes against the stark truth staring him in the face. "No. Enough of that. It—it hasn't given me any peace." He gritted his teeth and shook his head as if he could shake off these vulnerable emotions coursing through him. Yes, he had power and authority now, but at what cost? His father and brothers had been plotting against him from the beginning, and now the realm was on the verge of destruction. It had all been for nothing.

Cyrus had been using his power and anger to shield himself from what he truly feared: the mortal realm. Though he would never admit it to anyone, he feared what that place could do to him. How it could change him.

Evander watched him for a long moment before his mouth spread in a smile. “I appreciate you refraining from making false promises of rank and authority. It’s what Father would’ve done.”

Cyrus chuckled. Yes, Aidoneus would have promised a high-ranking position, maybe a seat alongside his own throne. But Cyrus knew Evander well enough to know his older brother didn’t desire such things. Evander was the most level-headed of all the princes of hell. Even Cyrus. *Especially* Cyrus.

His power had made him blind. To everything and everyone.

And now, the mortal realm was about to claim him. The one thing he thought he could trust—his own magic—was betraying him, just like everyone else had. And it rattled Cyrus. What *could* he trust? Not himself. Not his brothers. Not his father.

He felt lost. He was drowning in a sea of confusion and fury.

Evander seemed to sense the conflict in his gaze. "I hear you, brother. For the sake of this realm and whatever sliver of your soul is left, I will look after this place as best I can."

Cyrus glanced up when his brother touched his shoulder. Evander's eyes were earnest.

"But I am not as powerful as Marcellus or Vasileios," Evander continued. "So, I cannot promise that I can hold them off for long."

"Any help you can offer will be appreciated, even if I return to find this whole place in cinders."

Evander's gaze turned speculative. "Why, Cyrus?"

"Why what?"

"Why do you want to protect this place?"

Cyrus's brows lowered. "What kind of question is that?"

"Just answer. That is my price in exchange for helping you: honesty."

Cyrus scowled, biting down a foul retort. He shouldn't have been surprised. Evander had always seen more than the other brothers had. Cyrus had certainly never treated this realm as something to preserve. Something to defend. It was a valid question. Why would he bother protecting a home he resented?

Cyrus huffed a breath as he considered. "This is the only home I've ever known. And . . . it's the only place where I can truly find out who I am and the full extent of my powers." His brows furrowed as he realized he wasn't making much sense. "I can't explain it. I know I am drawn to the mortal realm, but down here, I can be myself. Whoever that is."

Evander nodded, despite Cyrus's ramblings. "I had to ask. I know you're not like them, but I had to know your reasons."

"I've seen what happens when the souls roam free," Cyrus said. "It can't happen again. It would be catastrophic."

Evander shuddered. "If this place is destroyed, I hate to think what that would do to both realms. All those souls . . ."

A tremble of foreboding rippled down Cyrus's spine. He knew how dangerous the souls of the Underworld could be if they were unleashed. If freed, they had the power to devour the Underworld completely. Cyrus couldn't believe his father and brothers hated him enough to risk destroying their home.

A strange whisper brushed against Cyrus's skin. He stilled, his whole body prickling with a foreign energy.

"Oh gods." He crammed his eyes shut, but even in his mind, all he saw was the amber eyes and soft smile of the woman who'd nearly destroyed him.

Then, a piercing scream rang in his ears. So familiar and haunting, so full of agony. At first, he thought it was a tormented soul from Acheron, and he was taken back to those miserable days when he'd been the overseer of that wretched place. Before the mortal realm and his explosion of power.

But as the screams intensified, a sickening dread built in his chest. Those were not human screams.

The images in his mind melted away, and a book came into view. The Book of Eyes. It quivered from the intensity of those screams.

It was time.

SAMHAIN

PRUE

THE TOUGHEST PART was enchanting the pomegranate seeds.

Never mind the hassle of cutting open the damned fruit and extracting the seeds with her fingers. After Prue's fingertips were raw and throbbing, she resigned herself to turning the halved fruit pieces upside down and whacking them with a wooden spoon.

Because, *of course,* the spell called for every single seed from a freshly picked pomegranate. Prue couldn't afford to leave any behind. And she didn't have time on her side.

Sweating and covered in pomegranate juice that refused to be washed out, Prue gathered the ingredients, including every single precious seed, and followed the forest path that led to the village crypt. Once she descended the stairs, she knew she wouldn't be disturbed. No one came down here except the coven necromancer, and even that was rare. When witches died, their ashes were spread at sea, not buried. It was considered offensive to the Goddess to bury bodies where no one would ever see them.

But the crypt held the ancestors of the coven, those who founded the village of Krenia. It would've been disrespectful to destroy the place, so it was left to wither away.

The air was damp and smelled of rotten flesh and decayed corpses, but Prue finally felt she could breathe because she could take her time now. Everyone was in the square, and even if they sent witches looking for her, no one would think to look here.

With a deep breath, Prue lit a torch and swiped cobwebs away from her face. Her bare feet pressed against rocks and roots, and something sharp dug into her heel that she desperately hoped wasn't a human bone. But the feeble flame of her torch didn't light the path at her feet.

I really should have worn shoes, she lamented. But there hadn't been time. Mona and Prue had spent their lives running around the village barefoot, as earth witches were known to do. Prue couldn't remember the last time she'd put on a pair of shoes.

Heart pounding, Prue searched for an adequate place to cast her spell. The first few chambers contained massive sarcophagi taking up the entire space, but the third one was entirely empty. Perfect. Her throat felt dry as she hauled her ingredients and lay them on the dusty floor, careful not to spill any pomegranate seeds. With painstaking precision, she withdrew her chalk and sketched a pentagram on the ground, having to pause often to pull up roots and knock dust and debris out of the way. Her hands shook as she lit thirteen candles and spaced them around the pentagram, then cut her palm with her athame and spread her blood on each point of the shape.

Wiping her forehead with the back of her hand, Prue took a steadying breath, her body tingling and her nerves thrumming at the prospect of what she was about to do. She turned to the least appealing condition of the spell: presenting the Book of Eyes.

This cursed book was the same one that had attacked their village. The same entity that had taken Mona's life. The elders claimed it was bound to the river Acheron, located in the Underworld. When the tortured souls had been unleashed, only a blood sacrifice could stop the carnage.

Mona had paid the ultimate price. And now, Prue would use the very same book to bring her back. Her throat knotted with emotion as the memories of that awful day came flooding back.

The book hadn't been easy to steal. It had been spelled, warded to protect the village from any further harm. Prue had had to call upon the Triple Goddess

Herself to grant her power to break the enchantment. She knew without a doubt if she hadn't been blessed with the Maiden's power, she never would've been powerful enough to steal it.

Power had always belonged to Mona. She would have made the perfect Maiden. Hope crept through the anxiety wriggling in Prue's gut, and she clung to it. *I'll bring you back, Mona. Everything will be right again.*

The wards on the book were still intact, thank the Goddess. Otherwise it would've burst open and tried to devour Prue alive. She hefted the massive grimoire in her hands and dumped it unceremoniously in the center of the pentagram. Even when she turned her back on it, she still felt a presence watching her, as if the book did indeed possess eyes.

Suppressing a shiver, Prue opened the Donati grimoire, which belonged to her own family and was much less threatening, and found the page she'd marked. After reading over the conditions and ensuring she'd done everything correctly so far, she withdrew the sack of pomegranate seeds. Her eyes closed, and her hands hovered over the sack.

"*Incantare*," Prue whispered. Her third eye blinked open, and a burst of power flared to life in her chest. Vines emerged from the ground, a sign of her grace coming to life from the power inside her. They coiled at her feet like serpents seeking their master. The bag of seeds hummed in her hand. When she poured a few into her palm, they felt warm to the touch, and a golden glow surrounded them.

They were ready.

Prue sprinkled the seeds along the edges of the pentagram until only one remained. She returned to her ingredients and found a long, gold chain. She pressed it against the final pomegranate seed, closed her eyes, and whispered the spell.

"*Hoc semen fascinare,*

Ligabis ad librum,

Et factori intus contento."

A roar burst from the Book of Eyes, and Prue jumped with a yelp. The ground quivered, and dust rained from the ceiling. Prue sucked in a sharp breath, her skin prickling with awareness. Her third eye remained open and waiting, and the otherworldly presence of her magic was still unnerving. Even after six months of being the coven's Maiden, she still wasn't accustomed to all this power.

Her hand shook as she opened her fist to find the pomegranate seed encased in a waxy film and welded to the gold chain. It now resembled a small ruby instead of a fruit seed. It shone in the candlelight, gleaming like a jewel.

Preserved forever in her enchantment, this seed was now bound to all the others. As long as Prue wore this around her neck, the magic of the summoning spell would be contained. Her fingers still trembled as she clasped the chain around her throat. The seed settled comfortably against her collarbone.

Goddess, she was really doing this. Her heart thundered in anticipation, and her palms felt sweaty and clammy. From outside, a faint howl pierced the air. Urgency flared in her chest. She was out of time. The ceremony had already begun, and the sounds of the drifting spirits echoed from the village square.

Was Mona there now? Prue wondered how the people were reacting. How her *mother* was reacting. A small, guilty part of her regretted not being there for Polina. This would be so hard for her . . .

It'll all be set right again soon, Prue told herself. Whatever grief Polina was enduring tonight would be nothing compared to the joy of seeing her daughter alive and whole once more.

"Goddess above, grant me power," Prue murmured. The hairs on her arms stood up in response, and a whisper of assent brushed the back of her neck. She shivered. It took her a long moment to gather her strength, to summon the courage she needed to proceed with the final step. Her breathing turned ragged, and she wiped her sweaty palms along her dirt-smeared skirt. With slow steps, she approached the pentagram and clutched the pomegranate necklace in both hands.

"God of the Underworld, I summon you," she said. Her voice was loud and clear, and she was grateful her words didn't come out as a croak.

For a long, agonizing moment, nothing happened. Prue held her breath, and even the air itself seemed to stop and wait. No whispers. No cries from the spirits on the other side. Nothing but empty stillness.

Then, the Book of Eyes started screaming. Prue gritted her teeth against the shrill sound grating against her ears, her eyes watering as the painful memories of her sister's death came rushing through her. When the souls of Acheron had been unleashed, the book had screamed then, too. The sound brought an onslaught of grief and agony slicing through Prue's chest, but she forced herself to remain upright, to keep holding onto the seed hanging around her neck. Her fingernails dug into her palm as she clutched it tighter.

I will not let go, she told herself. *I will be strong.*

The earth cracked, and more vines snaked along the ground from the opening. They crawled forward, coating the floor until all Prue could see were those wretched green leaves, as if an explosion of plant growth had taken over the crypt.

Dust floated in the air, surrounding the Book of Eyes. The particles swirled, forming a small funnel cloud around the grimoire. It spun and spun with vicious intensity until Prue's eyes stung, and she had to shut them. Then, a violent white light burst from within the book, searing and excruciating. Tears streamed down Prue's face from the force of it, so stark compared to the faint candlelight she was accustomed to.

When she was ready to sink to her knees—to keel over and weep from the raw, brutal power coursing through the air—the light finally faded, receding back inside the Book of Eyes. The screaming stopped, leaving Prue's ears throbbing. She gasped for breath, trying to stifle the flow of tears, but once they started, she couldn't stop them. Her chest heaved with unrestrained sobs, but she kept her eyes pinned on the center of the pentagram where the dust still swirled.

When the particles finally fell like a curtain, they revealed a figure contained within the pentagram. Prue's breath lodged itself in her throat as she laid eyes on the god of the Underworld.

He was a huge, hulking figure, and—Goddess above, he was completely naked. Before she could stop herself, Prue's eyes landed on his cock, lengthy and unrestrained and just *there* in all its glory. Then, she snapped her attention to something else. Anything else. Strange swirls were inked on half of his muscular body, from his face and neck, all the way down to his bare feet. Oddly enough, the tattoos only covered the left half of his body. They stopped right in the middle as if the artist had been interrupted before finishing. At a distance, the markings almost resembled vines, which made Prue's heart stutter in fear. Vines were her grace. Her specialty. Why did the god of the Underworld have them tattooed all over his body?

The man's hair was silver, save for a single stripe of

black on the left side. Two black ram horns protruded from his temples. His eyes were a luminous silver, two glowing orbs that bore into hers as if he could see into her very soul.

His expression contorted with fury. He bared his teeth, looking every bit like the demon Prue knew him to be. “Witch,” he spat, his voice a deep growl. “Do you have any idea what you’ve done?”

BOUND

CYRUS

CYRUS WAS FALLING, his body spinning out of control. A dizzying array of lights and shapes blinded him, and then, just as suddenly, it all stopped. A suffocating warmth pressed in on him, making it hard to breathe. The air smelled of dust and moisture and decay.

He knew without looking that he was in the mortal realm. His lungs strained with each inhale. Gods, it was stifling in this horrible place.

And even so, the magic within him sang with recognition. That restlessness, that agitated presence inside him, finally settled as if to say, *At last. I'm home.*

As Cyrus's eyes adjusted to the bleak darkness surrounding him, he made out a woman standing before him. Alarm mingled with the familiar sense of betrayal he'd harbored inside him for so long. For one awful moment, he thought it was *her.* The one who'd betrayed him. He was back in that village, and the witch was entrapping him again . . .

But no. This woman was different. Her eyes were lavender—such a strange shade in a human. And unlike the brilliant red hair of the witch Cyrus remembered, this woman's hair was dark and mussed with curls. Her brown skin was streaked with dirt and blood.

No, not blood. Cyrus inhaled deeply. It smelled like . . . *fruit.* Her fingertips and forearms were stained a deep red that must have been some kind of jam or juice. Cyrus almost laughed at the absurdity until he sensed the power emanating from her.

She was a witch. And a powerful one.

A snarl built up his throat. He would've stormed toward her and ripped out her throat if not for the spell binding him in place. He could easily sense the restraints of her magic holding him there. Trapping him. Shackling him.

She had caged him, just like the other witch had. And he would kill her, too.

"Witch," Cyrus growled. "Do you have any idea what you've done?"

The woman lifted her chin. To her credit, she didn't seem at all alarmed by his horns or nudity, though her gaze flicked down to his cock for the briefest of seconds. "Assuming you're the god of the Underworld, then, yes, I know exactly what I've done."

His whole body trembled from the authority

emanating from her voice. Gods, this woman had *power.* It almost made him drunk with envy. How? How could a mortal possess this much magic?

And how could he extract it from her and use it for himself? Surely that much power could undo whatever Aidoneus had done to Acheron . . .

Cyrus closed his eyes momentarily. *No,* he chided himself. This same power-hungry lust was what had gotten him into trouble in the first place. No, what he needed to do was convince this witch to send him back immediately. The sooner the better.

Cyrus opened his eyes and spread his arms. "Well, my lady, I am yours to command. What would you have me do?"

The woman blinked, no doubt caught off guard by his sudden complacency. Suspicion crept into her gaze as she surveyed him. "I want you to bring my sister back from the dead."

Cyrus schooled his features into something neutral, though he was certainly startled by this request. Yes, mortals often wished to resurrect their loved ones. But ordinarily, witches knew better. They understood the barrier between life and death wasn't so easily crossed.

"What makes you think I can do this?" Cyrus asked quietly.

"You are the god of the dead, are you not? And tonight is Samhain."

Ah, Samhain. The humans' pitiful explanation for

the resurgence of death magic. Whenever the magic of the Underworld seeped into the mortal realm, the humans had to come up with some reason for it. Something to explain the unexplainable.

But some things could not be understood. Even Cyrus did not understand the full extent of the death magic floating in the air.

"Let me rephrase," Cyrus said at last. "What makes you think I *would* do this for you? Surely, you understand there are laws I cannot break." His mouth curved into a smirk. "Even for witches as beautiful as you."

He expected her to blush, but instead, she lifted her chin, her eyes flashing with indignation. "Spare me your flattery. It won't get you anywhere."

Cyrus only lifted his eyebrows. Fair enough. Though, he couldn't deny she *was* beautiful. Despite the mess of dirt and fruit juice along her hands and skirts, her soft curves and ample bosom were quite pleasing for him to look at. Not to mention her smooth skin, full lips, and luscious curls. Yes, she was certainly prettier than the other mortals he had encountered. No doubt about that.

But he shouldn't find her pretty. She was his captor. She had entrapped him. She was nothing more than his enemy.

"Stop looking at me like that," she snapped.

"Like what?"

"Like you want to devour me."

A wicked smile spread across his face, and before he

could stop himself, he said, "Maybe I do." Let her feel unsettled—taken aback by his forwardness.

But to his surprise, she matched his expression with a grin of her own. "I'd like to see you try."

For a moment, they glared at each other in a silent battle of will. But Cyrus had to admit she had the upper hand. As long as he was contained within this circle, he couldn't do anything. Despite how his fury churned within him, demanding him to end this witch's existence, he sighed and said, "If you're only going to make useless requests of me, you might as well send me back."

The witch gritted her teeth. "You're not going anywhere until you bring her back."

"I am not some demon you can summon at your will and pleasure. I am the god of the dead, and you will treat me with respect."

"Really." She crossed her arms and smirked. "Because it seems to me that I *can* summon you at my will and pleasure."

Cyrus had had enough of this. He called upon his icy cold power, letting it flood his chest and rise higher and higher. Then, he unleashed his black flames. Even if he couldn't cross the summoning circle, perhaps he could frighten her into submission. Or lure her closer so he could scorch her.

But the flames that burned within him suddenly . . . died. As if someone had doused the fire with a bucket of water. Shock rippled through him, and he went very still, his insides feeling just as empty as the last time he'd been in the mortal realm.

The satisfaction in the woman's eyes brightened. "Looking for this?" She lifted one arm, and black flames —*Cyrus's* black flames—erupted from her fingertips.

TRUTH

PRUE

PRUE HONESTLY HADN'T EXPECTED to channel the devil's magic.

But when his anger had brimmed, she'd felt it swelling inside *her*, too. And her magic had known there was another presence lingering inside her. It felt exhilarating. And terrifying.

"What's your name?" she asked him. The more she watched him, the more she realized he seemed younger than she'd anticipated. His silver hair had been misleading; he had no facial hair or wrinkles, and his voice, while deep, lacked the gravelly undertones of old age.

"Cyrus," he said, then clamped his mouth shut, his eyes widening slightly. He quickly masked his expression into something apathetic, but not before Prue caught sight of the alarm in his face.

He couldn't lie to her. He was bound to answer her

questions. Good. At least that aspect of the spell was working.

"Cyrus as in . . . Osiris?" Prue asked.

"You're a smart one, aren't you?" he snarled.

Prue laughed. "And you're a prickly one, aren't you?"

"You don't work with the dead for thousands of years without getting a bit prickly," Cyrus said, his luminescent, silvery eyes gleaming. "That darkness becomes a part of you."

Prue crossed her arms, trying to ignore the rising panic inside her. How much longer did she have before one of the witches found her? Had Mona provided her distraction yet? What if the veil closed before Cyrus could bring her back?

She took a deep breath and said, "So, will you help me? Or will I have to coerce you?"

Cyrus's expression took on a hungry glint. A challenge. She regretted her words instantly as she realized he would love nothing more than for her to try.

She summoned his black flames again, igniting her forearm with the inky, rippling waves of fire. "Let's not forget that I have magic. And you don't."

"Exactly why I can't help you," Cyrus said, spreading his arms. "How do you expect me to raise the dead when you've taken my powers?"

Prue smiled and retracted the flames, still amazed that her arm didn't feel hot at all. "Give me your word you'll do as I say, and I'll release you from the circle."

Cyrus clenched his teeth, and a muscle worked in his jaw. Fury blazed in his eyes. "No." The word seemed wrenched from him, almost by force.

Prue almost laughed again. "I knew it."

Cyrus swore. "How are you doing this? How are you making me respond?"

"You and I are bound, Cyrus. It's how I can use your powers." Prue lifted the pomegranate seed hanging around her neck. "Earth magic."

Cyrus squinted at the necklace, then glanced down at the pomegranate seeds lining the pentagram. He crouched, leaning over and sniffing deeply.

Prue wrinkled her nose. Why was he *smelling* the pentagram?

Then, to her surprise, a low chuckle rumbled in his throat. It intensified as he stood, his eyes crinkling as he laughed raucously.

"What?" Prue snapped, struggling to quench the alarm racing through her. *What went wrong? What is it? What did I miss?* Not for the first time, she wished Mona was truly here. She'd always had a perfect intuition when casting spells, knowing exactly how to meet the conditions and use magic properly. Prue often made mistakes. And this spell, of course, was no different.

"Oh yes, we are certainly *bound*, as you say." Cyrus's face was still split with a wide grin. She couldn't shake the feeling that he was laughing *at* her.

Prue's eyes narrowed. She was overwhelmed by the

sense that she was missing something vital. “Yes,” she said slowly. “So, it would be in your best interest to work with me. I hold your fate in my hands.”

“That’s not the only thing you’re holding.” Cyrus choked on another laugh.

Prue let her hands fall against her thighs, her frustration mounting. “What are you talking about?”

“What’s your name?” Cyrus asked.

“Why?” Prue snapped. Names had power, and she didn’t want to give him anything to hold over her.

“I feel it would only be proper for me to know the name of my wife.”

The world seemed to stop for a full minute as Prue processed his words. She wanted to laugh. Or cry. Or scream. Instead, all she could do was stare at Cyrus, her mouth hanging open like a fool. He only watched her with mocking amusement, the glee evident on his face.

“Your . . . what?” Prue finally managed. A distant part of her brain registered that he couldn’t lie to her. Otherwise, she would have immediately dismissed it.

“Did you not understand the full extent of the spell?” Cyrus raised his eyebrows, but his silver eyes glinted knowingly. “You can’t access my power until our marriage is solidified.”

“No.” Prue shook her head. “No, that isn’t true. Look!” She raised a hand, conjuring the black flames once more. Triumph soared in her chest, melting away the panic that had started to suffocate her.

Cyrus crossed his arms, his muscles bunching together along his biceps, making his tattoos stretch. "Go on. See how long it lasts."

Prue's relief flickered, but she kept the flame aloft on her arm, wiggling her fingers to watch how the fire danced. *He's wrong,* she told herself. *He has to be wrong. Maybe he's convinced himself and that's how he's able to lie to me. If he believes it's true, then it isn't a lie. That must be it.*

But as the fire licked her arms, the tendrils of flame reaching toward the crypt ceiling, something within her shifted. Icy coldness bit into her, clamping down with unrelenting jaws. The fire sputtered and died, but the chill remained, seeping into her bones, choking her from the inside out . . .

Prue gasped, the sound horrid and rattling. "Goddess above, what *is* that?" Her voice was raspy as if Cyrus's magic had aged her sixty years.

Cyrus chuckled. "That would be my death magic. It hurts, doesn't it? It's certainly not the most pleasant feeling."

"How do you stand it?" Prue rubbed her chest, eager for that horrible icy presence to leave her. Even her blood felt chilled, like her insides were frozen solid.

"You of all people should understand the sacrifices we make for power."

The darkness in his tone made her stiffen. She dropped her arm and squared her shoulders, watching him through narrowed eyes. "It's not a sacrifice I made willingly."

"Such a shame. If you'd sought more power, I'm sure that would've been something to behold." He leveled a stare at her, that same hungry look sparking in his gaze.

Though her insides coiled from the intensity of his stare, she forced herself to meet it. He couldn't intimidate her. And she couldn't reveal her fears and anxieties. It was too dangerous.

"So, we are . . . married?" Prue practically choked on the word.

"In the eyes of your Triple Goddess, yes."

"How?"

Cyrus gestured to the pomegranate seeds. "Seeds from a newly ripened fruit. It symbolizes union and new life. I can feel the bond between them. And between yours." His eyes lowered to her collarbone, and she resisted the urge to clutch at her necklace.

Prue lifted a hand and tried summoning Cyrus's black flames again, but nothing happened. The strange coldness in her chest lingered and then faded away. She couldn't deny she was relieved to feel the comforting warmth of her own magic in its place. "So why don't I have your powers right now?"

"You have a remnant of my powers because of our bond, but it's only temporary."

"But if we are truly married, then . . ." She trailed off as an echo of that dark coldness resonated in her chest.

She wasn't sure she *wanted* his power to come back. But she needed it if she hoped to reach her sister.

"I said we are married in the eyes of your Triple Goddess. But in the eyes of *my* kind, we are not fully joined until the marriage is consummated." Once more, that lethal grin spread across his face.

Prue fought the urge to retch. "*No*! Absolutely not."

Cyrus shrugged, still looking amused. "Suit yourself."

Prue's mouth opened and closed. What game was he playing? Was he seriously suggesting this? There was no way—he had to be toying with her.

At long last, she found her voice. "Are you saying we have to make love in order for me to bring my sister back from the dead? You're insane!"

Cyrus's humor vanished, and something akin to anger flickered in his gaze. Was he . . . upset? As if she'd rejected him? "No matter whether we are fully joined or not, you will never be able to bring your sister back."

An entirely new wave of coldness crept into Prue's heart from the severity of his words. "Why not?"

"Several reasons. For starters, depending on what river she was sent to, I may not even have access to her soul. Besides, you cannot bring her back unless you go to the Underworld yourself."

"I know," Prue said at once. "I plan to." She had already anticipated this.

Cyrus stilled, his eyes meeting hers with an unreadable expression.

"And as for which river, I know she didn't go to Tartarus, if that's what you mean. Her soul was pure."

Cyrus snorted. "You humans and your concept of *purity*. It's pathetic. You have no idea the extent of darkness in someone's soul unless you can peer directly into it."

"I know my sister," Prue bit out.

"*Knew.* You knew your sister."

Heat flared in Prue's face as she took a step forward. Only when Cyrus's eyes gleamed did she stop herself, realizing she was inches away from entering the summoning circle.

"Let's say Mona's soul is in a river you can't access," Prue said, fighting to keep her fury at bay. "If I travel to the Underworld with you, can you find her?"

Cyrus's jaw worked as he considered this. "Perhaps. But I cannot guarantee your safety in my realm. It's very possible you won't be able to return."

"That's fine."

Cyrus arched an eyebrow. "So cavalier about losing your own life? I must admit, from a human, that's surprising. Usually your kind is desperate for an elongated lifespan."

"Well, I'm not." Prue rubbed her arms, unable to look him in the eye. There was this otherworldly sense about his eerie silver eyes that made her feel as if he could see directly into her soul. And maybe he could.

A shrill shriek echoed from outside the crypt. Prue

jumped, the noise much closer than the other haunting sounds from the ceremony. This one felt . . . different.

Cyrus's gaze suddenly sharpened, and he glanced around. "Where is the book?"

"What?"

"The Book of Eyes!" he hissed. "Where is it?"

Prue blinked, glancing at the dusty floor. The book had sat in the center of the summoning circle, but now it was gone. Perhaps it had vanished when Cyrus appeared. She almost suggested it had returned to the Underworld, but she knew that was impossible. Polina had explained that the book had to remain in the mortal realm as an access point to the Underworld.

"I—I don't know," Prue admitted. "It was here when I summoned you."

"Shit." Cyrus ran a hand through his silvery hair, his fingers brushing over his horns. "You really have made a mess of things, haven't you?"

"Where could it have gone?"

Another scream pierced the air, and awareness prickled along Prue's skin. Her third eye was already open, but it twitched slightly from the magic churning in the air. Whatever power lingered in the air was far more potent than an ordinary Samhain.

"I imagine it was sent back to the gate entrance," Cyrus said. "In Faidon."

"*Where*?"

A crash echoed above them, and Prue yelped,

covering her face with her hands. Dust and pebbles rained from the ceiling.

"Release me from the circle, witch!" Cyrus said, his voice taking on a panicked edge.

"You'll kill me!"

"I cannot. We are bound. Let me out!"

The ground rumbled, and Prue teetered, almost falling to the ground. "Swear to me."

"Shit, woman, we haven't time for this!"

"Swear it!"

Cyrus roared in fury and bared his teeth. "I, Osiris of the Underworld, pledge to you, my witch and my wife, that I will not harm you until we reach the gate to the Underworld." He spread his arms. "Satisfied?"

Prue didn't have time to consider his words, to analyze the power of his pledge to her. She drew her athame and pressed it into her palm, then extended her hand to him. "Seal it."

Cyrus nodded, stretching out his own hand. She pricked him, too, and a drop of silver blood welled from the wound. Their hands met, and a surge of power burst between them in an explosion of white light. Prue winced against the intensity of it, almost as severe as when she summoned Cyrus. But in a flash, it was gone. Magic crackled in the air, and Prue sensed the power leaving the summoning circle.

Just like that, Cyrus was free.

She waited for him to lunge for her, to burn her up

with his unholy flames. In her frantic desperation, she had no doubt she'd made a mistake making this bargain with him. But to her surprise, he touched her elbow. "Where is the way out?"

"This way." Prue led him out of the chamber, and they hastened up the steps. The ground continued to quake, and heavier rocks fell from the ceiling. Cyrus jerked her out of the way before she was crushed. She spared him a look of surprise before continuing onward.

A sinking sensation in her chest told her she knew what she'd find when they emerged from the crypt. Sure enough, when they surfaced, Prue sucked in a gasp at the sight before her.

Pearly white spirits floated through the air, streaking back and forth like birds of prey. Shouts echoed from the village square. Everywhere around them, people were sprinting as ghosts chased after them. Doors slammed shut, crates and barrels smashed as people carelessly crashed into them in their haste to escape the spirits.

Prue's spell had invoked a horde of ghosts. And they were attacking the village.

GHOSTS

CYRUS

"IF YOU WOULD JUST GIVE me back my magic, I could help with this," Cyrus said as he followed the dark-haired witch, relying on her to guide him through the forest and out of the path of restless souls. He cried out as his bare foot met something sharp and thorny on the ground.

"And undo our bond?" she said over her shoulder. "Absolutely not. You'd probably just magick yourself right back to the Underworld and leave me to deal with these ghosts."

Cyrus didn't bother telling her he could only go back through the gate in Faidon. But in a way, she was right. If he had full access to his powers, he would abandon her without a second thought.

Cyrus swore as something sliced through his foot again. "Gods, how do you get around without shoes?"

He eyed the witch's bare feet—though filthy, they seemed unharmed.

"I've lived here my whole life," she said. "Just step where I step."

Cyrus mumbled a string of swear words. She said it like it was easy. If he didn't also have to watch out for a wayward spirit careening toward him, then yes, he could easily just follow her steps.

At long last, they emerged from the dense wood, and Cyrus blinked at the scene before him. Tiny hovels lined the pebble road that wound uphill. The briny air smelled of salt and fish. Shrill cries echoed in the air, and Cyrus knew from pure instinct that it was the sound of screaming souls mingling with terrified villagers. Even as he stood there watching, a spirit consumed an old man, its pearly form vanishing inside the villager's chest. The man seized and twitched, his limbs jutting out at odd angles. His eyes turned a milky white, his expression smoothing into a look of cold apathy. His movements were jerky as he strode forward, no doubt looking to wreak further havoc on the village.

Cyrus expected the witch to halt and stare in horror, or perhaps to join in with the screaming, as women were wont to do. But instead, she surged into action, hurrying up the road to the home perched on top of the hill.

"Just what do you intend to do?" Cyrus demanded as he followed after her.

She didn't answer.

Just before they reached the front door, it burst open, and a wild-haired, blue-eyed woman appraised them. The delicate nose and full lips matched the witch's, and Cyrus assumed this was her mother.

"Prudence!" the older woman breathed in relief, sweeping her in her arms. "Thank the Goddess."

Prudence. Cyrus wrinkled his nose. No wonder the witch had been so reluctant to give her name. It was horrendous.

Slowly, the woman's gaze strayed to Cyrus, who was still stark naked. Her eyes lifted to his horns, and her expression hardened into something fierce.

"Get behind me," she hissed to her daughter.

But Prudence didn't move. "I summoned him."

Her mother went still. "You . . . *what*?"

"I don't have time to explain! But the spirits are here because of him. And I have to send him back. Do we have a map?"

But the older witch still stared at Cyrus with unrelenting fury. Something in him prickled with awareness. This woman was powerful, too. Like her daughter.

Who would have thought this stinking fish town possessed so much power? Perhaps Cyrus had stumbled on a treasure trove.

"Mama!" Prudence snapped. "I need a map!"

Her mother finally swiveled back to look at Prudence. "Follow me."

Prudence obeyed, and Cyrus made to follow, but

some invisible barrier slammed into him, sending him stumbling backward. "What the—"

"You. Stay." The older witch jabbed a finger at him threateningly.

"But I—"

"My home is warded against foul demons like you. If I let you through, I let the spirits through. Now *stay*."

"I am the god of the Underworld," Cyrus growled. "I have more power than you could ever dream of. And you dare to command *me*?"

The woman lifted her chin, unfazed by his words. "Yes. I do. I am the Mother of this coven, and it is my duty to protect my people from the likes of you."

For a long, tense moment, they stared each other down, neither one willing to give in. Only when Prudence tugged urgently on her mother's hand did she finally break contact and disappear into the house.

Cyrus slammed his fist against the door frame, his teeth bared in frustration. Once again, he searched within himself for those black flames, the well of power he often tapped into. But only a flicker of smoke remained. That witch—*Prudence*—had drained him completely. The conniving bitch. Cyrus would gut her as soon as he got the chance, bond or no. No one tampered with his magic and got away with it.

It didn't take long for Prudence and her mother to return, the former clutching a stack of parchment and the latter carrying a bowl that emitted steam. The sweet, fruity scent of whatever she held stung Cyrus's nostrils, and he recoiled from the intensity of it.

"Show me, Cyrus," Prudence said, crouching and spreading the parchment on the ground. "Show me where Faidon is."

"Faidon?" Her mother's face paled. "Goddess . . ."

"Polina!" cried a voice.

The older woman turned at the approach of another witch, this one thinner and darker-skinned. She stood a few inches taller than the first as they embraced each other. The newcomer took in Cyrus's appearance, her eyes widening slightly. But, to her credit, she did not address him, turning instead to Polina and taking her shoulders. "The Book of Eyes, it's gone."

Polina sighed, closing her eyes. "I know."

"You—you know?"

"It's in Faidon," Prudence said impatiently. "Cyrus, *now.*"

Cyrus had half a mind to strike her for speaking to him that way. "Why should I help you?" he snarled.

"You want to get home, don't you?" Prudence shot back. "I thought we'd been through this. We both need to get to the Underworld."

Polina and the other witch both started exclaiming at once, their words unintelligible.

Prudence raised her hand to silence them. "I bound him to me in order to bring Mona back. It's done, and I won't undo it. So don't bother arguing about it."

Polina's face turned bone-white, and the other witch stiffened, her mouth falling open. "How could you do this?" the taller woman whispered.

Cyrus rolled his eyes. They were wasting precious time with this pointless argument.

"How could I not?" Prudence shouted. Anger filled her gaze, even as her eyes shone with tears. "I can't just let her go, Sybil. I *can't*."

"Look at what you've done!" Polina cried, waving a hand at the spirits still raging down the road. "Have you learned nothing from the last time?"

Cyrus's eyes narrowed. *Last time*? This had happened before? His mind spun with the possibilities . . . How long had this coven possessed the Book of Eyes?

"We're prepared this time," Prudence said. "You've warded the house. The coven is safe if they stay here. I will go with Cyrus to retrieve the book and end this. And Mona will come back."

Uncertainty and longing stirred in Polina's eyes. But the other witch—Sybil—drew closer, her expression guarded. "But *you* won't."

It wasn't a question.

Even Cyrus stilled at those words. Though Prudence hadn't seemed concerned for her own safety in the Underworld, she had never explicitly stated she planned to remain there.

"Prudence," Polina murmured, her mouth trembling. Tears streamed down her face.

Prudence's jaw went taut as she met her mother's gaze. "Did you see her?" Her voice was a choked whisper. "Did you see Mona?"

Polina's mouth opened as a tear trickled down her cheek. She inhaled sharply. "Yes."

Prudence closed her eyes for a moment, her expression stricken with a mixture of agony and relief. "Then you know. You know this needs to happen."

Polina didn't argue, and Prudence nodded once as if this had settled it. She snatched Cyrus's wrist and tugged him to the ground next to her. "Faidon. *Now*."

Cyrus groaned and shuffled through her maps, grateful the magic ingrained in him allowed him to read all mortal languages. At least one thing his father had infused in him was helpful. Curse him and his love for all things human . . .

"Here," Cyrus said at last, recognizing the sloping peaks of the Askir Mountains. He tried to ignore the way his chest tumbled in recognition. Even on a map, the tiny village of Faidon still called to him. "It's not labeled, but Faidon is right here by these mountains."

"You're sure?" Prudence asked.

Cyrus scoffed. "*Yes*. You know I cannot lie."

"Well, you could be mistaken," Prudence grumbled, rolling up the map and tucking it into her skirt. "Mama, I'll need coins."

"I'll fetch them," Sybil said before disappearing.

Polina suddenly stood in front of Cyrus, raising the steaming bowl. "Drink."

Cyrus's head reared back as that same sickeningly sweet scent assaulted his nostrils. "I will do no such thing!"

"If you intend to travel anywhere with my daughter, you'll drink this."

"For all I know, it's poisoned."

Polina rolled her eyes, suddenly looking so much like her daughter that Cyrus couldn't help but stare. "Do you take me for a fool? If you die, these spirits remain. As foolish as Prudence has been"—she cut a scathing look at her daughter—"she is correct. We still need you in order to end this."

Cyrus peered into the bowl where a blood-red liquid churned of its own volition. "What is that?"

"Pomegranate tea, mingled with some other binding ingredients. It will prevent you from harming or abandoning Prudence. At least until you reach your destination." Her eyes darkened at the words, and Cyrus knew she still hadn't accepted that her daughter was about to be lost forever.

"I already made a blood bargain with her earlier," Cyrus argued. "I can't hurt her."

"Forgive me for not trusting your word," Polina said in a flat voice. "Besides, there are always loopholes in a bargain. But this pomegranate tea will ensure you don't renege your side of the bargain. If you do, the magic contained in the tea will destroy you from the inside out." A cruel smile spread across her face as if she would actually enjoy watching his demise.

"Pomegranates," Cyrus grumbled. He was learning to despise that wretched fruit.

"Yes." Polina was staring at Prudence now. "I know exactly what pomegranates represent." Polina's gaze hardened, and in that moment, Cyrus realized she knew. She knew her daughter was married to the god of Hell.

Prudence rose to her feet and gnawed on her lower lip, avoiding her mother's gaze. "Mama . . ."

"Save it," Polina said tightly. "What's done is done. Now, go fix it."

Prudence only nodded, still not looking at Polina.

Sybil returned with a large pouch that jingled with each step. She pressed it into Prudence's hands. "Be careful, sweet." They embraced, and Prudence blinked tears from her eyes.

Polina shoved the bowl more incessantly toward Cyrus, and he groaned before accepting it. He only allowed himself a moment's hesitation before thinking to himself, *I am not a coward.* He would do whatever it took to return to his domain. Just as Prudence would do anything to retrieve her sister.

Bracing himself, he tipped the contents of the bowl into his mouth and swallowed it down. The tart flavor burned down his throat, and he smacked his lips, struggling to get the thick nectar as far from his tongue as possible. When he was finished, he spat on the ground at Polina's feet, but she didn't even flinch.

She nodded once before accepting the empty bowl from him.

"Here." Sybil shoved a pile of clothes into Cyrus's arms. He wasn't sure when she'd disappeared, but at some point, she'd run off to fetch some clothing for him. He scowled down at the peasant garb that smelled of fish and dirt.

"Don't look so revolted," Sybil snapped. "It's better than nothing."

"Is it?" Cyrus arched an eyebrow. "I happen to know how good I look naked."

"Oh, Goddess help us all," Polina whispered, raising her gaze skyward.

"Mama." Prudence stared past them with wide eyes.

The spirits had multiplied. The wispy white auras now saturated the air so thickly that the village seemed to be ensconced in a dense fog.

"Almighty Goddess," Sybil breathed in horror. "They'll never stop."

Prudence's face had drained of color as she stared numbly at the souls that continued multiplying. Even Cyrus had never seen anything like it. His first journey to the mortal realm had been like a leak in the gate, allowing one soul at a time to slip through.

But this was as if an entire dam had burst,

unleashing a powerful flood that would sweep away everyone and everything.

"We're safe in the house," Polina insisted. "Prudence, you must go. *Now.*"

But Prudence continued to stare at the souls, her expression haunted. Cyrus sensed she was seeing something else; something that shook her to the core.

Prudence blinked, her eyes moist, before turning back to her mother. "I can't. I have to find a way to stop this first." She looked at Cyrus, her face hardening with grim determination. "Get those clothes on. We have work to do."

BANISHMENT

PRUE

WHILE CYRUS WAS busy dressing himself on the porch, Prue darted through her house, dodging various coven members and muttering her apologies as she elbowed them. The house, which had seemed large for only three people after Mona died, now seemed impossibly small with the entire coven crammed inside.

"It's unwise to perform a banishment," Polina chided for the fourth time, trailing Prue like an incessant shadow. "Especially after the massive spell you just cast, bringing *that* in my village." She gestured a hand toward the front door where Cyrus stood, cursing as he stepped into the borrowed clothes from Erasmus, an older man who lived next-door.

"Would you rather I abandon you all and let the spirits take you?" Prue snapped, snatching a jar of jimsonweed from the shelf in the kitchen and throwing it into her bag where it clinked along with the other ingredients. After a moment's hesitation, Prue opened a closet door and dug through various boxes and shawls and hats until she found what she was looking for: her mother's old pair of sandals.

Goddess, how long had it been since Prue had worn shoes? Wrinkling her nose, she stepped into the sandals, already hating the way they crowded her feet. But she couldn't exactly wander around the Realm of Gaia barefoot. Not all terrains were as easy to navigate as Krenia.

"Yes, I would!" Polina cried, waving her arms and accidentally whacking the shoulder of Beatrice, the Crone of the coven. "Sorry, Beatrice," she muttered quickly. "Prudence, the way to solve this problem is to dump that demon back to the gate where he belongs. *That* is what you can do for this coven."

Prue gritted her teeth, whirling to face her mother. "I am *not* leaving these people to fend for themselves. Not—not again."

Darkness clouded Polina's eyes for the briefest of seconds, and Prue knew their thoughts had turned to the same thing: Mona's death. Mona and Prue had unleashed the Book of Eyes once before, summoning a deathly magic that filled the village with ghosts intent on possessing innocent people and then killing their hosts.

Mona's sacrifice had stopped the carnage.

Prue refused to let it get that far. Not this time.

"You know this is different." Polina's voice was a low murmur.

Prue nodded. "I know." When Mona had been alive, the spirits had resembled inky black shadows slinking along the ground, far different from this pearly white mist filling the sky.

But even so, Prue couldn't doom her village to this. Not again.

Polina sighed heavily and wiped her hands along her skirt. "I'll come with you."

"What? Mama, no—"

"This isn't just one ghost we're trying to banish, Prudence. You saw how many spirits are out there. To banish all of them, we'll need the full powers of the Triple Goddess." Polina turned to Crone of the coven. "Beatrice? Will you join us?"

The older witch nodded firmly and strode toward them, not even balking at the notion of stepping outside where the ghosts surrounded them.

"Mama!" Prue shouted, grabbing Polina's shoulder. "You can't. The coven needs you *here*."

"Have you ever cast a banishment before?" Polina challenged, her gaze turning cold. When Prue said nothing, Polina nodded once as if this settled things. "Don't worry about the coven. The house is warded. My powers are needed elsewhere right now."

Prue opened her mouth to object when a heavy groan sounded nearby. At first, she thought it was the howling souls. But then the walls started quivering, and several witches shrieked in alarm.

"Goddess," Beatrice murmured in a low voice. "They're attacking the house."

Prue's heart flew to her throat. If her home was smashed to pieces, Polina's wards would no longer protect the coven. A lump lodged itself in her throat as she locked eyes with her mother, finally understanding that she couldn't do this alone.

"All right," Prue said slowly. "But we need Cyrus, too."

"That foul demon—"

"He has the magic to *control* the ghosts," Prue interrupted. "We need him."

Polina threw her hands in the air once more. "Fine! Have it your way. Let's go, Beatrice."

When the three of them stepped outside, the fog was so dense Prue could hardly see. Only when she bumped into a solid figure on the porch did she realize where Cyrus was.

"Watch yourself, witch," he growled.

"Silence," Polina snapped, appearing beside Prue. "Bite your tongue before I cut it out for you."

"Let's go," Prue urged, eager to get this over with before Cyrus and Polina ripped each other's heads off.

"*Accendo*," Polina muttered, and a burst of flame ignited along her fingers, piercing through the fog of ghosts. They seemed to hiss as the fire cut through, forging a path.

Prue felt Cyrus stiffen next to her, and when she cast a glance his way, she found his eyes aglow with an envious hunger. Every part of her body prickled with unease. This god yearned for power in ways that made her shiver. She instinctively clutched her pomegranate necklace, grateful for the thin tether she had over his power. But how long would it last? With her luck, she'd conducted some part of the spell wrong and Cyrus would find a way out.

Prue swallowed her unease and followed her mother down the path, sticking close to ensure the ghosts didn't press in on them before they noticed.

When Polina reached the main road, a safe distance from the house, she raised both hands, two beacons of light amidst the swarm of spirits.

"*Contego*!" Polina shouted, her voice formidable and resonant as it split through the air.

Prue's eyes widened as an invisible barrier sliced through the spirits, forming a transparent dome around the four of them. Even Cyrus's eyebrows lifted as he looked at Polina, obviously impressed.

"Show me what you have," Polina said, turning to Prue.

Prue held open her bag, allowing her mother to survey the contents. To her surprise, Polina nodded approvingly.

Prue wasn't sure there had ever been a time when Polina hadn't chastised her for getting something wrong in a spell.

Polina arched an eyebrow, a challenge in her eyes. "What's the first step?"

"Really?" Prue scoffed, gesturing at the souls around them, fruitlessly slamming into the barrier again and again. "You're using *this* as a teaching opportunity?"

"Everything is a teaching opportunity," Polina said, waving a dismissive hand. "Besides, you summoned *this* monster." She gestured at Cyrus, who scowled. "A simple banishment should be easy for you."

Prue huffed a sigh, her fingers itching to reach for a grimoire. But, of course, she'd left it in the crypt, which was probably nothing more than rubble by now. She crammed her eyes shut, struggling to remember the spell she'd glanced over years ago. Of course, she hadn't been paying much attention then. Or ever. Mona had always been the one to memorize spells for no reason.

"We—we spill blood, join hands, and . . ." Prue swore, struggling to remember. "Dammit, what is the phrase . . ."

"*Expelle animas*," Polina prompted.

"Yes, *expelle animas . . . defendat terra*," Prue said quickly, her memory snagging on the phrase at last. "*Defende populum nostrum ad nutum triplices deae*."

"Very good," Polina said. She pulled an athame from Prue's bag and pressed it into first Prue's palm, then

Beatrice's, and then her own. The three witches brought their palms together, one at a time, sharing blood. When Prue lifted her hand to Cyrus and looked at him expectantly, he cringed away from her.

"What the hell are you doing?"

"It's your turn," Prue insisted.

"Absolutely not."

Prue rolled her eyes. "You've already sworn a blood bargain with me. What's the harm?" When Cyrus continued to watch her as if she'd sprouted a second head, Prue growled, "You *will* do your part to protect my home, or I won't take you back to yours."

Cyrus's nostrils flared, his eyes burning with hatred. Prue had the distinct impression he would've slit her throat right then and there were it not for the oath and the potion Polina had forced him to drink.

Thank the Goddess for those precautions, she thought as Cyrus begrudgingly took the blade and dragged it along his own palm. Silver blood oozed from his skin as he pressed the wound to Prue's bleeding hand.

Once they'd shared blood, Prue felt the air around them hum. The spirits pressed more fervently against the domed barrier her mother had cast to protect them, as if they could sense the power of the spell about to be cast. Prue's third eye blinked open, her insides trembling from the energies pulsing in the air.

The witches all joined hands, and Prue clenched Cyrus's fingers a bit too tightly. He dug his fingernails into her skin in response, and she bit back a smile at the anger roiling off him. Goddess, it was so amusing to witness him so angry. He was like a raging toddler who refused to obey his parents.

"*Expelle animas,*" Prue murmured, closing her eyes. Beside her, Polina and Beatrice echoed her words. "*Defendat terra. Defende populum nostrum ad nutum triplices deae.*"

They repeated the words over and over. After a moment, Prue elbowed Cyrus, who snapped, "What?"

"I *know* you know Latin. It'll help if you say it, too."

"I'm no witch."

"It doesn't matter!" Prue hissed. "*You're* the only one with a legitimate connection to death magic." She leaned closer to him, hoping Polina couldn't overhear her whisper. "If I die, or if my plan fails, I can't guarantee this enchantment will hold. But if you bind your death magic to it, perhaps it will." She was tired of threats. She was tired of putting on a brave front. So, her resolve deflated as she breathed a single plea: "Please."

Cyrus blinked, something unreadable stirring in his silver eyes. For a moment, he stared at her, his mouth slightly open and his brow furrowing. Just when Prue thought he would spit at her or laugh in her face, he nodded stiffly.

Prue almost chuckled in surprise. But, thankfully, the sound was stuck in her throat.

Cyrus turned away from her and began chanting, his

Latin flawless. Prue exhaled in relief before she joined him.

The ghosts screeched, ricocheting off the barrier again and again. Energy thrummed in the air, tickling Prue's skin. She felt her hair stand on end, her curls rising. Sweat pooled in her palms and along her neck and back. On either side of her, Polina and Cyrus's grips tightened as if they felt the strain, too. Prue's arms shook, her bones quivering. Her teeth chattered as she continued uttering the spell, refusing to back down. A whisper of power brushed down her neck. The ghosts continued to scream and rage.

Then, a burst of gold light surrounded the barrier, igniting in the sky like a beam of heavenly light. Pain shot through Prue's limbs, and her palm felt scorching hot. Gritting her teeth against the intensity, Prue continued chanting.

Come on, she urged. *Just a little longer.*

The ghosts unleashed one last pitiful scream before they faded and dissolved entirely. The fog dispersed, revealing the midnight sky above them. When the gold light vanished, Prue blinked at the sudden darkness that swallowed them. The village was eerily silent, and for one horrible moment, Prue expected the screaming to start anew.

Cyrus released her hand, and a sudden rush of fatigue overcame her. Her form drooped, and Polina caught her by the shoulders, keeping her upright. On the other side, Beatrice wilted as well, her breaths short and feeble. Polina, however, wasn't even winded.

"Look," Beatrice breathed, raising a shaking hand to point toward the sea in the distance.

Prue squinted, making out a faint golden gleam highlighting the sky. With a gasp, she realized it was the spell—for on the other side of the gold light was that same ethereal fog, the horde of spirits waiting for them. Their magic had formed an enchanted dome of safety around the island, but on the other side, the spirits loomed, eager to devour them.

And Prue and Cyrus would be heading straight for them.

FLEE
CYRUS

CYRUS MIGHT LOATHE these witches with every fiber of his being, but he couldn't deny the raw and magnificent power emanating from them. Particularly the Mother, Polina. He'd never seen such powerful witch fire before—powerful enough to cut through the souls of the Underworld.

And Prudence . . . Well, he had already sensed her power when she'd summoned him. But something about watching the three witches as their magic converged knotted something inside Cyrus's chest.

He and his brothers and his father—they never had that. And they never would. They would always be rivals instead of allies.

"We need to go," Prudence said, tugging on Cyrus's arm.

He opened his mouth to berate her for addressing

him so callously, but before he could, Polina interjected, "Now? You need rest, Prudence. Look at you!"

Prudence did indeed look exhausted. Shadows framed her eyes, and her skin took on a sickly pallor.

"No, look at *that*," Prudence said, her voice surprisingly firm as she gestured to the souls on the other side of the barrier. "The spirits are still out there. Even if they aren't in Krenia, I can't doom the rest of the realm to this. We have to fix this. Now."

Polina's mouth opened and closed, her eyes filled with anguish. "Prudence, I . . ." She trailed off as Prudence looked at her with the same intense regret.

"I'm sorry, Mama," Prudence whispered. Tears spilled down her face. "I wish there had been another way. But it should've been me. It always should've been me. I know you believe it, too."

Polina released a small whimper of anguish before pulling her daughter into a fierce embrace. Polina stroked Prudence's hair with such affection and tenderness that Cyrus had to look away, his throat burning. He would blame it on the pomegranate tea, but he knew better.

Witnessing such emotion between a mother and daughter made Cyrus feel strangely empty inside. He had never known his mother, so how could he miss something he'd never known? When asked about it, Aidoneus would only say she was a goddess from another realm and leave it at that, refusing to elaborate further. Aidoneus himself had been far from fatherly.

A sudden surge of impatience flared in Cyrus's chest. Thinking of Aidoneus reminded him of the dangers awaiting him in the Underworld. He had to return as soon as possible before his father and brothers destroyed the entire realm.

"Are you quite finished?" Cyrus snapped.

The women pulled apart, and Polina shot him a glare before returning her gaze to her daughter. "There is always a way, my dear. Don't forget that. And promise me you won't stop searching for it."

Prudence pressed her lips together and nodded, though Cyrus caught the darkness that flashed in her lavender eyes.

She had no plans to survive this. Perhaps Polina noticed this as well, because she sighed heavily, closing her eyes against the steady flow of tears.

Prudence touched Beatrice's shoulder. The older woman offered a frail smile, pressing her forehead to Prudence's. "Be safe, dear," Beatrice whispered.

The younger witch only nodded before turning away, not bothering to check if Cyrus followed. But he wasn't about to linger in this decrepit fish town, surrounded by hateful witches, for any longer than he had to. With a heavy sigh, he hurried after Prue, finding it much easier to navigate along the road without the fog of souls to mask his view. Even in the darkness, his immortal eyes could still see perfectly, for which he was grateful.

Ahead of him, Prudence sniffed and wiped at her face, and Cyrus rolled his eyes. These witches might be powerful, but they were still delicate creatures, prone to emotion and weakness.

And this wretched woman had somehow bound his powers? No. Impossible.

Cyrus stopped in his tracks, going completely stiff. The rage and indignation roared inside him, and he could no longer hold it at bay. And why should he? He was not some puppet, some weapon to be wielded at the whims of some inexperienced witch.

Prudence seemed to sense his halting steps. She turned and glanced over her shoulder. "What are you doing? Come on, we need to leave!"

"No," Cyrus bit out. He was finished being ordered around like some slave.

Prudence's eyebrows shot up as she stomped toward him, closing the distance between them. "*No*? I'm sorry, do you have somewhere better to be? I was under the impression you *wanted* to return home."

"Not if it means being chained to you. I'd gladly roam this awful realm on my own if it means freeing myself from this bondage." He spat each word like it was a foul curse.

Prudence's eyes narrowed. "I don't give a damn what you want. You're bound to me, and you can't hurt me.

You vowed you wouldn't until we reached the gate. So you can either follow me to the docks or I'll drag you there myself."

Cyrus huffed a dry laugh as he scrutinized her tired gaze and frizzy hair. She was in no shape to drag a *god* anywhere. He crossed his arms and raised his eyebrows. "All right. Go on and drag me."

Prudence blinked, her face slackening in shock. Cyrus watched her smugly, amusement mingling with satisfaction within him. At long last, he had bested her. And he *reveled* in it.

Freedom at last.

Cyrus spread his arms. "I'm waiting."

"I don't have time for this," Prudence said through clenched teeth.

He scoffed. "I didn't have time to be yanked away from my home against my will, and yet, here we are."

"Cyrus—"

He took a step closer to her, baring his teeth. "I am not moving from this spot unless forced." He cocked his head and smirked. "Of course, you could always just run off to your dear mama and ask *her* to do the work for you."

Rage burned in Prudence's eyes, and Cyrus knew he'd struck a nerve. His smile widened.

"Why?" she snarled. "Why are you doing this? You hate this realm! Don't you *want* to go back home?"

"What I want right now is to inconvenience you the same way you inconvenienced me."

Prudence threw her hands in the air. "You are a child!"

Cyrus merely continued grinning at her, knowing he'd won.

Then she looked at him, the ire fading from her face as something cool and calculating took over. "Oh, I get it now."

Cyrus's smile faltered. "What?"

"You're the devil. Torturing people is your specialty." She waved a hand between them, a slow smile spreading across her face. "That's what you're doing right now. You're torturing me."

Cyrus frowned. He didn't like the gleam in her eyes. Not one bit. "For your information, I merely oversee the realm of the Underworld. Usually, the torture is reserved for lesser beings like demons."

"Regardless, you'd still have to be pretty skilled in order to be the ruler of all that, wouldn't you?" She tilted her chin and gazed up at him, adoration glowing in her eyes.

Suspicion bloomed in Cyrus's thoughts. What was she doing? "Yes," he said slowly, not trusting where this conversation was headed.

"You like toying with the mortals, don't you?" Prudence draped her fingers over his arm, tracing the length of one of his tattoos.

Despite his unease, Cyrus couldn't help the shiver that coursed through him or the way his skin prickled from her touch. "I—I don't . . ." His words faltered, stuck in his throat. Why couldn't he speak? Gods, she was standing so close to him . . .

She moistened her lips, and Cyrus's eyes were inexplicably drawn to the movement, tracing the curve of her mouth with his gaze. Heat churned in his belly.

"You must be very powerful, then," she murmured, her voice a soft caress in his ear.

A strangled noise climbed up his throat. He swallowed hard, feeling ridiculous. "Well, yes. I am." Thank the gods his voice remained level.

Prudence caught her lower lip between her teeth, and Cyrus had the strangest urge to do the same, to drag his teeth along that full lip and see just what kind of sounds he could elicit from her . . .

Her eyes burned with a heady desire that made Cyrus lean into her, yearning for more. "You like playing games?" she asked, arching a single eyebrow as if issuing a challenge.

"Yes," Cyrus said at once, though he couldn't remember the question.

Prudence looked positively eager as she leaned into him, her face alight, and whispered, "Well, I'm good at games, too. And you, *Your Highness*, have just been beaten."

Cyrus squinted, not understanding her meaning.

"What the hell are you—" He broke off with a strangled cry as something tugged at his feet, jerking him down until he crumpled to the ground.

Then Prudence was standing above him, grinning wickedly. "Enjoy the ride."

"What—" Cyrus's protests were muffled as Prudence's vines wrapped around him, coiling tightly as if they were serpents. He choked on his breath as one vine in particular squeezed the air from him. The ivy felt like ropes around his ankles and wrists, pinning him to the ground.

"Let's go then!" Prudence called over her shoulder, setting off down the road.

Cyrus struggled and writhed, but he was thoroughly tied down. Reality crashed into him as he realized he had been played. Prudence had been toying with him. Manipulating him. Like the lying, conniving witch she was.

He was a fool. An utter fool. He deserved this for letting his guard down and falling for such a devious ploy.

The ivy underneath him started to shift and glide as if he were on a leafy sled and Prudence was the horse pulling on the reins.

A string of expletives burst from his mouth, but then the vines covered that, too, cutting off his curses as he careened down the road after Prudence.

SEAFARERS

PRUE

THE VICTORY of triumphing over Cyrus's little temper tantrum was fleeting. Prue couldn't shake the hauntingly devastated look of her mother from her mind even as they reached the docks.

But her thoughts of parting from Polina quickly fled from her mind when she found the chaos awaiting them. A crowd of people surrounded the *Daybreaker,* Krenia's largest ship, but no one was climbing aboard.

After ensuring Cyrus was still safely tied up in her vines, Prue strode forward until she found the captain, a tall, muscular man named Davies.

"What's going on?" Prue demanded, putting as much authority in her voice as she could muster.

"We were going to set sail, and then *this* happened." Davies gestured to the open sea.

Prue followed his gaze to the shimmering gold

barrier surrounding the island—and the mass of ghosts waiting on the other side.

"The crew are too afraid to leave," Davies continued. "And I can't blame them!"

"I have to board a ship," Prue said insistently. "If I don't, the ghosts will only keep multiplying."

Davies only spread his hands, a helpless look on his face. "I can't man the ship on my own."

Prue chewed on her lower lip in deliberation. Then, she straightened and lifted her chin. "I'll protect the ship."

Davies raised an eyebrow. "You will?"

"Yes. I will enchant the ship with the same magic." Prue waved a hand to the barrier. "Everyone on board will be protected."

When Davies continued to watch her dubiously, Prue gritted her teeth and hissed, "I'm the Maiden of the coven of Krenia. Do you doubt my abilities?"

Davies' spine straightened, his face smoothing. "Of course not."

"Then, assemble your crew. Tell them to prepare to set sail."

Davies nodded quickly. "Of course, my lady."

Ignoring the weariness settling into her bones, Prue stood next to the still-bound Cyrus as the crew hastened to prepare the ship. Some outright refused, glancing warily at the ghosts hovering by the barrier. But, thankfully, enough crew members agreed to sail in exchange for Prue's protection.

She had no idea *how* she would protect the entire ship and its occupants. But she had to try. There were no other options. She *had* to leave this island.

When at last the captain called for the passengers to board, Prue waved a hand, summoning her vines to urge Cyrus forward. At their approach, Davies raised an eyebrow at Prue's prisoner, still tied down to the bed of ivy.

In answer to his unspoken question, Prue said, "This is my prisoner. He's responsible for the ghost attack on the village."

A muffled outburst signaled Cyrus's indignation, but she ignored him.

Davies cast a wary look at Cyrus. "Are you certain it's wise to bring him aboard?" A flicker of fear shone in his eyes.

"I have him contained." Prue's voice was thick with authority and power. "He won't cause you or your crew any trouble."

Davies cleared his throat and nodded. "Very good, my lady." He waved them aboard.

As Prue climbed onto the ship, her limbs throbbed, the cost of using so much magic finally wearing on her. She took a deep breath, but it did nothing to fortify her drained body. Behind her, her vines eased Cyrus on deck, then receded back to the ground.

It was just as well. Her vines wouldn't survive

without something rooting them to the earth. But Cyrus didn't need to know that.

Prue knelt at Cyrus's feet while he spat leaves from his mouth. "Did you enjoy the ride, darling?" she asked sweetly, batting her eyelashes at him.

"Bitch," he choked, spitting a chunk of ivy at her.

Prue only smirked at him. "I've been called worse." She traced a finger along the raw welts on his wrists from her vines. He snarled, jerking away from her, and her grin widened. "Don't test me, Cyrus. Or I'll tie you up again."

Cyrus's eyes were blazing, his jaw taut, but he said nothing.

Ignoring his murderous looks, Prue stood, tying her long curls behind her in a messy braid. As the crew prepared to set sail, she peered over the crowd of passengers, longing for one last look at her beloved island. The palm trees swayed in the unearthly breeze that whispered over the island, a product of the death magic now coursing through the entire realm. Even though the island was still, the air was thick with magic, pulsing and waiting for them on the outskirts of the barrier.

I did this, Prue thought. A knot developed in her throat. Did this mean Mona's sacrifice had been for nothing? Her sister died so the village would be safe from undead spirits. And now they were back, threatening the *entire realm*—as if Mona's death hadn't happened at all.

I'll bring her back, Prue vowed. That was, after all, why she was aboard this ship in the first place: not just to return Cyrus to his realm and rid the mortal world of these ghosts, but also to bring back her sister.

Prue glanced over her shoulder, ensuring Cyrus wasn't causing any trouble. Sure enough, he stood behind her, arms crossed and a scowl on his face as he refused to look at her.

Still sulking, I see, Prue thought to herself, biting back a smile.

The ship set sail, the crew shouting to each other as the boat shifted forward. Prue placed a hand along the wooden beam of the ship, murmuring a quick prayer to the Triple Goddess as the vessel sailed along.

Please give me the strength to protect the boat from the spirits, she thought, her eyes closing. *Please.*

She bit down on her lip, her eyes opening as she turned to face forward, watching as they drew nearer and nearer to that shimmering gold barrier. She called on her magic, waiting for her third eye to open . . . But nothing happened. Warmth filled her chest, but the aching in her limbs made her go stiff, her magic faltering.

No, no, no . . . The ship was practically at the barrier now. Prue drew on every last drop of strength, struggling to summon her magic.

"*Contego,*" she whispered in desperation. Energy prickled at her fingertips, but it died as if a candle had been snuffed out.

Come on! Prue sank to her knees, gasping, pleading with the Triple Goddess. Her hands pressed into the wooden floorboards beneath her, urging her magic onward. *Please.*

Then, she sensed movement around her. Panting, she looked up to find the other passengers moving about the deck, some descending the stairs while others chatted away merrily.

Prue's mouth fell open. What the hell? She looked toward the barrier and flinched. The gold light gleamed brightly, burning against her eyes. Her stomach lurched as a tremor rocked the boat, making it quiver as it passed through the magic.

Prue held her breath, waiting. Dozens of white ghosts appeared, hovering and floating around the boat like elegant dancers. Prue's blood chilled at the horrific and yet beautiful sight. Her heart hammered painfully in her chest as she waited for the spirits to dive for them, to start attacking the crew.

But they didn't.

Prue slowly rose to her feet, gaping at the harmless ghosts in the air. Stunned, she glanced over the crew and passengers, but none of them even noticed the ghosts.

Had her magic protected them after all?

A low chuckle drew her attention. Turning, Prue found Cyrus smirking at her.

"What's so funny?" Prue demanded.

"Do you really not know?" Cyrus taunted. "Is your mind so simple that you can't figure this out?"

Prue raised her hand. "Tell me or I'll tie you up again." It was a feeble bluff, especially if he had seen her fall to her knees earlier.

But the reminder was enough. Cyrus scowled again, his eyes darkening with fury. "Mortals can't see ghosts."

"But the mortals in my village—"

"Are exposed to magic on a daily basis. The farther they are from that magical influence, the less they can see. By now, the glamour has probably taken effect and shielded their minds."

Prue's eyebrows lifted as she looked around the ship with a new perspective. The crew and passengers puttered about, unbothered by the presence of magic around them. And the spirits were equally unperturbed.

Relief filled Prue as she realized the souls and the mortals were completely ignorant of each other. And with Prue's magic drained, she hopefully wouldn't draw the ghosts' attention.

"Thank the Goddess," Prue breathed, sinking backward against the gunnel, allowing herself to relax for the first time in hours.

"The Goddess has nothing to do with it," Cyrus snapped. "The glamour comes directly from *my* kingdom. The Underworld is what fuels that particular brand of magic."

Prue only arched an eyebrow at him, too tired to

even be irritated by his snobbery. Truth be told, she *hadn't* known this, and it was fascinating information. But she wouldn't tell him that.

A familiar copper-haired crewman approached, removing his hat and inclining his head politely toward the two of them. His name was Bernard, and Prue recognized him as a fisherman who often sold the most delicious bass in the market.

"I beg your pardon, but you two should probably go belowdecks, just to be safe." He gestured to the thinning crowd as the families descended, no doubt eager to find a free cabin to sleep in for the night.

"Shit," Prue blurted, then clamped her mouth shut. But a smile tugged at the corners of Bernard's mouth. "Sorry," she muttered. "Thanks, Bernard."

She was so worried about what would happen when they crossed the barrier that she hadn't even considered finding a place to sleep. By now all the more private cabins were probably filled. Despite how exhausted she was, she doubted she would be getting much sleep anyway. Between casting the summoning spell, binding herself to the god of the dead, finding out they were *married,* unleashing the souls of Acheron—*again*—and the prospect of seeing her sister alive in the flesh, Prue's mind was racing with endless thoughts and questions. Her insides felt so agitated she thought they would spill from her and erupt on the ship.

But Cyrus was already attracting curious glances

from those who remained on deck. Not to mention the spark of recognition in the eyes of those who identified her as the Maiden, followed quickly by hostility and distrust. Prue had no doubt they were wondering why she was abandoning her people and her village. That was certainly what it looked like. It was unheard of for someone blessed by the Triple Goddess to flee from the island.

Gritting her teeth against the blatant stares of those around them, Prue snatched Cyrus's arm and hauled him belowdecks, ignoring his grumbling and idle threats. He stumbled down the stairs, struggling to keep up with her. The ship lurched suddenly, and she and Cyrus collided, slamming against the walls with a thud. Prue's face pressed into his collarbone, and his chest smacked against hers.

In a flash, Cyrus gripped her shoulders and settled her a safe distance from him, as if her touch alone revolted him. She gave him an equally repulsed look, happy to part from the cold, unyielding stiffness of his body. Goddess, it was like he was made of stone. Well, perhaps he was. He certainly wasn't human.

"This one will do," Cyrus grunted, gesturing to the nearest cabin. He stormed inside, and a woman yelped at his unannounced entrance. "Out," he commanded her.

"Cyrus!" Prue hissed, grabbing his arm and tugging

him out of the room. "You can't just order someone out of their room."

"Why not? I'm the god of the Underworld and you're the Maiden of your coven. Surely, our authority warrants the best of accommodations."

Prue's nostrils flared. "No. We aren't throwing out helpless villagers just because you want a cozy bed for the night."

"Prudence—"

Prue recoiled at the sound of her given name and cast a horrified look at Cyrus. "What did you call me?"

Cyrus only frowned. "Isn't that your name?"

"It's Prue. Just Prue."

Cyrus nodded once. "Fine. *Prue.* I don't give a damn about these people, and you don't either. Don't pretend otherwise," he added when she opened her mouth to object.

Prue's jaw tensed, her nostrils flaring. "Regardless, I don't want to make a scene. I'm tired and I've fought enough battles today. If *you* want to throw people out of their cabins, be my guest. But I guarantee the crew will eventually intervene, and without your magic, I'm betting you won't be able to fight off seven sailors at once."

Cyrus's brows lowered as he glared at her, his silvery eyes unsettling. Prue resisted the urge to drop her gaze under his scrutiny. A storm raged in his eyes, and before he could lash out at her, she guided him farther down until they reached an open space filled with hammocks. Several individuals were already getting comfortable, swinging to the rhythm of the swaying ship.

“Take your pick.” Prue gestured to the empty hammocks on the left side, striding toward one without preamble.

“Gods, this is abysmal.” Cyrus’s wrinkled nose made his face twist into something almost animal-like. The more he made that expression, the more he resembled less of a man and more of something like a warthog. Prue bit back a laugh at the thought.

The boat lurched again, and Cyrus’s arms flew out to meet the wall before he fell over. His face took on a greenish tint.

Prue, already laying comfortably in her hammock, peered at him in curiosity. “You aren’t going to be sick, are you?”

“Of course not.” But Cyrus’s hollow voice betrayed his discomfort.

This time, Prue *did* laugh, and Cyrus shot her a glare. “We don’t have oceans in the Underworld,” he said defensively. “I am unaccustomed to sea travel.”

“Well, if you vomit, make sure it lands in the bucket over there.” Prue gestured to the opposite side of the room and leaned her head back, closing her eyes. She didn’t feel relaxed, but Cyrus didn’t have to know that.

Indeed, his snarl told her she was agitating him. She smiled. *Good.*

She listened to his awkward sounds with amusement. An "oof" indicated he had collapsed into a hammock, and his sharp intake of breath signaled he was quite uncomfortable with a bed in motion. Well, he would have to get used to it.

"How long will we be on this godsforsaken vessel?"

"The Salwaki Islands are about a day's journey from here. We'll stop there, then continue onward toward Voula City, which is another day."

"Hmm."

Prue opened one eye to look at him. "What?"

"When I looked at your map, it seemed there was a more direct route. Through the Manos Sea."

Prue raised her eyebrows, unable to hide how impressed she was at his memory. "Yes . . . if you want to get caught in the whirlpool."

"Whirlpool?"

"Yes, it's like a spinning vortex of death that will swallow anyone and anything."

"I *know* what a whirlpool is."

Prue smirked again. "Just checking."

"Even so, I'm a god and cannot be killed by mortal means. And you are the Maiden. Surely, between the two of us, we have enough magic to navigate safely through a simple whirlpool."

Prue's smile melted into a scowl. "I'm not sending a ship full of innocent humans to their deaths just for our convenience."

"Why not? I can assure you they'll be well taken care of after they die." Cyrus flashed a mischievous grin.

Prue scoffed. "You're a bastard."

"Probably. I never met my mother."

Prue blinked, and Cyrus did, too, as if he hadn't intended to reveal this truth about himself. *Thank the Goddess for that truth spell,* Prue thought. If she had to suffer his company *and* his lies, she might just jump overboard.

"I never met my father, either," Prue said shortly before leaning her head back and shutting her eyes again.

"Why?"

"He wasn't a witch. He was just a man who sired witches. A nobody." Prue kept her tone even and refused to open her eyes, even as her gut twisted from the words. She'd asked her mother on multiple occasions who her father had been, but Polina had claimed he'd been a soldier passing through on a long journey and she'd never seen him again. When Prue prodded her for more answers, Polina brushed them off. It was her magical heritage that mattered, not the male seed that had created her. Polina had always believed men to be less than nothing; an irritant to endure on Gaia's great earth. Nothing more than flies to swat at.

Prue knew witches were powerful and important, but she'd never go as far as saying men were worthless.

Mercifully, Cyrus said nothing as the ship continued

on, rocking with the lapping waves underneath them. Prue's eyelids felt so heavy, and the motion was soothing, reminding her of childhood journeys with Polina, Sybil, and Mona. Her limbs ached with such intensity she thought she could sleep through an entire day. The thought sounded wonderful.

Just before she drifted off, she thought of Mona—was her spirit safe? Would Prue see her ghost again? But she supposed it didn't matter. Soon, Prue would resurrect Mona, which would be so much better than the frail echo of Mona's spirit.

With that hopeful thought, Prue fell into a deep sleep.

MONA WAS SCREAMING. Crying out for her. Prue reached for her sister, but Mona's shouts faded. Frantic, Prue scrambled forward, arms outstretched . . .

But a shadowy figure snatched Mona around the waist and tugged her away. Prue only caught a glimpse of inky black hair and a single streak of silver before darkness consumed her.

Gasping, Prue woke, her heart racing. She clutched her chest, only to find the pomegranate necklace warm at her throat. Gradually, her panic subsided and her eyes adjusted to the darkness of the room. Her hammock still swung with the ship's rocking motions as she wiped sweat from her face.

Goddess, that dream had seemed so real . . . As irresponsible as Prue was, she was never one to push aside premonitions. Even she knew better than that. Her mouth twisted as she tried to recall details, which slipped from her hands like droplets of water.

The figure who had snatched Mona—who was he? The streak of silver in his hair was similar to Cyrus's, but the opposite; Cyrus had nearly all-silver hair with a single black streak. And this figure had been taller and leaner. Plus, he lacked the distinct tattoos on his skin that Cyrus had.

Whoever the man was, it wasn't Cyrus. As easy as it was to believe the god of Hell was her enemy, that much was clear.

Prue's nerves were frayed. She was on edge. Restless. Agitated. It quite easily could've been a normal nightmare.

But witches didn't get normal nightmares. Especially not her, who was blessed by the Triple Goddess.

Prue sat up, peeling her sticky curls off her forehead and neck, struggling to breathe deeply. But it was so stifling belowdecks. The air reeked of sweat and seaweed.

Without another thought, she swung out of the hammock and climbed the stairs to the surface, already enjoying the wisps of fresh sea air that coiled around her with each step she took. A midnight sky full of stars greeted her, accompanied by the gentle spray of sea water from the hull as the ship pressed onward. A breeze whipped at her hair, cooling her from the sweltering terror of her dream.

Yes, this was much better.

She maneuvered toward the bow until she was close enough to the edge to rest her arms against the gunnel, allowing the splash of the ocean to soothe her anxiety.

"You humans always were a restless bunch."

Prue might've jolted at the sound, but thankfully, the rush of water underneath her provided a calming background noise that almost drowned out Cyrus's voice entirely. She could even pretend he hadn't spoken at all.

But then the heat of him behind her sent her body spinning. Unwilling to let him approach without her watching him, she whirled to face him, eyes narrowing.

"What are you doing up here?" she accused. Her eyes roved over his form. He was shirtless, but at least he had the decency to keep his trousers on. "Don't you immortals sleep?"

"Actually, we don't." Cyrus smirked at her, leaning casually against the gunnel alongside her. Despite the tattoos and unusual hair and eye color, his confident swagger made him seem like he belonged here and no one could tell him otherwise. Prue envied that confidence, though she would never admit it. *Self-assured bastard.*

She forced herself to turn away from him, though the back of her neck prickled from the presence of someone powerful and otherworldly behind her. "Well, I came up here to be alone. So, if you don't mind . . ."

Cyrus huffed a laugh. "We may be bound, but you certainly do not have authority to give me orders."

Prue flinched at the word "bound." Well, at least he hadn't said *married.*

"What happened in your village . . ." Cyrus took a breath before continuing. "You said it had happened before."

Prue remained silent, waiting for him to ask his question, though it wasn't hard to guess. Even so, she wasn't keen on sharing the circumstances of her sister's death with him.

"When?" Cyrus finally asked. "How?"

"Why does it matter?" Prue snapped.

"It's the Book of Eyes," Cyrus said calmly, unfazed by her irritation. "My connection to this realm. I need to know how it happened before to better understand . . ." He trailed off, his eyes darkening slightly. He lifted his chin, resolve filling his face. "To better understand what tethers me here."

Curiosity prodded Prue's mind, pushing out all thoughts of Mona and the nightmare. She half-turned to face him again. "How does that work, exactly?"

Cyrus scowled. "I believe I asked you a question first."

It was Prue's turn to smirk. "Answer mine, and I'll answer yours."

Cyrus's eyebrows lowered in clear annoyance. It only made Prue's smile widen. Funny, how his displeasure stoked her glee like fuel to a fire. But, to her surprise—and slight disappointment—he relented. He shifted, pressing his back to the gunnel and crossing his arms. Prue tried not to stare at the way the ink on his biceps twisted with the movement.

"It is the source of my power," Cyrus said. "But it binds me to the mortal realm. The book serves as a gate to my world. An access point. And the power within the book is fueled by my soul."

Prue's eyes widened. "Your *soul*?"

He nodded grimly. "The price of power is great, as I told you."

"But . . . why? Why would you do that? I mean, you seem to really detest this place." Prue spread her arms at the ocean around them. "So why would you bind yourself here?"

Cyrus's eyes darkened. "You do not understand what I endured to get where I am. The shame and humiliation of being the youngest of six powerful princes of Hell. The mockery and torment of knowing they would never respect me. That my own father would never acknowledge me."

Prue stilled at his words, and something twisted inside her chest. Surely, it wasn't *sympathy* for this monster. But . . . perhaps it was. "Wait. Hang on. You're the *youngest*? And somehow you're the god of the Underworld?" When Cyrus nodded, she sputtered, "But . . . your father? Your brothers? Are they. . ."

"They are still gods, yes. But I have the authority of the throne."

Prue frowned as she considered this. Goddess, six princes of Hell? She couldn't imagine . . .

"It's your turn." Cyrus arched an eyebrow at her, though the shadows hadn't fully left his eyes. "What happened before?"

Damn. Truth be told, Prue was hoping he'd refuse to reveal anything about the Book of Eyes so she wouldn't have to answer. She sighed, facing the bow of the ship once more. If she stared, unfocused, at the dark, lapping waves bathed in moonlight, maybe she could pretend she was somewhere else.

"I don't know how the Book of Eyes was opened the first time," she admitted. "The Crone of our coven unlocked it somehow. We think the book itself lured her to do it. It seems to have a mind of its own. And when the darkness within was unleashed, it was . . . black as night. Different from the white spirits we saw yesterday. It seeped into the earth like ink and blood. It possessed people, taking over them completely until they were nothing more than husks." She took a shuddering breath. "Only when a blood sacrifice was offered—my sister—did it finally stop."

Cyrus remained quiet as she spoke. When silence fell between them, Prue focused on the rushing water beneath her, willing it to drown out the memories of screams and terror from that horrible night.

At long last, Cyrus said, "That is strange."

Prue's eyebrows knitted together. She'd just revealed the nature of her sister's death, and all he could say was that it was *strange*? Well, she shouldn't be entirely surprised. What did she expect from him, sympathy? The idea made her want to laugh.

"What is?" Her voice was harsher than she'd intended.

"I think you're right that the book has a mind of its own," he said. "I only encountered it once. But it seems in the three instances when it's been used—granting my power, terrorizing your village, and summoning me—it performs differently. I never saw black magic pooling from it as you described. But I *have* seen spirits possess humans. I wonder . . ." He broke off, rubbing his chin, his silvery eyes contemplative.

"What?" Prue asked, genuinely curious.

"I wonder if, each time it's opened, it infuses itself with souls." He met her gaze. "All the souls that are lost, that are possessed or obliterated . . . What if the book absorbs them? What if those souls *fuel* the magic in the book? The magic . . . in me?"

MURANE

CYRUS

PRUE HADN'T SAID anything about Cyrus's speculation. She'd merely looked at him with haunted eyes, accusation blaring in her gaze, before stalking off. Cyrus, however, preferred solitude to the company of mortals—especially that nuisance of a witch—so he remained above deck, enjoying the breeze and the crashing waves around him.

He hadn't *wanted* to share his speculation with Prue . . . but he needed her to trust him. Because he knew exactly what the marriage bond entailed. If they consummated their bond, Cyrus would access *her* powers, too.

And then he could take back the throne to the Underworld once and for all. He would have plenty of power to counteract what Aidoneus had done to Acheron. Prue was an earth witch, after all; she possessed the magic of life. If Aidoneus had poisoned the river, intent on killing the life within it, then Prue's magic would be able to restore it.

If he had to bed Prue in order to access her magic, then fine. He had bedded far worse and far uglier. But first, he had to gain her trust—because he absolutely refused to take her by force. Monster that he was, even he wouldn't lower himself to such a level. Earning the witch's trust was a slow game, a manipulation—one he'd fallen victim to once before. Playing the role of the deceiver left a foul taste in his mouth. But he had to. He had to save his home. Whatever the cost.

He shuddered at the thought of making love to the earth witch. But then, as his thoughts wandered, the shudder turned into something else. Something wilder. He pictured her nude, which wasn't hard to imagine given her curves and the size of her breasts. He imagined the sounds he could elicit from her, how she would moan as he caressed between her legs, coaxing raw and feral pleasure out of her . . .

Cyrus suddenly blinked, finding himself out of breath. His cock strained within his trousers, responding to his strange fantasy. Gritting his teeth, he ran a hand through his hair and took a deep breath, struggling to calm his thoughts.

He was being absurd. Bedding the witch would bring him no pleasure at all. It had just been far too long since his last dalliance. That was all.

Still. He couldn't shove away the tiny, minuscule part of him that *wanted* to consummate his marriage with Prue. If only to see what it would be like. She was powerful. What would that power be like, manifesting itself against him? *Through* him?

Just after dawn broke, the ship docked at the Salwaki Islands, a bustling port filled with ships, merchants, and traders. Some of the crew disembarked to exchange goods, but Cyrus remained aboard, glowering toward the sea and the destination that loomed ahead.

A few hours later, the ship was in motion again. He didn't bother trying to track down Prue. Between their bond, her earth magic, and the concoction her mother had forced him to drink, he knew he couldn't escape her for long, so he saw this temporary absence as a blessing. He already tired of her company after a single day. He couldn't imagine enduring her for the several days it would take them to arrive in Faidon.

And he was supposed to *woo* this infuriating witch, too. Gods, the mere thought of it . . .

Cyrus knew his mortal form didn't require rest or sustenance, but it was still unpleasant. His body felt fatigued and his insides hollowed. He munched on an apple, practically gagging with each bite, only because he knew he would function better with food on his stomach. He even forced himself to sway in that ridiculous hammock for a few hours, wondering if his body would eventually grow weary enough for sleep. He had never slept, not even during his first journey here. There hadn't been time. But he had no doubt this wretched place would alter him somehow if he stayed for too long.

He didn't fancy another midnight discussion with the witch, so instead of lingering by the bow, he moved to the stern, watching the tiny islands wink out of existence as the ship progressed. He didn't like watching from behind. He preferred to look ahead, to envision the next step. Lingering in the past served no purpose.

This would be the longest he'd ever been away from home. The longest *any* of his brothers had. They'd told him they'd always kept their visits to the mortal realm brief, simply because no immortal being could survive for too long there.

Cyrus shuddered at the thought of testing that theory. How long before he, too, faded away into nothingness, just like the Salwaki Islands?

"Did she run, then?" came a gruff voice.

At first, Cyrus didn't register the question was directed at him. Only when he felt a presence behind him, accompanied by the lingering stench of rotten fish, did he turn. A sailor with a graying beard and squinty eyes appraised him.

"What?" Cyrus bit out. How dare this simpleton address him?

"The Maiden. Did she run from those spirits?" His voice was thick with accusation.

Cyrus's eyes narrowed. "How is that any of your business?"

"My family grew up in Krenia. Those witches protected us when no one else did. We didn't *want* to leave, but we have no magic, see? But it's downright cowardly for the coven's own Maiden to abandon her people at a time like this." He spat on the ground.

Coils of black fury rose up in Cyrus's chest. In a flash, he had the man by the throat and lifted him off the ground. The sailor's eyes bulged, his face purpling as he choked, clawing uselessly at Cyrus's unrelenting grip.

Cyrus couldn't explain the fiery rage that consumed him. Wasn't he just thinking bitter thoughts about Prue himself? But there was something about this stranger ridiculing Prue when she was on a mission trying to *save* his sorry ass that incensed Cyrus.

Or perhaps he was merely feeling defensive because they were bound. Because even though she was a conniving witch, she was *his* conniving witch.

He didn't care. Either way, this scumbag deserved to die.

"You dare insult my wife?" Cyrus hissed, his voice soft and lethal. "You dare spit your pitiful accusations at me? I don't give a shit about you or your family. I'll snap your neck without another thought, vermin."

The man's limbs flailed as he struggled to breathe, his body flopping like a fish. Satisfaction swelled in Cyrus's chest.

"Cyrus, *stop*!"

Cyrus froze as Prue appeared behind the man, her lavender eyes wide with shock and anger. "Release him. *Now*!"

Cyrus gritted his teeth before obeying, letting the man fall into a heap on the deck. The man inhaled shuddering gasps, massaging his throat and shooting horrified looks between Cyrus and Prue.

"Your . . . wife?" he wheezed.

"Dammit all," Prue said with a groan, lifting her gaze to the moonlit sky. "Really, Cyrus? Have you been telling the entire crew we're married?"

"He spoke against you," Cyrus said, as if this explained everything.

Prue laughed harshly. "And what, you sought to defend my honor? People will always talk, Cyrus! I don't care about idle gossip."

Cyrus only frowned, bewildered by this. He was a god and she was the Maiden. This man was lower than scum. Cyrus had done the sensible thing in threatening him. In fact, the world would have improved without such a man to taint its existence.

"Get out of here," Prue snapped, waving a hand at the man.

He didn't need to be told twice. Muttering foul curses, he scrambled to his feet and hobbled away from them as fast as he could.

Cyrus's scowl deepened as the man vanished. "Why did you do that?"

"Because I don't enjoy watching others getting strangled by the *devil*. What the hell's the matter with you? You can't just go around killing people."

"Why not?"

Prue threw her hands in the air. "Goddess, you're impossible!" She stepped closer to him, her eyes widening with emphasis. "While we're in the realm of Gaia—"

"The *what*?"

"The human realm!"

"Just call it that."

"No." Prue sliced her hand through the air, cutting him off. "If you're going to travel with me through this realm, you're going to respect how we humans do things. And for starters, we are named after the earth goddess Gaia. She blessed us with these lands. I don't give a shit what you and your stupid brothers believe in, but that's what *this realm* believes in."

Cyrus opened his mouth to argue, but she interrupted again.

"Second," she said, her voice rising, "we believe in justice according to the monarch of said lands. If you believe someone has committed a grievous crime—more grievous than a mere insult or whisper of gossip—then you report him to the proper authorities instead of exacting punishment yourself. Understand?"

Rage burned in his chest at her patronizing tone. "I am a *god*—"

"And that's another thing," she said, talking over him again. "You can't go around parading yourself as the god of the Underworld. It will cause mass chaos. Let's make this journey as seamless as possible, without drawing too much attention. We'll get you back to your world, and everything will continue as it was before." She spread her arms, her eyes distant as if she were convincing herself more than him.

Silence fell between them. Cyrus crossed his arms, summoning all his restraint not to take *her* by the throat, too. Instead, he watched her, eyebrows raised in expectation.

Prue finally looked at him, recoiling at the fire in his eyes. "What?"

"Is that all?" Cyrus asked.

"I—well, yes. I think so."

"Good. Now it's my turn. I will respect your foolish demands if you respect mine. I will tell whoever I like that you are my wife because it is the truth. I don't enjoy deceiving anyone, even pathetic humans like that weasel you just let go."

"But—"

Cyrus drew closer to her and growled, "I'm. Not. Finished."

Prue's mouth clamped shut. He expected her to

argue, but something in his face must've startled her into silence. Sweet, blessed silence.

"Second, I am a *god.* An immortal being. I don't belong here and I don't want to be here. Let's not forget you summoned me against my will and trapped me here. So, I will abide by your rules if you abide by mine. No more tying me up. No more dragging me around like a prisoner. You will treat me with the respect I deserve instead of treating me like your worthless servant." He spat the words, recalling the days when his brothers treated him the same way. "Are we understood?"

Prue's lips grew thin, her eyes raging at him. "Perfectly," she said through gritted teeth.

For one tense moment, they stared at each other with venom and loathing. The power rippling off her made Cyrus grateful he stood much taller than her, otherwise he'd be tempted to cower from the force of it.

Prue broke eye contact first. With a disgusted huff, she turned and stormed away from him.

Well, so much for wooing her, Cyrus thought bitterly. At this rate, it would be a miracle if they didn't rip out each other's throats before they reached Faidon.

At her retreat, Cyrus exhaled heavily, deflating from the pressure of asserting himself against that much magic. He wasn't even sure she'd noticed the glowing cords of gold magic trailing after her.

PRUE AND CYRUS skillfully avoided one another until they finally reached their destination: the kingdom of Murane. Cyrus knew nothing about this place other than what he'd seen on the map—a mountain range separated it from the Thanassian Empire, which was where Faidon was.

Cyrus followed Prue and the other passengers as they disembarked the vessel. The port was far different from the one in the Salwaki Islands. The islands had been minimal but full of life, a bustling hub of activity and culture. But this place was massive and overwhelming. Several docked ships surrounded them, and hordes of people rushed this way and that as if they were in a hurry and couldn't be bothered to slow their pace. The women wore elegant gowns while the men wore expensive suits and smoked cigars. The area reeked of wealth and self-importance, so much that Cyrus wrinkled his nose.

These humans thought they knew power and authority, but they were clueless. Every single one of them.

Prue kept shooting nervous glances at the sky, where several wispy ghosts floated about, roaming aimlessly. After a while, Cyrus murmured to her, "Don't worry. No one can see them."

"I know." But Prue bit her lip, glancing upward again as if expecting the ghosts to suddenly dive down and devour her. "But . . . why aren't they attacking?" Her voice was barely above a whisper.

"They are drawn to powerful magic. Otherwise, they're harmless. I imagine there aren't many witches or mages in the city. Or, if there are, they are keeping to themselves."

Prue's throat bobbed as she swallowed. A wrinkle formed between her brows, and her frown remained.

As they walked, several eyes fixed on Cyrus, widening in alarm at the stark color of his hair and eyes, along with the tattoo markings all along his body. But, thankfully, none of their gazes drifted to the horns atop his head. Which meant the glamour from the Underworld was doing its job, thank the gods. Just like with the ghosts, these mortals were clueless about what truly lurked around them.

"Come on," Prue said stiffly, tugging on his arm. She was clearly unperturbed by the disgusted glances the other women shot her, no doubt offended by her torn and stained skirts. "We're only staying in Voula City for long enough to get supplies, and then we're moving on."

Cyrus said nothing. He certainly wouldn't regret leaving this place. But he bristled at the command in Prue's tone, as if *she* was in charge.

The two of them maneuvered through the throng of passengers and sailors, along with vendors and merchants shouting their wares and low prices. The stench of perspiration and human greed thickened in Cyrus's nostrils. Humans were disgusting creatures, always lusting for wealth and riches and notoriety. Ignorant fools. How could they not see that all of this was meaningless?

"I can feel your judgment," Prue said over her shoulder. "Wipe that scowl off your face or we'll attract too much attention."

Cyrus stiffened. *He* was the one being unreasonable? He hadn't even said a word. "Need I remind you of our bargain?" he hissed. "Because if you continue to bark orders at me like a servant, I'll be tempted to slit the throats of these filthy mortals."

Prue shot him a look of disgust but said nothing else.

Cyrus expected the crowd to thin as they ventured farther from the dock, but bodies continued to press against him, the chatter and commotion grating against his ears. They reached a bazaar filled with tables and stands displaying the most vibrant jewelry and clothes. The smell of spiced meat and ale filled the air, no doubt coming from a nearby tavern. Beyond the crowd, Cyrus could make out the peaks of towering buildings that stretched toward the darkening sky. The wrought-iron balconies and ornate pillars spoke of the supposed grandeur of Voula City, and it made Cyrus want to laugh.

This city might have been more elegant and populous than Prue's tiny island village, but it was certainly not grand or impressive. Not compared to his throne in Styx.

"There," Prue said, pointing to a sign on one of the buildings. "An inn. We can stay there for the night."

"I thought you said we would only be getting supplies."

"It's almost dusk. Even if we wanted to travel overnight, there would be very few carriage drivers willing to make the journey for us."

Cyrus sighed. What he wouldn't give for his magic, which could easily whisk him from one domain to the next without a thought.

But, unfortunately, Prue still had complete control of his magic. The frustration and fury that rippled through him only fueled his determination: *Seduce the witch. Consummate the bond. Get your magic back.*

They elbowed their way past the throng—Cyrus wanting nothing more than to blast these incessant humans into oblivion with his dark flames—until they finally reached the inn. A bell tinkled as they opened the door, and blessed silence greeted them when they stepped through. The air was warm and near stifling, but at least there weren't any people around. Cyrus strode deeper, examining the foyer with interest. Architectural paintings hung on the walls, and several armchairs surrounded a small fireplace. On the opposite side of the room sat a desk, behind which an elderly, portly man sat, watching them in curiosity.

"Good evening," he said, his voice smooth. "How can I assist you?"

"We'd like a room please," Cyrus said before Prue could answer. He drew closer to the desk, sensing Prue's alarm behind him.

"One room?" The man's eyebrows raised as he glanced between them.

"Yes." Cyrus forced a smile, and the expression felt foreign on his face. He gazed at Prue with what he hoped was a look of fondness and admiration, ignoring the thunderous anger burning in her gaze. "We've just gotten married, you see."

Prue's face paled, but the man's eyes widened, his face splitting into a wide grin. "Oh, my! Congratulations to the happy couple. I have the perfect lodgings for you." He bustled through some drawers before removing a large brass key. He shuffled out from behind the desk. "Follow me, please!"

Prue swatted Cyrus's shoulder and hissed, "*Married*?"

"We are, aren't we?" Cyrus shrugged, fighting back a smile at the outrage in her expression as they followed the innkeeper down the hall. He led them up two flights of stairs and down another narrow hall, past several rooms, before they reached a large oak door, much grander than the ones they'd passed before. Without preamble, the man unlocked the door and swung it open with a flourish.

A massive canopy bed took up most of the room, decorated with delicate white curtains and a heap of fluffy pillows. An antique wardrobe rested opposite the bed, and along the wall stood a wide window displaying a perfect view of the city, the buildings twinkling in the light of the setting sun.

Cyrus couldn't help but feel impressed. Yes, the room was small, but the furnishings were elaborate, and he imagined the view was quite spectacular during the day.

"The room is ten gold pieces, if it's to your liking." The innkeeper adopted a humble expression, but Cyrus detected the greed in his eyes.

Prue shot Cyrus a look that said, *This is your fault*, before she withdrew her coin pouch and paid the man. The innkeeper bowed, offering a sly grin—as if he was imagining exactly what they would be up to tonight—before departing from the room.

LOVERS

PRUE

"MARRIED," Prue grumbled. "Honestly."

"I believe I was perfectly clear with you how I felt about lying," Cyrus said.

"Yes, but if you had let *me* do the talking, I could've told the man we were siblings or something."

"Siblings?" Cyrus laughed and gestured between them. "Who in their right mind would believe we were siblings?"

Prue scowled, refusing to admit he was right. Between his white hair and paleness and her brown skin and black curls, they couldn't have been more different. But her stubbornness took over, and she said, "Regardless, if you'd let me handle it, I could've ensured we hadn't spent so much money on this ostentatious lovers' suite!"

Cyrus raised his eyebrows with a smirk. "A lovers' suite? Gods, you mortals . . ." He chuckled, shaking his head.

"What?" Prue demanded, uncertain if it was his condescension or his ploy with the innkeeper that infuriated her more. "Do you not have lovers in the Underworld? Because that sounds like a rather sad life to me."

Irritation flickered in his eyes. "Of course we have lovers."

Prue snorted. "With whom? Demons?"

Cyrus's gaze turned cold, but he said nothing.

Prue's mouth fell open. "I'm right, aren't I? You sleep with *demons*!"

"I don't see how it's any of your business." Cyrus's tone was clipped as he turned his gaze away from her, pretending to stare out the window instead.

"And you have the gall to turn your nose up at humans?" Prue barked out a laugh. "That's pitiful indeed, Cyrus."

"In case it escaped your notice, *witch*," Cyrus spat, "the options for bedmates in the Underworld are rather slim. Unless I wish to bed my father or one of my brothers, then it's the demons I must settle for."

Prue stilled at the bitterness in his voice. He still wouldn't look at her, but she detected resentment and grief in his silver eyes. She knew by now he used anger to deflect his emotions. But what exactly was he hiding?

Had he loved someone once before? Did he miss her? Or him? Prue honestly couldn't tell what his preference was, though judging by the way he'd looked at her when she'd first summoned him, she assumed he preferred women.

"What's it like?" Prue forced herself to ask. "Being with a demon, I mean. Do they . . . have human bodies? Like you?"

"My body is not human. *Your* mortal forms are mirrored after the gods, not the other way around. But . . . yes. Some demons have bodies like mine. Many of them have horns. Some have tails and claws and snouts." He cut her a dark look. "Taking a lover is not nearly as romantic as you humans wish it to be."

"Well, obviously, when you have so few options," Prue said with a scoff. "I mean, it can't be pleasant to kiss a woman with a *snout*."

"Who said anything about kissing?" Cyrus seemed genuinely confused.

Prue's stomach turned as she pictured Cyrus taking a tumble with a woman with tusks and a snout like a boar. A bedmate and nothing more. Someone to offer momentarily release. To satisfy a carnal need. That was all it was.

Prue's throat felt tight. She'd only had one lover, but their time together had been . . . passionate. Liberating. Intoxicating. With each dalliance, she'd only wanted more of him.

She couldn't imagine Cyrus's life—to seek out a bedmate out of necessity only, not pleasure or desire. Nothing more than a task to accomplish.

"Don't look at me like that," Cyrus growled.

"Like what?"

"Like you pity me."

"Maybe I do." Prue shrugged, turning away from him.

"You know *nothing* about me or my life," Cyrus spat. "I have—"

"Yes, yes, I know, you have heaps of power, an abundance of unholy magic and authority," Prue said in a bored voice. "You've mentioned it a few times. But I don't care how much power you possess, Cyrus. That still seems like a sad life to me."

"You speak to *me* of a sad life? What about you, the supposed Maiden of a powerful coven, blessed by the Triple Goddess? But you can't even cast a summoning spell without botching it. You can't perform a banishment without assistance. So, where is all this *great power* you supposedly possess? Why are you so useless? So incompetent? Oh, yes, I know—because you're plagued by guilt because *you're* the reason your sister is dead."

Prue went utterly still, her insides chilling in horror and anguish. Silence screamed inside her mind as time seemed to freeze for a full second. Nothing moved. She couldn't even breathe.

When her heart finally started beating once more,

she turned to look at him. His eyes were dark with fury and venom. She supposed she'd brought this upon herself in provoking him. She already knew he was ruthless and unfeeling.

Even so . . . his words rang true. She *was* useless and incompetent. Mostly because she had no desire to explore the extent of her magic. Once, she had yearned to expand her powers, to learn new gifts, to strengthen her grace. But when Mona had died, her magic had been absorbed by Prue, fueling her power as the Maiden.

And ever since then, every time Prue cast a spell, she felt sick to her stomach, knowing her dead sister's aura was fueling each enchantment, each incantation, each simple conjuring. How, in good conscience, could she continue to perform magic as if it were her own? As if it didn't belong to someone else?

At long last, Prue found her voice, and it sounded hollow to her ears. "You don't know anything about me, Cyrus." It was all she could manage before she disappeared into the bathing chamber, blocking him out entirely.

AN HOUR LATER, after Prue had bathed and washed her tangled mess of curls, she emerged from the bathing chamber in nothing but her underdress, only to find Cyrus stretched out on the bed.

Completely naked.

Of course. Had she really expected anything different? This man, this *god*, believed he owned everyone and everything. Why should he have to worry about anything like decency or respect or chivalry?

Prue should have balked at his nudity and all the parts she did *not* wish to see—particularly the lengthy breadth of his manhood, which was far bigger than she thought possible for anyone, god or no. But instead, she strode right up to the bed and reclined alongside him. To her immense satisfaction, Cyrus stiffened beside her.

"What are you doing?" he asked, his voice low and dangerous.

"What does it look like I'm doing? I'm going to sleep." Prue nestled herself into the sheets, her body turned away from him as she sighed against the softness of the pillows beneath her. At least the bed was large enough for them not to touch. Even so, she could feel his warmth emanating from the other side.

When Cyrus didn't answer, Prue added, "Did you expect me to lie down on the floor? Or perhaps spend the night in the bathing chamber?"

Cyrus grumbled something unintelligible. The bed shifted as he turned, no doubt to face away from her like she was. Without another word, Prue lifted her head to blow out the candle on the table beside her. Cyrus's, however, remained lit. But that was fine. Prue could easily sleep even with the light gleaming from the other side of the room.

As Prue's breaths fell into a steadier rhythm, she buried her face deeper into the pillow, wishing more than anything to block out the image of her sister's vacant and lifeless expression. It haunted her daily. A never-ending reminder of her failure.

"How did you know?" Prue whispered, unable to stop herself.

Cyrus didn't answer for so long that she wondered if he'd fallen asleep, despite his claim that gods didn't sleep. But after a long moment, he murmured, "Know what?"

"That I'm responsible for her death. I never told you that."

Cyrus exhaled a long, slow breath before responding. "I can smell her death on you. You keep it shrouded over yourself like a cloak. Like you don't know who you are without it."

Prue's chest hollowed out at his words. His voice was so soft, almost tender, that it didn't sound like him at all. As if the arrogant ass she'd been stuck with for the past day had vanished, to be replaced by this all-knowing and yet gentle being beside her. She wasn't sure what to say. For one thing, she had underestimated his power, despite how often he reminded her of it. He perceived more than she realized.

Because he was right. Prue kept her grief close because she needed it. It was the only thing keeping her going. Keeping her alive.

Prue sniffed, her eyes feeling hot. "I thought you didn't sleep." Her voice was thick, and she swallowed hard.

"I don't. But it doesn't mean I don't desire rest every now and then."

Prue nodded, even though he couldn't see her. She crammed her eyes shut, willing her mind to be silenced so she could sleep. Though her body was weary down to her bones, her mind was a chaotic swirl of emotion and thought.

"You were right," Cyrus said suddenly.

Prue cleared her throat. "About what?"

"I *do* live a sad life. An isolated life. And I do envy you humans in that regard. You . . . are never alone. I wish I could have that, too."

Prue's mouth opened, her heart jolting in surprise at his words. It was the most earnest thing he had ever said to her. And the spell that bound them together told her he wasn't lying. She was absolutely dumbfounded that he would expose this side of himself.

Before he could lash out upon discovering he'd made himself too vulnerable, Prue said, "Sometimes we *are* alone. Even when we're surrounded by other people, we can still be utterly and completely alone." She paused, then went on, "Like my mother. We both lost Mona. You'd think that would bring us together, but it only drove us farther apart."

"How so?" Cyrus seemed genuinely intrigued.

"Mama and I never got along. She always accused me of not taking my gifts or my responsibilities seriously. I know in her heart she wishes I'd died instead of Mona. She's never said so, but somehow I can feel her resentment and disappointment in the daughter I've become. That presence stretches between us, growing more every day. We had a strained relationship before, but now it's . . . intolerable."

"Hmm." The sound was a low rumble in Cyrus's throat. "I know a thing or two about insufferable relatives."

"Your brothers?" Against her better judgment, Prue found herself shifting so she lay on her back, her eyes fixed on the ceiling. She didn't dare turn her head to look at Cyrus, though he seemed much closer than he had been before.

"Yes. And my father."

Prue waited for him to go on, but he said nothing.

"It's okay," she murmured, "to be vulnerable once in a while. I won't judge you for it."

Still, Cyrus said nothing, but she felt his steady breaths beside her.

"I'll still think of you as the same powerful, arrogant asshole I know you to be," Prue added.

Cyrus laughed. The sound was so rich and deep that Prue couldn't help her own smile. She hadn't heard him laugh like that since he'd been in the crypt with her, having just realized they were married.

Goddess. *Married.* And here she was, sharing a bed with him for the first time. Her cheeks heated at the thought. Obviously, nothing would happen, but . . .

Prue frowned as she realized something. "You do realize that if we . . . you know, consummate our marriage, then you'll have access to your powers again, right?"

"I know."

"Then . . ."

He turned to look at her, but she couldn't meet his gaze. She heard the amusement in his voice when he asked, "Are you offering?"

Her face was on fire now. "*No.* I'm just saying, you strike me as someone who takes what he wants without asking. So . . ."

"Are you asking me why I haven't raped you?" His voice turned cold.

Prue flinched at the words. "Obviously, I'm glad you haven't. But *why*? I'm nothing to you, right? I know you're already sick of this arrangement."

"There are some lines even I wouldn't cross." Cyrus's

voice was still sharp, as if he were offended that she was even asking this.

"But you would slit the throats of random strangers? Your lines are really vague, then."

"There is a difference between death and pain. To me, death is not so much a punishment as a passage to another realm. It can be painless. My thoughts of murdering others were not as cold-hearted as you would believe. More than anything, I just wanted to ensure they were out of my path for the foreseeable future. That is all. But . . . pain? Trauma? No. I would not inflict that on anyone." He paused. "Unless they deserved it."

Prue would have laughed, but his voice hardened with a sharp edge that made her believe he had someone specific in mind for that kind of torment. He was the god of the dead, after all; torture was his specialty.

Her mouth went dry as she finally turned her head on the pillow to look at him. His luminescent eyes shone in the darkness, two glowing orbs that burned brighter than the fading candle behind him. She had briefly wondered if it was uncomfortable to lie down when he had horns, but they rested comfortably on the pillows behind him.

For just the briefest of moments, she let herself imagine what it would be like to hear him growl her name in that low, throaty voice he often used when angry, to run her fingers along his horns, to feel his hands caress her body, or to feel his cock moving inside her . . .

Startled, Prue blinked, realizing she'd gone too far with her thoughts. Blushing, she shifted slightly on the bed, trying to ignore the ache between her legs as she forced her thoughts elsewhere.

Suddenly, Cyrus was looking at her, too, his eyes burning as if he could read her thoughts. She sucked in a breath, every inch of her aware of how close he was to her. If she moved slightly, her bare foot would touch his. Or her arm might brush against his chest.

The thought of his skin on hers made her stomach turn to knots, so she quickly looked away. Her breathing was sharp and fast as she whispered a hasty, "Good night."

"PRUE," a voice murmured.

Prue's eyes flew open, her heart thundering. For one wild moment, she thought Cyrus was whispering to her. But when she turned to look at him, her mouth fell open.

He was asleep. His bare chest rose and fell with long, slow breaths. Prue wasn't at all surprised to find he even scowled in his sleep.

So much for gods not sleeping, she thought with a smirk.

"Prue," the voice said again.

Now fully awake, Prue could finally place the voice, and she shot bolt upright as awareness flooded her mind. Sure enough, standing at the foot of the bed, her pearly form transparent and haunting, stood Mona.

"Mona," Prue breathed, relief flooding her chest. She'd feared something had happened to her sister's spirit during Samhain. "Are you all right?"

Mona's form flickered. "N-no. Prue, something is . . . happening."

Alarm flared in Prue's body, making her blood chill. "What's wrong? What is it?"

"I can't get to you as often as I could before. And . . . down here, things are . . . bad." Her luminescent figure rippled again as if she were a flame amidst a storm, on the brink of dying out entirely.

"Bad *how*?" Prue had complained often of Mona's inability to articulate when she was frightened. This instance was no exception. "Mona, I need you to tell me more. What's going on?"

"The Underworld . . . is dying. The s-souls are fading. *I'm* fading."

"Mona." Prue's voice rose with panic. "What does that mean? What can I do?"

"The gods here, they are toying with forces that should not be meddled with. The delicate fabric binding this realm together is coming apart from their scheming." Mona's voice gained strength, her studious tone returning as she described the realm.

Cyrus's brothers, Prue thought in realization. They were destroying his home while he was stuck in the mortal realm. "I'm on my way to you, Mona. Just hold on."

Mona shook her head. "It's happening *now*, Prue. Here. They are coming for you."

HUNT

CYRUS

A WHITE GLOW burned against Cyrus's eyes. The orb of a wayward soul floated before him, capturing his attention. This soul was . . . different. He could sense power emanating from it, unlike the souls of most mortals. A witch perhaps?

Gods, he was so sick of witches.

But that wasn't it . . . This soul was untethered. Unbound. Instead of being linked to the Underworld, as most souls were, this one was free.

And it was dying.

Well, not so much dying, as fading. Souls were already dead. But their essence, their aura, continued to live on after their mortal death. This one, however, had an aura as feeble as a feather.

"What happened to you?" Cyrus murmured.

A cry resonated from the orb, burning through

Cyrus's skull until his ears throbbed. He groaned, shutting his eyes against the tormented wail, the screams of anguish . . .

Cyrus's eyes flew open. Light streamed in through the curtains, bathing the room in a soft morning glow. He blinked, his mind strangely muddled. His limbs felt stiff and awkward. He shifted, then froze.

Prue lay atop him, her head resting against his chest, her curly hair sprawled around them both. Her steady, slow breaths indicated she was still asleep.

Oh, gods. Not only had Cyrus actually slept, but he had slept with Prue. Like this. Like *lovers*.

Uncertain if he should be mortified or furious, he carefully extricated himself from her embrace. His skin felt warm and sticky, and he wanted nothing more than to cleanse himself. How could this have happened? He was an immortal. He wasn't supposed to need things like sleep or sustenance. This wretched place must have been rubbing off on him.

Cyrus tried moving as gently as possible so as not to wake the witch—though he had no idea why—but his efforts were in vain. She moaned slightly in her sleep, eliciting a coil of heat in Cyrus's belly. He glanced down at his nakedness and swore at the stiff member that Prue would certainly taunt. He snatched his trousers and hoisted them up just as she rubbed her eyes and squinted at him.

"Mona?" Her voice was a croak, but it wasn't entirely

unpleasant. It was raspy and deeper than her usual timbre. Then, her eyes widened and she sat bolt upright. "Mona!"

Cyrus stared at her, frowning as she brushed strands of hair out of her face. Her shoulders rose and fell with heavy breaths as awareness settled in her expression. "It was . . . a dream. Just a dream." She sagged backwards with a deep exhale, then turned to scrutinize Cyrus. "You're awake."

"Astute observation," he said dryly, while fetching his shirt. Just before donning it, he sniffed it and recoiled. "That's awful."

"I know." Prue yawned and sat up. "That's why we'll be stocking up on supplies while we're here. We need more than just one outfit."

"Well, hopefully we can get something more fitting. These peasant clothes itch like hell."

"You're such a snob."

"I'm a *god.*"

"Are you?" She pressed a hand to her chest in mock surprise. "I had *no* idea."

Cyrus just shook his head, his brain too muddled to manage a snarky reply. He finished buttoning his trousers and noticed Prue staring at the window, her gaze solemn and distant. She gnawed on her lower lip, her expression troubled.

Cyrus wanted to ask what was wrong, but he worried

he would seem affectionate if he did so. But it wasn't affection that urged him; it was burning curiosity. A dark, haunted look shadowed her gaze. Her mindless blathering about her sister and a bad dream made him wonder if *his* dream had actually been real. *Had* something happened last night? Had that strange orb visited them both?

Had it been Mona?

Prue blinked, suddenly waking from her stupor as she caught Cyrus staring at her. "I—" She broke off, as if changing her mind about speaking.

"What is it?" Cyrus tried to put as much softness in his voice as he could muster.

Prue took a breath, paused, and then tried again. "Is something . . . wrong in the Underworld?"

Cyrus went perfectly still, though his chest thrummed in response. His throat closed, and he couldn't speak or breathe for a moment. After swallowing hard, he managed, "What makes you say that?"

Prue bit her lip again and dropped her gaze.

Cyrus tried another approach. He took a step closer to the bed and dropped to his knees so they were at eye level. "Prue, that's my home. If you know something, I beg of you to tell me." Did it have to do with Aidoneus poisoning Acheron? Was it worse? What else were his father and brothers up to?

He thought of Vasileios, his oldest brother—the one he had stolen the throne from. If anyone had a right to hate Cyrus, it was Vasileios. How far would he go to take his revenge on Cyrus?

Prue stared at him, her eyes shining. Shock crossed her face as she glanced over him, kneeling before her. “You’re . . . *begging* me?” A touch of amusement filled her voice.

Cyrus suppressed a groan. Of course she would take this moment to tease him. “It’s my home,” he said again.

Prue’s humor faded, and she nodded in understanding. Cyrus knew she thought of her own village being terrorized by ghosts. Certainly a sobering thought. With a deep breath, Prue said, “My sister’s ghost visited me last night. In a dream.”

Cyrus’s skin prickled, and an echo of his magic pulsed inside him as if responding to the knowledge that a spirit had indeed been here. A million questions raced through his mind, but he forced himself to ask, “What did she look like?”

“A transparent version of my sister.” Prue’s voice sounded incredulous.

Of course. Cyrus forgot that to mere mortals, spirits looked different. To him, they were orbs. But they could manifest themselves into different forms depending on the sight of the beholder. “And . . . did she do or say anything?”

Prue wet her lips and dropped her gaze, wringing her hands together on the bed. But she didn’t answer.

Cyrus tried a different question. "Prue, has she visited you before?"

Slowly, Prue nodded.

Shit. "How long? How long has this been happening?"

Prue looked up at the alarm in his voice. "I—I don't know. A few weeks? Maybe a month?"

Cyrus ran a hand through his hair, his fingers grazing over his horns. Gods, this was bad. This was very bad.

"What?" Prue demanded. "Cyrus, what does this mean?"

"It means something *is* wrong with the Underworld. If your sister's spirit is still here, then she didn't pass over as she should have. Either something is broken in the rivers of Hell, or . . . something is wrong with your sister's soul." He didn't want to tell her what he knew—that Acheron was already broken, if not destroyed. Was that why Mona's spirit was visiting Prue? Because of what Aidoneus had done?

Was this Cyrus's fault? If his father hadn't been trying to overthrow him, this wouldn't have happened.

Prue jumped to her feet, her hair wild and massive around her head. Her eyes grew wide, and her face drained of color. "W-what? My sister's *soul*? What does that mean? How do we fix it? I—I—"

Her face crumpled, and Cyrus couldn't stop himself. He closed the distance between them, then faltered.

What was he about to do? Embrace her? The thought was absurd. Already half-committed to the idea, he settled with placing his hands on her shoulders instead, which shook with trembling sobs. This fierce, stubborn, powerful witch seemed broken before him, and he couldn't stand it. He would much prefer she yell or throw insults at him. But not this. His insides twisted at the sight of her. His throat tightened, his chest constricting as if he couldn't breathe.

Why did he feel like this? Perhaps he was simply horrified by her pathetic show of weakness. Disgusted, really. That was all. That was why he wanted to put a stop to it. Nothing more.

His thumbs traced circles along her shoulders, the motion almost unconscious, as he said softly, "We will fix this. We are heading to the gate already. We can't do anything about it in this realm, but once we are there, we can fix this. I promise."

Prue covered her face with her hands and wept further. Between sobs, she whispered, "She s-said . . . the Underworld is d-dying. And she's . . . fading."

Panic welled in Cyrus's chest. His home was *dying*? "What else did she say?"

Quickly, Prue filled him in on all her sister had spoken the night before, though it hadn't been much. But Cyrus's attention snagged on one thing: *they are toying with forces that should not be meddled with.* His brothers were indeed destroying their home just to punish Cyrus. They were willing to go that far.

Evander, the brother closest to Cyrus, would never do anything to harm the Underworld. Romanos wouldn't, either. They were both far too reasonable for that.

But the others? With the strength of Aidoneus and the wrath of Vasileios—yes, they certainly could. A force like that could easily tear apart the Underworld.

Prue lowered her hands, her face streaming with tears as she looked at him. "What's going on? What are your brothers doing?"

Cyrus closed his eyes and heaved a sigh. "They poisoned the river Acheron. It was the one thing linking me to the Underworld. They hope to sever me completely from my home. But . . . in the process, the river of souls is dying."

Prue's mouth fell open. "So . . . you can't get back home?" She took a step back from him. "Have you been lying to me this whole time? We're here traveling together, and you can't even get *in* to the Underworld?"

"No, no," Cyrus said hastily. "I can still get in, I just . . . may not be able to stay for long. The Book of Eyes must remain in the mortal realm. And with the river poisoned, that book is now the strongest anchor attached to me. I will be pulled to the mortal realm the instant I set foot in the Underworld. But I will fix this, Prue. I will find a way to tether myself to the rivers again." He shook his head. "I haven't lied to you. You know I can't."

Prue swallowed and drew in a shuddering breath. "All right." She blinked, awareness crossing her features. She took in his arms, still outstretched as if to grasp her shoulders again. Then she glanced down at herself and took another step back.

Cyrus abruptly dropped his arms, realizing what she had: he had touched her. He had *comforted* her. Not a drop of animosity between them. What the hell was the matter with him?

Cyrus cleared his throat and rubbed his jaw. "Right. Well. We should go get those supplies, then."

"Yes," Prue said quickly. Too quickly. She snatched her dress from the floor and disappeared into the bathing chamber, leaving Cyrus feeling like a damned fool.

VOULA CITY WAS JUST as tiresome during the day as it was at night. Even with the morning sun illuminating the rise of buildings around them, it didn't erase the stink of the passersby or the cramped feeling of walking alongside thousands of people on the street. Gods, Cyrus missed his isolated domain in the Underworld.

Prue kept a swift pace as if hoping to lose him in the

crowd. Cyrus got the feeling she was embarrassed by what had happened in their room, though he wasn't even sure what *had* happened. They'd shared a bed, but somehow she was more mortified that he had comforted her than anything else. Then again, he couldn't blame her. He *was* a monster. Practically a demon in her eyes. Even if he was a prince where he came from, the horns and the overall frightening facade he wore would be enough to make anyone recoil.

It only made him harden his resolve. She might have technically been his wife, but he didn't care what she thought. Yes, it would have been easier to woo her if she didn't see him as something revolting, but that was only a minor obstacle. All he needed was one moment of weakness, one night with too much wine and seduction . . . and her power would be his.

Then, he would get back through the gate without issue. He just knew that with her power, he would be unstoppable. Never mind what his father and brothers were doing to his realm. Never mind that he was no longer tethered to Acheron. Nothing would stop him. Nothing.

Not even Vasileios and his petty idea of vengeance. Cyrus could silence him for good, ending him from existence so he would never be a threat again.

Once they reached a men's clothing shop, Prue pressed several coins into Cyrus's hands. She snatched his wrist before he walked off.

"I'm not giving you any more than this, all right? Find yourself some decent clothes, but nothing too extravagant." She raised her eyebrows as if knowing he planned to buy the finest suit he could find.

"You know, I could just frighten the shit out of the shop owner to coerce him into giving me what I want." He offered a roguish grin.

Prue rolled her eyes. "Be inconspicuous, remember? Do you really want the mortals coming after you?"

"Let them try."

"Yes, and it will make our journey even *slower* if the authorities are searching for us." She fixed a stern gaze on him.

He lifted his hands in mock surrender, half his fingers still curled over the coins she gave him. "I'll be the picture of civility."

She gave him a doubtful look before turning and leaving for the dress shop across the street. Cyrus watched her for a moment, the way her curls bobbed behind her with each stride. He wasn't sure why he was so fixated on her departure. After a moment, he shook his head and strode into the shop.

An hour later, he emerged, grumbling at the persistence of the shop attendants trying to squeeze every last coin from him. It was a miracle he escaped with a suit and two tunics without shedding any blood.

He scanned the crowd for Prue. Something tugged within him, and he groaned, clutching at his chest.

Ignoring the odd looks of the passersby, he glanced around more urgently. Where was Prue?

The pull inside him yanked more insistently, drawing him forward a few steps. He staggered, and several women in fine dresses gasped loudly at his jerky movements.

Cyrus straightened, alarm pulsing through him. Something was wrong.

Without another thought, he sprinted forward, shoving past the clueless mortals who kept getting in his way. He reached the dress shop, but that unknown *thing* tugged him onward, past the shop and toward the alley where the two buildings met. He didn't hesitate; didn't even question this feeling inside him. He darted into the alley to find a hooded figure slashing daggers at Prue, who wielded vines from her fingers as if spinning string. Her vines wrapped around the man's ankles, holding him in place while she shoved her elbow into his gut, then stomped on his foot.

Cyrus's eyebrows lifted. Well, at least she wasn't *completely* helpless.

But the man spun, ducking to avoid another one of her jabs. A few of the vines at his feet tore with his movement, and he slid his foot under Prue's legs, tripping her. She came crashing down, and a pallet of soft grass rose up from the ground to soften her fall. The daggers glinted in the sunlight as the man's fingers spun with finesse and skill. Regardless of the power of Prue's magic, she lacked the fighting skills to best him.

Dropping his bags, Cyrus surged forward, tackling the man from behind. The assailant grunted as Cyrus held him in a chokehold. Prue's knee connected with the attacker's groin, but he didn't even flinch.

Was this thing even a man at all? Unless . . .

Just as Cyrus put the pieces together, shadows bled from the ground, snaking toward Prue.

"Prue!" Cyrus shouted, but it was too late. The inky blackness reached her toes, and she fell to her knees with an anguished scream. The darkness climbed up her foot, trying to claim the rest of her body.

Cyrus knew this darkness well. It would eat at her flesh and bones until it had consumed her entirely.

"My magic!" Cyrus bellowed. The man wriggled, trying to get free, but Cyrus held fast. "Give it to me, Prue!"

When she continued to do nothing but scream, Cyrus roared, "*Now!*"

"It's yours!" she screamed. "Take it! Just take it!"

Cyrus swore. How could she give him his magic back if she wasn't even coherent enough to use her own? But, miraculously, fire swelled in his chest as if responding to her words. And with his power came something . . . else. A roar of anger and resentment rumbled in Cyrus's mind, making his vision go dark for the briefest of moments.

Cyrus didn't know how, but he somehow knew it was his death magic. His own powers were raging against him, as if angry they had been restrained for too long.

What in all the realms of Hell was going on? Since when did his magic have a mind of its own?

But he didn't have time to focus on it. Mercifully, his vision cleared, and he snapped into action. He shoved the assailant forward before unleashing his dark flames on him. Fire pooled from his hands like water, smothering the attacker's body. A feral growl, followed by a shrill scream, filled the air as Cyrus's magic scorched the man. Cyrus bared his teeth, reveling in the hungry roar growing inside him with each push of his flame. The magic yearned to be let out, to burn this man to a crisp until he was nothing more than a smoking husk.

Prue let out a cry of anguish, snapping Cyrus out of his vengeful haze. He halted his attack on the man, who whimpered feebly in response, and hurried over to Prue. The shadows had crept past her ankle and were now climbing up her shin. She clutched her leg, clawing at the darkness as if she could pry it off her skin by force, but Cyrus knew it was impossible.

Only one thing could chase away the darkness: Cyrus's fire.

Cyrus shot a jet of black flame straight at Prue's foot. She screamed again, her face contorting with agony and pain. Tears streamed down her face. But, just as he expected, the shadows receded, repelled by Cyrus's magic.

As soon as the darkness disappeared, Cyrus was inspecting her foot, his movements slow and gentle so as not to exacerbate the injury. He hadn't sent a full blast of power, so, thankfully, her skin was still intact. Just singed. It would heal.

"Are you all right?" he murmured, looking into her eyes to ensure the shadows hadn't claimed her elsewhere.

Prue didn't answer. Her face was wet from crying, and she hissed a breath through her teeth. Though her eyes swam with tears, they drilled into him with all the force of her fury.

Scuffling footsteps drew his attention to the mouth of the alley. The assailant had scrambled to his feet and darted away, but not before Cyrus caught sight of the tail slithering from underneath his cloak.

Shit. It definitely *hadn't* been a man. It had been a demon from the Underworld.

FEARS

PRUE

HE BURNED HER. He'd actually *burned* her. As soon as he'd gotten his magic back, he'd used it on her.

Goddess, she was so stupid.

"I can heal that," Cyrus muttered.

"It wouldn't need to be healed if you hadn't burned me," Prue snapped as she hobbled along the sidewalk toward the apothecary. "Besides, I already took your magic away again. I'll heal it myself once we find a carriage driver."

Cyrus opened his mouth to argue, but Prue silenced him with a scathing look. She wasn't sure how his magic could come and go with nothing but a word from her, but she wasn't about to question it, not when she could render him powerless with a mere thought.

After spending several minutes haggling and emerging from the apothecary with far less than she'd hoped to buy, Prue found herself in an even worse mood than before. Curse this wretched place and its high prices. She yearned for the simple markets in Krenia, where everyone offered their wares for a fair exchange. Voula City, however, was full of nothing but greed and deception.

Just like Cyrus.

Prue was a fool. An utter and complete fool.

"You saw those shadows, right?" Cyrus asked in an undertone.

"Not now," Prue hissed, glancing over her shoulder. Truth be told, she just wasn't in the mood to discuss this with him. But it *was* smart to keep quiet just in case other assailants lurked nearby.

Prue used the last of her coin to secure passage in a carriage headed for the Emdale Mountains. She stared for a moment at her now empty coin pouch, wondering how in the hell they would make it all the way to Faidon when they had no money. But as the coachman readied their carriage, she shook away her fears. Even if they had to go without food for a day, they could make it. Faidon was on the other side of the Emdale Mountains.

They could make it. They had to.

Cyrus helped her into the carriage, and the pain in her ankle was so severe that she didn't object. When she collapsed in her seat, Cyrus clambered in after her before shutting the door. To her surprise, he took the seat right next to her instead of the one across from her.

Startled at his sudden nearness, she tried to scoot away from him, but he stared at her intently.

"I didn't burn you to hurt you," he said, his voice earnest. "I did it to frighten off the death shadows."

Prue stared at him. The coachman above them shouted something, and the carriage lurched into motion. Prue's arms flung out in alarm, one of them catching Cyrus's shoulder. But as the vehicle settled into a more soothing rhythm, she relaxed, only to find Cyrus smirking at her.

"What?" she snapped. "I don't suppose you've been in many carriages in the Underworld, have you?"

He only snorted, shaking his head at her.

"Death shadows," she repeated. "What is that?"

Cyrus immediately sobered. "Essence of a particular demon. A wraith."

Prue went very still, the color draining from her face.

"You've heard of them?"

Slowly, she nodded. "The wraith is what came out of the Book of Eyes just before . . . just before Mona died." She closed her eyes, gritting her teeth in frustration. She should've recognized those shadows immediately. That same eerie darkness had chased after them in Krenia, too.

It had killed so many. Including Mona.

Prue shivered and rubbed her arms, gazing out the window at the brick buildings they passed. "So, what does this mean? Did it come from the Underworld, or from the book?"

"I'm not sure." Cyrus hesitated, and Prue looked at him with suspicion. When he caught her gaze, he added, "Vasileios, my eldest brother, often uses wraiths as his subordinates. My first thought was that he sent one after me."

"You mean after *me*."

Cyrus froze, his eyes widening slightly.

"That wraith cornered *me* in the alley."

Cyrus rubbed the back of his neck. "Shit, you're right." His gaze turned distant, his jaw working back and forth. "Why would he be after *you*?" The words were nothing more than a whisper, as if he were asking himself more than anything.

"Maybe he's threatened by our bond? Maybe he knows I could potentially gain your power?"

Cyrus rubbed his chin. "It's definitely a possibility. But it would make more sense to kill *me* instead. I'm powerless, and then our bond would die, too." He shook his head, frustration glinting in his eyes. "It doesn't make any sense."

Prue heaved a sigh and sank backward against the cushions. "I'm sorry. You know, for assuming you were trying to attack me."

Cyrus shot her a rueful look. "I would've assumed the same. All is forgiven." He held her gaze, his silver eyes probing as if searching for more in her face. She met his stare head-on, unabashed and unafraid, trying to ignore the restless stirring in her stomach at the intensity burning in his eyes.

Prue wasn't sure which one of them looked away first, but they both turned to gaze out their respective windows as the buildings melted into open plains and vast farmlands. Prue stared wistfully at the rows of crops, reminiscent of the small farming lands in Krenia. Were her mother and Sybil all right? Was the magical barrier still protecting the village?

A long while passed, and when the agony pulsing from her ankle was too much to bear, Prue sifted through the ingredients she'd bought from the apothecary. She dabbed her ankle with the lavender oil, hissing in pain as the wound throbbed, then sprinkled rosemary and sage over it. When she waved her hand over her foot, vines crept in from the corners of the carriage. How they managed to grow and follow a *moving* vehicle, Prue had no idea.

"*Integro,*" Prue whispered. The space between her hand and her ankle shimmered, and heat burned into her foot. She gritted her teeth against the intensity of it, staring instead at her vines, which had multiplied, creating almost a thick carpet of ivy along the carriage floor. Her magic swelled, and rosebuds popped up among the ivy.

Prue sucked in a breath, thinking immediately of her sister. Roses had been Mona's grace.

Gradually, the heat in her foot subsided, her magic receding back into her. The ivy snaked out of the carriage, and the rosebuds vanished, leaving a hollow feeling inside her chest.

"Remarkable," Cyrus murmured.

Prue blinked and turned to him. She'd completely forgotten he was there. He watched the last of the vines slither away with a look of awe on his face.

Prue didn't know what to say. She'd never seen him look like that before. Power-hungry, yes. Smug and satisfied, yes. Enraged, yes. But never . . . *awestruck.*

He turned to look at her, fixing that strange new emotion on her face. She resisted the urge to fidget under his gaze.

"Your magic is incredible," Cyrus said. "You know that, right?"

Prue felt even more uncomfortable. "I suppose." Truth be told, she'd never liked her magic, even when Mona was alive. The constant presence of vines was an irritant, completely unhelpful in every way. And then, after Mona's death, the sudden appearance of roses seemed like a mockery, announcing to the world that Mona was gone and Prue had stolen her magic.

She couldn't stand any of it.

"I've never seen a witch perform a healing spell so effortlessly," Cyrus said, staring at her ankle as if expecting it to suddenly start spasming.

Prue frowned. "You can't have met many witches, then."

Cyrus scoffed. "How would you know? I've been around plenty. Many of them had to rely on other coven members to perform *that* kind of healing." He gestured to her foot.

Prue shrugged without meeting his gaze. "My mother does it all the time."

"Does she?"

Prue looked at him. Cyrus had a single eyebrow arched in obvious doubt.

She crossed her arms. "What's that supposed to mean?"

"I just think it's strange that you and your mother possess this great source of power, but no one finds it odd. Your coven simply goes along with it as if it's ordinary."

"I'm the Maiden and she's the Mother," Prue said as if this explained everything.

"Yes, yes, the Triple Goddess, I know." Cyrus sounded exasperated. "But she wasn't always the Mother, right? And you weren't always the Maiden."

Prue's frown deepened. Cyrus didn't know what he was talking about. He didn't know anything about her coven.

And yet . . . Prue remembered the previous Mother of the coven, before Polina had been blessed with the title. Polina definitely possessed more power than her predecessor. Even as a child, Prue witnessed grand acts of magic, before Polina stepped into her role as Mother. Once, Prue had fallen out of a tree and broken her leg. Instead of sending for the healer, Polina had acted quickly, summoning her own magic to bind and mend the wound, setting the bones back into place. At the time, Prue had been so consumed by pain that she hadn't paid much attention. But Mona had gushed all night about Polina's ingenuity and powerful magic, making the event impossible to forget.

Prue hadn't thought of that incident in years. And yet, Polina hadn't gathered any herbs or used any grimoire spell to heal the broken bones. So . . . how had she done it? Polina didn't even have an affinity for healing. It should have been impossible.

Prue shut her eyes and shook off thoughts of Polina. She didn't want to think about her right now. Instead, she dropped her gaze, fixing her attention on her foot. She rolled her ankle one way, then the other. No pain. Thank the Goddess.

"Are you afraid?" Cyrus asked suddenly.

"Of what?" Prue didn't break her gaze from her foot, worried he would bring up Polina again.

"The wraith. My brothers. Whoever's coming after you."

Thank the Goddess he changed the subject. Prue considered his words. She took a steadying breath as she sat up, assessing her emotions. To her surprise, she didn't find any fear—at least, not for her own well-being. Mona, yes. But not herself. "No," she said at last. "Some of it may be a bit frightening. But this mission—bringing back my sister, sending the ghosts back to the Underworld—is more important."

She sensed him watching her, but she refused to meet his gaze, afraid his eyes would capture hers again.

He asked, "Then what *do* you fear?"

Prue chuckled. "You won't trick me into giving away my secrets, Cyrus."

"No trick. I'll share mine if you share yours."

Now, she *did* look at him, if only to assess his sincerity. His eyes were solemn, but half his mouth quirked upward in that familiar teasing manner that frustrated her to no end.

"All right," she said slowly. "I fear for my family. For my sister's soul. I fear I'll be too late to help her." Though the words rang true, she uttered them without emotion or emphasis, hoping to brush past that small kernel of truth. "What about you?"

Cyrus inhaled deeply, his eyes growing distant. "I fear the mortal realm. I fear being powerless. I fear losing my home and being enslaved by my brothers."

Prue arched an eyebrow. "You fear the mortal realm?"

Cyrus shifted in his seat. "Yes."

Prue laughed. "Why? You're this powerful god. You

could slaughter everyone in the city with one thought. What would you have to fear?"

"I fear losing myself to this place. Each time I am here, I feel this realm takes more and more of my soul. I fear that if I'm here for too long, I won't be able to go back home because I'll be anchored to mortality. That eventually . . . I will *become* mortal myself." He shuddered.

Prue stared at him, her smile fading. Fearing the Realm of Gaia was laughable compared to how powerful he was, but as he spoke, she saw the reality of his words. It was certainly a valid fear to have, especially given how much this realm had already taken from him.

"Well," Prue said, forcing her voice to remain steady. "It's a good thing you'll be returning to your realm shortly. You won't have to be here much longer."

Cyrus's gaze dropped as he fiddled with the cuffs of his shirt, his fingers dancing over the inked markings on his hand.

"Why do you have vine tattoos?" Prue asked suddenly.

Cyrus blinked and looked at her in bewilderment. "What?"

Prue touched his wrist, her finger tracing over one swirling vine. She could've sworn Cyrus shuddered again. "These vines . . . what do they mean?"

"They aren't vines. They're flames." He looked at her as if seeing her for the first time. Surprise and awareness lit his features. "But you're right. They do look like vines, don't they?"

Prue sucked in a breath as their eyes locked once more. A distant part of her brain registered her fingers were still tracing circles along his wrist, and the contact sent a trail of fire through her hand and up her arm. Heat coiled in her belly, and this time, she couldn't look away from him. Her eyes roved over his luminous eyes, his silver hair, the dark horns protruding from his temples. He was a monster, in a sense, and yet, he was still vulnerable. Still *human*, even if he was immortal. He had vulnerabilities and fears, just like her. Yes, he was different, but so was she. She was a witch, after all, and her lavender eyes, dark skin, and wild, curly hair probably drew as much attention as his horns would have, were it not for the glamour.

"The markings came after my first journey to this realm," Cyrus said, his voice a low rumble that made Prue's toes curl. "I imagine that, once I return, the markings will take over the other half of my body." He said the words with a hint of regret.

"I like them," Prue blurted. She wasn't sure why she said it, but he seemed disappointed at the prospect of being inked on his entire body. She raised her hand, tracing the waves of flame that curled along his throat and collarbone. "They tell a story."

Cyrus's breath hitched as her fingers traced the curves down to the muscles of his chest that peeked out from under his loose tunic. "And what story do they tell you?" His voice had grown husky.

Prue chewed on her lower lip, and his eyes darkened as they dipped to her mouth. Trying to ignore the heat in her face, Prue said softly, "They tell a story of darkness and power. Loss and grief." Her eyes lifted to his once more. "They speak of a man who sees himself as a monster."

"Isn't he?"

Prue shook her head. "Not entirely. Not as much as he thinks he is."

She uttered the words without thinking, without truly considering what they meant. Why had she said that? Didn't she believe him to be a monster?

But the honest truth was . . . no. She didn't. He did monstrous things, but so did all humans. Everyone was capable of despicable things. Here was a god who loved his home, who would do anything to save it, even at the expense of others. He was willing to commit vile acts to get what he wanted, but Prue finally understood that he didn't do it callously or carelessly. He did it out of necessity.

He was tortured, haunted by a past she couldn't quite understand. But he was certainly not a monster.

The space between them had shrunk to mere inches. Their faces were so close they were sharing breath. Prue's heart thundered loudly in her chest, and she swore he could hear it, that even the coachman outside could hear it. But she couldn't break away. This shared space, this connection, was so fragile that if she broke it, she feared it would never grow back. And despite the roiling uncertainty churning inside her, a strange part of her needed to preserve this link with him. It was so new, so fragile and surprising, that she clung to it in desperation.

Cyrus's lips parted, and he leaned in, his nose brushing against hers. Prue's eyelids fluttered closed, and her body arched toward him.

A loud thump sounded atop the carriage, and they both jumped, jolting away from each other. It took Prue's muddled brain several moments to figure out what had happened. But then she realized the carriage had come to a stop. They must have reached the mountains already.

She should have felt relieved. Eager to continue with their journey. So why did she feel disappointment instead?

LAUGHTER

CYRUS

THE CHILLED air nipped at Cyrus's face as he stepped out of the carriage, extending his hand to Prue to help her out as well. To his surprise, she took it. He'd expected her to snap at him, or claim her ankle was fine and she didn't need help.

A fierce wind billowed around them, swirling Prue's skirts and whipping at their hair. Prue's curls rippled around her like waves in the ocean while Cyrus's hair just fell forward over his face, blocking his vision.

The carriage rattled away, returning down the path toward Voula City, as Prue and Cyrus faced the snow-capped mountains before them.

Emdale Mountains. Already, the fierce coldness of the towering peaks seeped into Cyrus's bones, making him shiver.

"We should get going," Prue said, glancing over her

shoulder. Her hand went to the pomegranate necklace at her throat, almost subconsciously. "I'd like to make as much progress as we can before nightfall. But we'll probably have to make camp within the mountains somewhere." She shuddered, biting her lip as she gazed upward toward the peaks, a look of hesitation and unease crossing her features.

"Have you ever climbed a mountain before?" Cyrus asked.

She shook her head. "Have you?"

"No." Even if there were mountains in the Underworld, it would've been an illusion and nothing more. Nothing to prepare him for the reality of this. "But we both have magic." At a significant look from Prue, he amended, "*You* have magic. And I am immortal. I think we'll be fine."

"But what about the ghosts?" Prue pointed to the sky. There were more ghosts now, probably a dozen or more.

"They didn't seem to notice your healing spell earlier," Cyrus muttered thoughtfully. "Perhaps it's only large and powerful spells that pull them in. Like the summoning spell you cast."

"Or the wards around Krenia," Prue mused. Then, she shook her head. "Regardless, I'm not taking any chances." She set down her bag and started wriggling out of her dress, her hands fumbling as she undid the buttons along her back.

"Um," Cyrus said uncertainly. "What are you doing?"

"Changing," Prue grunted. "I don't fancy freezing my ass off in that thin dress." She gestured to the pile of fabric on the ground, now ripped and stained with dirt and blood. The floral pattern was barely visible beneath the stains.

Cyrus arched an eyebrow and crossed his arms as he watched her struggle to reach the lower buttons, her fingers shaking from the cold. His mouth twitched in amusement.

At long last, Prue huffed in exasperation and dropped her arms. "Could you help me?"

Cyrus laughed. "I thought you'd fight for hours with that monstrosity before asking for help."

"I considered it," she grumbled.

As Cyrus approached, Prue suddenly went stiff, shooting him a sharp look. "Don't try anything."

All amusement fled from him, replaced by a cold chill. "I thought we'd been through this. I would never do anything like that to you, Prue."

She surveyed him through narrowed eyes as if she didn't believe him. He couldn't blame her. He *was* a monster, after all, regardless of her statement in the carriage. She only said that because she didn't really know him. In truth, there was nothing he wasn't capable of.

But eventually, her expression softened, and she nodded once before turning away from him. Cyrus squinted at the neat column of buttons along the fabric.

Gods, they were positively miniscule. Whoever designed this gown must have intended to torture women.

"How did you even get this dress *on*?" he asked.

"My hands weren't nearly as cold when I got dressed this morning," Prue said defensively.

"Hmm." Cyrus's brows furrowed, but he was too focused on the damned buttons to argue.

"Probably should have changed back in town," Prue admitted, her teeth chattering.

"Yes," Cyrus agreed. "But there was a demon after us, so . . ."

Prue huffed a laugh at that. Cyrus's fingers were numb with cold by the time he finished undoing all the buttons. He stood back as Prue hobbled out of her dress, now in nothing but her shift. It wasn't anything Cyrus hadn't seen before, but for some reason, his eyes were drawn to the way the thin, sheer fabric hugged her curves. He couldn't stop staring at the stark shape of her nipples visible from underneath, no doubt stiff from the chilled air.

Prue caught him staring, and her cheeks reddened. "You should change, too. You'll want to be in something warmer."

Cyrus blinked. "Right." He shuffled through his bags until he found the suit he'd purchased earlier. It certainly wasn't conducive to hiking up a snowy mountain, but the clothing shops hadn't exactly provided practical gear. Voula City seemed more focused on fashion—comfort be damned.

As Cyrus rummaged through the different pieces of clothing, trying to figure out which to don first, he couldn't resist glancing over at Prue. The dress she'd picked was a deep plum that brought out the purple in her eyes, and Cyrus couldn't help but notice it scooped low, revealing much of her bosom. Had she chosen such a dress on purpose?

He shook his head quickly, trying to rid himself of such foolish thoughts. But he caught her peering at him with curiosity as he stripped out of his worn and ragged clothes. Her eyes roved over his bare chest and the tattoos all over his skin. Her words from earlier rang in Cyrus's head: *I like them.*

Prue blushed when their eyes met, and they both quickly turned away.

After what felt like an eternity, they were both dressed. Cyrus couldn't deny the wonderfully clean feeling of dressing in new clothes, even if they were ridiculous. And his suit came with a coat, thank the gods.

To his surprise, Prue withdrew a few hats and scarves from her own bag and tossed the bigger ones toward Cyrus. His eyebrows lifted in surprise and admiration. She'd had the foresight to prepare for their mountain climb. He cursed himself for not even considering it.

For the first time, he thanked the gods Prue was with

him on this journey. He might be immortal, but that didn't make him immune to the elements. He could still experience cold, and the idea of freezing his ass off on that mountain was most unappealing.

Cyrus wrapped himself in the scarf and tucked the hat over his head, but it wouldn't quite fit over his horns. "Shit," he muttered.

"Here," Prue said with a laugh, drawing closer. She'd wrapped a thick wool shawl around herself, covering the exposed parts of her skin. Cyrus wasn't sure why this disappointed him.

Prue removed the hat and inspected it. After holding it up to his temples, her mouth twisting in concentration, she tugged at two points in the fabric until they tore. Then, she handed it back to him. "Try again."

Frowning, Cyrus slipped the hat on. His horns fit through the misshapen holes perfectly. He huffed in half surprise, half gratitude.

Prue smiled. "I hope your horns are impervious to the cold."

Cyrus snorted. "They are."

Prue's grin widened, her eyes twinkling with amusement as she looked over his appearance.

"What?" Cyrus asked.

"Nothing." She shook her head, biting back her smile.

Cyrus crossed his arms and sighed. "Tell me."

Prue burst out laughing, unable to contain it any

longer. "I'm sorry. I'm sorry, it's just—with the hat and the suit, you look like some well-dressed satyr posing as a professor." Her words dissolved into a fit of giggles. She slapped a gloved hand over her mouth, her face reddening with each peal of laughter.

Anger and embarrassment flooded Cyrus's chest. But the longer Prue laughed, the more it seemed to melt away, until, to his surprise, his own face split into a smile. Seeing her double over with laughter, clutching at her ribs as tears streamed down her face, made it impossible for him to hold on to his anger. And then, he was laughing, too, the feeling so foreign and delightful that he clung to it, eager for more. The way his stomach contracted and his shoulders shook was strange and . . . *human*. But he didn't mind at all.

After their chuckles faded and Cyrus's stomach was sore, he wiped a tear from his eye and met Prue's gaze. Silence fell between them, punctuated only by their panting as they caught their breath.

"I'm surprised you didn't remind me for the millionth time that you are a *god* and should be treated with *respect*," Prue said, pitching her voice low in a poor imitation of his.

Cyrus's brow furrowed. "Yes, well . . . I . . ." He trailed off, unable to find words.

Prue snorted at his stammering. "I've rendered you speechless? Well, that's a first. We should take advantage of this rare silence and get moving. You know, before you get the sudden urge to lecture me." She winked before striding past him toward the base of the mountains.

Cyrus stared after her, alarmed at the flutter of emotion burgeoning in his chest. Had she just *winked* at him?

And what was more shocking: he *liked* it.

"Come on then, O Wise and Benevolent God of the Dead," Prue called over her shoulder.

Cyrus hurried after her, fighting back another laugh. "When did I ever call myself benevolent? If anything, I'm the opposite."

"Oh, there he goes again. I guess the blissful silence only lasted a moment, then."

Cyrus laughed again, finding it surprisingly easy to smile, as if his face was designed for it.

Gods above, what was happening to him?

"Come on!" Prue gestured impatiently, and Cyrus realized he'd been lagging behind. "We've got a mountain to climb."

Cyrus's expression sobered as he quickened his pace, eager to cross the mountain pass as quickly as possible.

CLIMB

PRUE

IT WAS SLOW WORK, climbing the mountain pass. Thankfully, it was so well-traveled that the path was evident, even in the snow, but the climb was slippery and perilous.

When the path grew rockier and more unsteady, Prue's pulse raced, her anxiety spiking. She glanced down at her boots, suddenly regretting purchasing them in a dress shop. If she'd only bought men's boots like Cyrus had, she would've felt more confident in her steps.

But these dainty, heeled contraptions around her feet would do no good. Especially since Prue was uncomfortable enough wearing *any* kind of shoe. She was out of practice and woefully unqualified to make this climb. Not to mention her toes were throbbing, the shoes merciless as they pinched, biting into her flesh. She would surely have blisters by the time they reached the end of the mountain pass. How did women *wear* these torturous things? Were they just accustomed to suffering, or was Prue doing it wrong? Maybe she bought them in the wrong size.

"What's wrong?" Cyrus asked from a few paces ahead of her.

Prue's wide eyes were fixed on the rocky path before her. "Um. Nothing." She shivered, wishing that ridiculous shop had sold thicker material than the shawl she'd purchased. It had seemed like a warm, thick fabric when she'd put it on, but now it was feeble compared to the blistering cold around her.

She took a step and found the ground so slick with ice that she nearly fell. Her arms spun about wildly as she struggled to keep her balance.

Goddess above, I'm going to die here. She gulped, glancing over the cliff's edge. It was only steps away from her. One tumble was all it would take to send her crashing to her death.

"Don't look at it," Cyrus said, his voice firm and demanding.

Unwittingly, Prue's gaze snapped to his. His fierce tone jolted her, shaking loose some of the lingering fear.

"Remember why you're here," Cyrus said. "You're here for Mona."

Mona. Prue pictured her sister's face and nodded, taking a shaky breath. She tried to move forward, but her gaze snagged on the ice beneath her, and she froze again.

"Ignore the cliff," Cyrus went on. "Just look at me."

"Why would I want to do that?" Prue snapped.

For some reason, Cyrus's mouth twitched. As if her insults amused him. "Because I am a *god*, Prue. Now take another step."

Irritation burned in her chest, and she huffed as she took a step, her legs wobbling. But she didn't fall. "There it is again," she muttered. "The *I'm a god* speech."

"Maybe you wouldn't need a speech if you showed me some respect. Take another step."

Prue gritted her teeth, continuing onward. Her boots slid slightly, and her heart hammered in her chest again.

"Here." Cyrus stretched his hand out to her.

Prue's eyes narrowed. She didn't for one second trust him. But . . . she trusted him more than she trusted the slick, icy path underneath her. She lunged forward, reaching for his outstretched hand . . .

Only to slip on another patch of ice. The ground shifted, and with her body already leaning halfway over to reach for Cyrus, she didn't have time to right herself. Her knees crashed to the ground. Rocks bit into her kneecaps, and she cried out. But the mountain wasn't finished with her yet. She kept tumbling, her shoulder hitting something sharp and pointy. The ground wouldn't stop rolling. A scream built up her throat. She was falling, falling, falling . . .

Firm hands latched onto her, gripping her by the

arm. Prue's head was spinning, her entire body weightless as if she had, indeed, fallen off the cliff.

"Prue!" Cyrus shouted. "Hold on to me!"

Prue blinked, trying to see past the dark spots dancing across her vision. Her knees and shoulder throbbed, the pain pounding through her skull.

As her head cleared, she realized why she felt so weightless. She was dangling off the cliff's edge.

A petrified gasp burned in her throat, stealing her breath. Raw and brutal terror gripped her, freezing her completely. If it weren't for Cyrus's firm grip on her arm, she would already be plummeting to her death.

"Dammit, Prue!" Cyrus bellowed. "*Take my hand!*"

His command pierced through the haze of her fear, and she blinked up at him. His expression was strained, his teeth bared and his face red with exertion. Something about the sight of him struggling to hold on to her jolted her into action. With great effort, she swung her other arm up to meet his, gripping his gloved fingers tightly. He grunted, hefting her upward. Her legs were still dangling over nothingness, but she tried not to think about it, remembering Cyrus's words: *Ignore the cliff. Just look at me.*

Her eyes locked onto his, pulled in by the silver gleam that often entranced her. This time, she let it. She welcomed it. She needed the distraction. As he pulled her upward, she fell into the depth and intensity of his eyes, finding herself wondering what the silver meant.

Silver hair, silver eyes, silver blood . . . Was it significant? Or was it random, in the same way that human blood was red? Did different gods and goddesses bleed different colors? She made a mental note to pepper Cyrus with questions when they got through this.

If they got through this.

No, don't think about that. Just focus on him.

Prue's eyes strayed to his horns. What did they feel like? Did they hurt, protruding from his head like that? Could he wiggle them, like some people could wiggle their ears?

Prue almost laughed at the ridiculousness of her thoughts, but the clarity in her mind meant the distraction was working. The muscles in her arms strained as she tugged, trying to hoist herself upward.

With their combined efforts, Prue was able to push off from the cliff's rocky edge, launching herself into Cyrus. The two of them fell backward, sprawled together in a tangle of limbs. Prue found herself atop him, with his back pinned to the ground.

A pained groan burst from Cyrus's mouth. "Thanks for that," he croaked.

"Sorry," Prue said with a wince, realizing she nearly impaled him on rocks. She scrambled to get up, but Cyrus gripped her elbows, stopping her.

"Be careful," he said, his voice earnest and full of warning.

Prue stilled, her lips parting as she gazed at him. Her

pulse still thundered in her ears, every part of her trembling, but now that she was safe, her thoughts swirled in realization.

Cyrus had just saved her life. Without him, she would've fallen off the cliff.

He'd intentionally goaded her earlier, taunting her with his claims of being a god who deserved respect—because he knew her irritation gave her confidence.

I am a god, Prue. Now take another step.

He'd found a way to reach her through her fear. To coax her courage back to life.

And when it hadn't worked, when she'd still managed to slip and fall, he had caught her. As if it was the most natural thing in the world.

As if they weren't enemies.

"Why did you do it?" Prue breathed. With her chest flush against his, she could feel his own heart pounding just as rapidly as hers.

"Do what?" His eyes were guarded, indicating he knew what she was asking.

"Save me. You could've just let me die."

Cyrus's breath hitched. An unreadable emotion stirred in his gaze. He moistened his lips, then swallowed. At long last, he said in a husky voice, "No, Prue. I couldn't have."

Before she could respond, he was shifting, easing her off him as he sat up. He rolled his shoulders back and stretched his arms, flexing his back muscles.

"Are you hurt?" Prue asked.

"No, just bruised. I'll live." He wouldn't meet her gaze as he climbed to his feet, then extended a hand to help her do the same.

I'll live, too, Prue thought. *Thanks to him.*

A knot of emotions tightened in her chest. Gratitude was strongest, but it mingled with unease and apprehension, confusion and utter shock. Why had he done it? Did he expect her to owe him some kind of favor now? Was there an ulterior motive to rescuing her?

Perhaps he only needed her to get him to the Book of Eyes so he could return home. Or perhaps the binding spell or Polina's pomegranate tea had forced him to save her. Those thoughts made more sense than any other alternative.

Cyrus looked at her expectantly. "Shall we continue?"

Prue nodded quickly, her steps more certain with her hand linked with his. "Yes. The sooner we get off this mountain, the better."

HEAT

CYRUS

AFTER THE INCIDENT at the cliff's edge, Prue and Cyrus found a steady pace, a collaborative rhythm as they climbed. Cyrus wasn't sure if this was due to Prue's confidence in herself, or her confidence in *him*. In truth, he hadn't expected to dive for her when he found her plummeting to her death. He hadn't even thought about it—it had been instinct to grab her.

Perhaps that was what bothered him the most. Why was it instinctual to save her life? If he'd let her die, his problems would've been solved.

Or maybe, with their bond and Polina's strange pomegranate brew, *he* would've died, too. It must have been some innate sense of self-preservation that had urged him to save her. That was all, surely.

When they reached the first mountain peak, Prue

paused to catch her breath and then exhaled sharply. "Wow."

Cyrus followed her gaze and turned, his own mouth opening in awe. Past an expanse of plains and trees, he could just make out the skyline of Voula City against a backdrop of a sunset. The rays winked at him from behind the buildings, which were small shapes in the distance. So feeble compared to the magnificence of the city itself.

Atop here, everything seemed smaller. So much smaller.

"Beautiful," Prue whispered, wiping sweat from her brow. Her eyes were filled with joy and wonder as she beheld the scene below. Cyrus stared at her for a long moment, admiring the way the stray curls clung to her face and her pink cheeks added warmth to her expression. Her eyes were alight with exertion, her nose red from the chill.

"Beautiful indeed," Cyrus murmured, but his gaze never strayed from her.

Prue blinked and looked at him. He could've sworn her cheeks flushed a deeper shade of red, but she looked away quickly. "We should find shelter for the night. We won't want to be out here after sunset. The cold will be brutal."

Cyrus nodded quickly. "Yes. I spotted several caves during our climb. Perhaps we can find one nearby."

They set off with purpose and determination, knowing their time was limited. Cyrus's stomach growled louder with each step, and he gritted his teeth against the mind-numbing cold and the rippling pain of hunger. He could make it a few more steps. Just a few more . . .

"There!" Prue's voice sounded as weak as Cyrus felt as she pointed, using her other hand to clutch her shawl more firmly around herself.

Cyrus followed her gaze, his teeth chattering, and found the mouth of a small cave just ahead. "How d-do we know there's not an animal inside?" he asked between shivers.

"We won't know if we don't check," Prue said, continuing forward.

"Prue!"

She ignored him and pressed onward before disappearing inside the cave.

Cursing, Cyrus staggered after her, his limbs stiff and frozen. When he crept inside, he blinked rapidly, trying to adjust to the darkness. He was so accustomed to the blindingly white snow burning against his eyes.

"*Detego*," Prue muttered, waving her hand in the air.

Nothing happened.

"Damn it," she hissed, removing her glove and gesturing more insistently toward the dark abyss in front of them. More firmly, she said, "*Detego*!"

Gold sparks emerged from her fingertips, swirling in the air and illuminating the space before them. The cave was much smaller than Cyrus anticipated. It extended for a few paces before it disappeared into a wall of rock. Certainly too small for a large creature to take shelter. He exhaled in relief.

But Prue wasn't finished. She curled her fingers together, and the gold dust shimmered and swirled together before shooting toward the opposite end of the cave. It circled around the perimeter and then returned to Prue's outstretched hand. The sparks hovered in front of her for a moment before she nodded and dropped her hand. The magic vanished.

"What was that?" Cyrus asked.

"Witch dust. It reveals truth and identifies any threats lurking nearby. The cave is safe."

"I'm not sure if I should be flattered or offended that I'm not considered a threat."

Prue smirked. "Of course you aren't. I own you, remember?"

Ordinarily, her words would've ignited his anger and indignation, but for some reason, they sent a thrill shooting up his bones.

Careful, he warned himself, trying to school his features into apathy. *You cared about a witch once before and it didn't end well for you.*

Instead of returning Prue's smile, he turned away from her, facing the cave opening where the wind still howled. “If you would be so kind as to return my magic to me, I can get a fire going.”

“With what kindling?”

Cyrus raised an eyebrow at her.

“Ah. Magic. Right.” Prue gestured nonsensically at him. “I, uh, grant you your powers back. *Temporarily*,” she added, widening her eyes in warning.

A swell of power burned in his chest, loud and terrible, churning with a ferocity that made his bones quiver. Cyrus closed his eyes against the intensity of it, waiting for it to pass like it had last time. But his magic was even angrier this time. *You’ve neglected me,* it seemed to say. *Don’t let that happen again.* His magic raged and thrashed inside him, and he struggled to calm it. He took several deep breaths, but the foreign sensation didn’t leave him until he promised, *I won’t.*

Cyrus swallowed hard, his chest filling with unease as his magic receded. Gradually, the familiar cold sensation settled in his chest, rhythmic and soothing. It felt as if he couldn’t breathe before, but now he could withstand anything. Any chill or fatigue, exhaustion or injury. He didn’t feel hunger or aches. He felt nothing but power.

Yes, this was normal. Ignoring the strange rise of anger from his death magic, Cyrus knelt to the ground and dug through snow and rock. He didn’t make much headway, but it was enough. He pressed his fingers into the cold ground and closed his eyes, summoning his heat. Rock melted from underneath him, giving way to his pressure until a small cavity formed underneath him. He waved a hand, and his black flame filled the crevice. He sat back to admire his craft. The flame continued to burn, as only death magic could. It wouldn't extinguish until Cyrus pulled it back into himself.

He turned to face Prue, who was watching him with an odd, wary expression. "What?" he asked.

"I—Nothing." Prue looked away quickly, but not before he spotted fear flickering in her eyes.

Cyrus stood to face her fully. "You—Did you think I would attack you?"

"Wouldn't be the first time," she said stiffly.

Cyrus groaned. "If I hadn't burned your foot, the death shadows would've consumed you."

"I know, I know." She waved an apologetic hand at him. "I'm sorry. I'm just exhausted, that's all. I'll, uh, work on creating a sleeping space for us."

Cyrus's body instantly warmed at the thought of sleeping next to her, but he shoved the feeling down, angry with himself for letting this witch affect him so. Why was he becoming so soft around her? It was ridiculous.

Instead of watching Prue, he knelt by the fire to warm his hands and face. From the corner of his eye, he watched Prue weave her hands through the air. Vines snaked toward them, crisscrossing to weave a net that thickened with each twist. Eventually, the pattern of foliage grew so thick that there were no gaps, and now it resembled a massive quilt. It would be prickly, yes, but it would certainly block out the cold.

Cyrus thought she was finished, but then she angled her arm toward the cave opening, and a curtain of vines formed, blocking out the wind. The area felt significantly warmer after that.

When Prue was finished, she deflated, her shoulders hunching over as her frame sagged. Cyrus resisted the urge to rush over and catch her before she collapsed. Thankfully, she only teetered for a moment before regaining her balance. She removed her hat and scarf and gestured feebly toward the vines.

"Well, hop in," she said in a tired voice.

"With you?" Cyrus asked hesitantly, his insides squirming at the thought.

"*Yes.* Body heat will keep us warm." Now she was removing her shawl.

Cyrus went perfectly still. "Why are you undressing?"

"My clothes are wet from the snow. I'd like them to be dry by morning. Besides, we'll share more body heat if we're naked."

Naked. Dear gods.

Prue must have noticed his stricken expression because she halted, her mouth quirking upward in a smirk. "Unless . . . that makes you uncomfortable, for whatever reason." Her eyes glinted with amusement. "I mean, I know I'm no *demon* or anything."

Anger flushed in his cheeks. "I'm acquainted with the bodies of nude women." He had no idea why he said it, but he suddenly felt defensive.

Prue's eyebrows lifted. "Are you, now?"

Cyrus clenched his teeth. "I'm not uncomfortable. You are right; it is the best way for us to keep warm."

"All right then." She still smirked at him.

Growling, Cyrus stood and practically ripped off his coat and shirt. Shivers quickly overcame him as he stepped out of his trousers. Prue was already completely undressed, shift and all. Cyrus's mouth turned dry at the expanse of her warm brown skin before she disappeared under the blanket of ivy.

Cyrus approached her warily. "Is it thorny?"

"Merciful Goddess, are you afraid of *plants*? It's Algerian ivy. Harmless." Her teeth chattered even as she taunted him.

Cyrus scoffed before joining her under the earthen covers. To his surprise, it wasn't as prickly as he feared. It wasn't soft, but it was sufficient. He couldn't feel the wind against his skin anymore, but he still shivered uncontrollably.

"Here." Prue scooted closer to him until her chest was pressed against his arm. He could feel the rise of her breast and the brush of her nipples against him.

Gods above . . .

He crammed his eyes shut. This was utter foolishness. She clearly felt nothing for him. And he shouldn't feel anything for her. So this arrangement shouldn't be a problem.

If anything, this would be the perfect opportunity for him to seduce her. Why hadn't he thought of that earlier? He needed to take advantage of this moment.

With a deep, fortifying breath, he turned to face her more fully. "May I?" he asked.

"Y-yes, go ahead," she said, teeth still chattering.

Cyrus wrapped an arm around her, feeling the rise of goose flesh on her arms from the chill. He summoned just a kernel of heat and pressed it into her skin.

Prue gasped suddenly, her body arching in ways that drove Cyrus mad. He shoved the sinful thoughts from his mind and asked, "Did I hurt you?"

"N-no. It was just a surprise, that's all. I didn't realize you still had your magic."

"I do. If you're afraid, you can take it back."

She looked up at him, her eyes gleaming. "I'm not afraid."

He held her gaze. "Good." He should have told her to cling to that fear; that letting her guard down around him was the stupidest thing she could do. But he couldn't bring himself to break this moment.

Silence fell between them, and gradually, their shivering ceased. Prue shifted against him, her leg grazing his cock, and he stiffened. Her eyes went wide as a blush spread across her face.

"Oh, shit," she whispered. "I—"

Cyrus cleared his throat. "Right. Um. Sorry."

Prue laughed, then covered her mouth. "No. It's not funny. That's my fault. I won't—"

Cyrus groaned, closing his eyes. "Save it, Prue. Yes, I have human parts. Yes, being naked with you is awakening certain . . . parts of me. There's no avoiding it."

Prue bit her lip and arched an eyebrow. "So . . . you're aroused?"

Cyrus shot her a flat look. "Don't flatter yourself. Demons, remember? I've bedded demons before."

"Right." She looked unconvinced.

Gripped by a sudden boldness, Cyrus shot her a smirk. "But it's not just me, is it? You're clearly affected by my body as well."

Prue snorted. "Certainly not."

Cyrus's brows lifted, accepting the challenge. "Really? You are indifferent to my body pressed against yours?"

Her chin lifted at the challenge. "I am."

"Truly?"

"Truly."

"Well, then you wouldn't mind if I did this." He shifted until his cock was pressed fully against her.

Prue's breath hitched, her body arching again. Her

jaw tensed. "Nope." Her voice was strained. "Still not feeling anything."

"Right," Cyrus said, echoing her doubtful tone from earlier. Slowly, he splayed his hand along the small of her back, drawing her flush against him. A ripple of pleasure rolled over him as his arousal rubbed along her thigh.

Prue's eyes closed, and a guttural sound rose up her throat.

"What was that?" Cyrus asked. "I couldn't hear you."

"Nothing," Prue said through clenched teeth. "That was nothing."

"Still not aroused?"

"No."

"Hmm." His hand lowered until he cupped her ass.

Prue stiffened, nostrils flaring.

"Too much?" Cyrus asked in a low whisper. "Does this make you uncomfortable?"

"You're *groping* me. Even the filthiest of creatures would make me uncomfortable if they did that."

Cyrus arched an eyebrow, easily sensing the lie. "Ah. Well, here I was concerned about your body heat." He removed his hand, calling her bluff. "I'll stop, if that's what you wish."

"I—" Prue's mouth clamped shut, irritation flaring in her eyes. Cyrus's body was still lined up with hers, her curves perfectly molded against him.

Cyrus smirked at her, delighting in the blush that crept up her cheeks.

"Stop it," she snapped.

"Stop what?"

"Looking at me like that."

Cyrus chuckled. "I didn't realize I was looking at you a certain way. If you're so unaffected by my presence, all you have to do is shut your eyes and go to sleep."

"I don't want to go to sleep," Prue said suddenly. She pressed her lips together tightly, as if she hadn't intended to say this.

Triumph roared in his chest. "What is it you would like to do?" His voice was barely a murmur. He leaned in and whispered, "What do you want *me* to do?"

Prue only stared at him, her lavender eyes beckoning. In that gaze, she seemed to say, *Everything.*

A thrill shot through him as he placed his hand on her ass once more. Desire stirred in her eyes.

"If you're uncomfortable," Cyrus said again, "tell me to stop."

"Don't stop," she rasped. Then, she blinked, her face reddening again. "I mean, I'm not uncomfortable. It's fine."

"So . . . this?" Cyrus nudged his leg between hers, satisfied to feel slickness there. "This is all right?"

"Yes," she breathed, her eyes closing.

His hand found her thigh. "And this?"

"Yes." The word sounded like a plea.

He inched upward, his fingers climbing higher and higher until he met that pool of wetness between her legs. His cock twitched in response.

“Goddess above,” Prue moaned.

“Should I stop?”

“Don’t you dare.”

He slid one finger inside her. Then another. She gasped, throwing her head back. Her hands clawed at his shoulders, her fingernails digging into him, but the sharp sting only ignited his arousal further.

When Cyrus halted his movements, she raked her nails down his back in silent command.

Cyrus leaned closer until his nose brushed her ear. He whispered, “Perhaps I should make you beg.”

A small whimper escaped her lips.

“Do you want more?” he breathed. “Or are you still *unaffected*?”

“Cyrus,” she gasped.

Heat flared in his chest at the desperate way she said his name. She started to move against him, grinding along his fingers, urging him to continue.

“Well?” he prompted.

“Please,” she begged. “Please, Cyrus.”

There it was again, his name on her lips. Gods, he could listen to her whisper his name like that forever.

“As you wish.” Cyrus’s fingers started moving again, plunging into her, then out, pumping more and more. She writhed against him, groaning and crying out with each movement as she neared her climax. He moved faster and faster, spurred on by the growing wetness inside her. And when the pleasure overcame her, it claimed him, too, and they tumbled over the edge together, both gasping and moaning, sharing breath and heat and satisfaction. They were both panting as their bodies relaxed against the ground, neither of them feeling cold anymore. Cyrus glanced over at her, but her eyes were still closed, a look of contentment on her face. She seemed relaxed. Completely at ease.

Strangely smug at the thought of satisfying her, Cyrus leaned his head back. A small, nagging part of him told him to keep going; to finish the deed. Just a few more steps, and he would have her magic. All that power would be his. He had no doubt Prue would consent. She had all but begged him to continue.

She would let him. He knew it.

And yet . . .

He couldn't. He couldn't do it.

It isn't the right moment, he told himself. *We have time. I don't want to rush it. If she pushes me away now, the plan will fail.*

But his excuses seemed feeble to him. He knew the real reason. It wouldn't feel the same. The sheer bliss, the indescribable pleasure they'd both felt . . . If he continued with her, it wouldn't be real anymore. It would be a game. A lie.

Why did that matter so much to him?

It doesn't, he thought. *It isn't the right time. We're both tired. I know I can seduce her again. Tomorrow, we'll consummate.*

He nodded to himself, believing the lie. He was playing a patient game with her, and it would take time.

With that thought, he relaxed against the makeshift bed, allowing his mind to unwind. It wasn't long before sleep claimed him.

DENIAL

PRUE

WHEN PRUE AWOKE, her body felt sticky and warm. It wasn't unpleasant, but it was unusual, and it took her a moment to get her bearings and remember where she was.

As soon as she did, her head snapped up, her heart racing.

Sure enough, her body was sprawled over Cyrus's, one leg draped over him. Her head had rested against his chest, which still rose and fell with deep breaths.

Oh, Goddess. Not again. Why was it so easy for her body to curl into his?

Her face burned at the memory of his hands on her the night before . . . and his fingers *inside* her . . .

Shame mingled with embarrassment, and she shut her eyes against the onslaught of unwanted desire burning up inside her. Goddess, why did she want him so badly? He was the *devil*. He was a ruthless killer.

And, technically, he was her husband. Which made this all the more complicated.

Biting her lip, Prue eased out of the blanket of ivy, extracting herself from Cyrus's firm grip. Unfortunately, at the last second, her arm jostled his, and he startled awake, his eyes flying open. Prue turned away from him, snatching at her clothes that lay by the still-burning black fire. Thankfully, her shift was dry, and she slid it on quickly.

"It's nothing I haven't seen before," Cyrus drawled, his voice low and husky from sleep. It made Prue's stomach coil with heat.

"I'm freezing," Prue said without looking at him. "I'd rather be dressed."

"Maybe you should've stayed next to me. You know, for body heat." She heard the amusement and smugness in his voice.

Gritting her teeth, Prue snatched her dress before tugging it on and wrestling with the buttons. "I'd rather not."

Leaves shifted as Cyrus stood. The back of her neck prickled from the intensity of his stare, but she took her time fastening her buttons and continued to avoid his gaze.

At long last, he spoke. "Did I do something to offend you?"

Prue winced, grateful she had her back to him so he couldn't see her expression. "Not at all."

"Then, why won't you look at me?"

Prue sighed, finally done dressing. With no more excuses to avoid him, she turned to face him, eyebrows lifted. She raised her arms. "There. Happy?"

Cyrus's eyes narrowed as he scrutinized her. She tried not to let her gaze wander to the rippling muscles along his torso and arms or the stiff part of him that she longed to run her hands over.

Stop it, Prue, she ordered.

"You are angry," Cyrus observed, still watching her. Assessing her. She didn't like the way he looked at her. She felt if he stared long enough, he would unravel her soul piece by piece.

"I'm not," she insisted.

Cyrus cocked his head. "Last night . . . Did it not please you?"

"No. Yes. I—" She groaned and ran her hands through her tangled hair. "It was a mistake. It shouldn't have happened."

Cyrus crossed his arms, his muscles bulging. "And why not? We *are* married."

"*That* was also a mistake." She shot him a dark look.

"Why?"

"Do I really need to explain this to you?"

"*Yes,*" he said insistently. "Because as far as I'm concerned, we are both attracted to each other. We engaged in passionate intercourse that left us both satisfied. And, if we were to properly consummate, we would both benefit from it. So, what's the problem?"

Prue's nostrils flared as she took a steadying breath. The space between them was tense and stifling, and she couldn't suppress the desperate urge to flee.

She had to sever this . . . *thing* between them. Before it grew into something neither of them could contain.

She had to run, to end this. She had no desire to be attached to *anyone,* especially the god of the dead.

Cyrus might not be able to lie—but *she* could.

"The problem is, I *don't like you,*" Prue said through clenched teeth. "You're evil incarnate. You're the *devil.* Do you honestly think I *want* to be married to you? We're only traveling together so I can send you back home and life can go back to normal. Last night was a moment of weakness. I was cold and lonely and pretended that you were a normal man. But we both know you aren't. I'm on a mission to bring back my sister. That is the most important thing, and the only reason I haven't run as far away from you as possible. I can't afford distractions, especially with vile monsters like you."

Agony flared in his eyes, so raw and vulnerable that it made her heart twist. She'd never seen such fragility in his expression. He'd always been so hardened and calloused, impervious to emotion and weakness. But here he was, laid bare before her.

She was hurting him.

She couldn't take it anymore. Her throat burning, she grabbed her shawl and scarf and fled from the cave, ignoring the way his anguished expression lingered in her mind.

PRUE STOOD OUTSIDE THE CAVE, shivering in the falling snow as she waited for Cyrus to dress and emerge. A few minutes later, she sensed his approach and turned to find him fully dressed, even wearing the cap with holes for his horns. He handed her the hat she'd forgotten, and she took it wordlessly, offering a nod of thanks before donning it.

"Ready?" she asked.

"Ready." He wore his mask again, the cool and calculated expression of apathy and disdain. Her chest tightened at the sight of it. It seemed like all the progress they'd made, all they'd shared together, had vanished, and they were back to that first moment when she'd summoned him.

But perhaps that was for the best.

After all, Prue wasn't capable of loving anyone more than she loved her sister. There was just no room in her heart for more.

And even if there was, Prue had *lost* Mona. She

couldn't survive a heartbreak like that again. So why risk it? Why risk another earth-shattering loss?

It was better to seal herself off from all attachments now. Before it was too late.

Prue turned and continued down the mountain pass, feeling his presence behind her. Their journey resumed with a chill between them that had nothing to do with the weather. In fact, Prue welcomed the biting cold, the sting of snow and ice. It distracted her from the pain inside.

This is the right thing to do, she reminded herself. *For Mona.*

But a tiny voice inside her insisted Mona would want her to be happy, too.

I can't be happy with the god of the dead. He doesn't belong here. He's dangerous and power-hungry and deceitful. It can't happen.

She repeated these words to herself the entire way, scaling up rocky peaks and easing down slippery slopes. Like before, Prue and Cyrus had to rely on each other, grasping hands and arms to keep from falling. But the way he dropped her hand immediately after—as if it were on fire—only made her feel worse.

Hunger gnawed at her body the entire way, bringing on the fatigue and soreness much faster than the day before. Her bones were tired and weary, and each step sent aches shooting up her legs. They stopped to rest much more frequently, and Prue summoned a patch of small berries for them to munch on, though it nearly drained her of what little energy she had left. Conjuring fruit-bearing plants tended to do that to her, which was why she didn't do it often. Vines were one thing—they were useless and irritating, so of course, they required little effort.

At long last, they glimpsed the castle turrets of the Thanassian Empire below. Spurred on by hope, Prue quickened her pace, ignoring the stiffness in her limbs and the clumsy stumbling that made her teeter.

"Prue," Cyrus said behind her, a warning in his voice.

Too late. Her foot came down hard on a patch of ice, and the ground slid out from underneath her. With a yelp, Prue went down, slipping and tumbling, her arms and legs crashing against rocks and snow. Pain lanced through her, sharp and cutting. Darkness seeped into her vision, blocking out the jagged rocks waiting to pierce her at the base of the mountain.

A burst of warmth surrounded her, stalling her descent. Though her entire body radiated with agony, the fresh scrapes leaking blood all over her new dress, she welcomed the relief. She seemed frozen, suspended in mid-air. Her eyes were closed, succumbing to the darkness. Perhaps she'd blacked out already. Or maybe she was dead. Either way, she didn't care. This was preferable to the biting pain.

Then, hands were on her, gentle and desperate, sending a surge of warmth through her. A familiar scent of cedar and ash filled her nose, and she knew immediately it was Cyrus. She never realized he smelled like that . . . Perhaps she'd grown too accustomed to notice.

"Prue," Cyrus said, his voice tinged with panic. "Can you hear me?" His fingers brushed the hair out of her face, and he swore. She flinched as his hands met a sticky gash on her forehead.

"Still alive," she grumbled, her voice a croak. "Just barely."

"I can heal you," Cyrus said. "But my power's run out. You need to give me more."

Prue almost sobbed at the thought. She had nothing left. No strength, no energy, no will . . . Nothing.

"Please," Cyrus begged. "Just say the words, Prue, and I'll take the pain away."

The promise almost seemed deadly, like he would hasten her journey to death. To the Underworld. Perhaps that wouldn't be so bad. It was where she was headed, after all.

Tasting blood in her mouth, Prue mumbled, "I grant you power. Take it, Cyrus. Take what you need."

She wasn't sure if it was enough, but when Cyrus exhaled loudly in relief, she knew it had worked. A strange, fuzzy warmth filled her head, and she gladly fell into it, drifting away to a hazy sleep.

ALTERED

CYRUS

CYRUS DIDN'T THINK. His mind receded so far into himself that nothing occupied his brain; it was only action.

After Prue had fallen down the mountainside, he hadn't hesitated; he'd used his magic to slow her fall. The sight of her, battered and bruised, covered in blood and wounds, her arm jutting out at an unnatural angle . . . It was too much for him.

When she'd granted him access, his dark power surged forward. But he cast it aside, worried that strange and unfamiliar rage would cloud his mind and slow him down. He needed his *other* power. The power of the gods.

He didn't use it often.

But what other choice did he have?

You could have let her die, said a voice in his head. But he pushed it away, focusing on action instead.

Get her to safety. Save her. He could dwell on those pesky thoughts later.

He gathered her in his arms, and magic came to life, encompassing her form in a gold glow. Pain wrenched through his body, jerking through him as if a dagger had been rammed into him from behind, dragging out his power by force. But he continued to hold on to Prue, waiting for his magic to do its work.

When the glow faded, she didn't wake up.

Cyrus stared at her, expecting her body to shift. He imagined those lavender eyes glaring at him as she pushed him away from her . . .

But nothing happened.

Prue's eyes remained closed. Her skin took on a grayish pallor. The large gashes on her shoulder and her forehead had sealed themselves up, no doubt from Cyrus's magic. And her arm was no longer twisted at an angle, indicating the bones had been mended. So why wasn't she waking up?

Dammit. He had to get her somewhere safe, somewhere away from the cold, otherwise the healing wouldn't work. That had to be it. He was so accustomed to using his magic in the Underworld, where the elements wouldn't disturb him, that he didn't want to imagine how the cold might affect her injuries.

His descent down the remainder of the mountain pass was achingly slow, and each step sent a fresh bolt of urgency through him, reminding him that Prue could be dying. Maybe his magic wasn't enough for her. Maybe she hadn't granted him enough power to heal her properly.

Maybe she was already dead. He was too terrified to check, trusting instead that his magic was knitting her back together as it should.

He didn't use his healing powers often. For one thing, rarely did anyone need to be healed in the Underworld; it mostly consisted of immortals or those who were already dead.

For another, the healing affinity came straight from the mortal realm. It was the one thing that took *from* him instead of empowering him. Healing was a human act because only mortals needed it. As such, Cyrus had to borrow from his own immortality in order to use it. It required a price.

The only other time he'd used it was to heal his brother after dealing him a fatal blow. But that had been utterly selfish; he'd wanted his brother to live, to suffer. And for Cyrus, the price was worth it. He would sacrifice a portion of his immortal soul for vengeance.

Other than that, he ordinarily refused to use that particular power. Because each time he did, he grew closer and closer to becoming a mortal himself. That magic would take and take until there was nothing left of his immortality. Until he was nothing more than a useless human.

But here and now, he didn't even need to think twice about it. Yes, he would do this to save Prue. He was startled by just how much he was willing to give up in order to save her.

It was only because of their bargain. Because he needed her magic to take back his throne. That was all.

Wasn't it?

He didn't let himself think about it.

At long last, he reached the bottom and followed the path winding toward the outer village of the kingdom. He hurried up to the first house, a tiny hovel with a roof buried in snow, and hammered incessantly at the door. Eventually, a wizened old woman answered, her eyes widening at the limp figure he held in his arms.

"Please," Cyrus panted. "Is there a healer nearby? She needs help."

The woman blinked, appraising him for one agonizing moment before gesturing down the road. "Healer Barrow is just down there. Brick house with a yellow flag attached to the door."

"Thank you." Cyrus bowed his head to her and rushed off, ignoring the strain in his muscles or the way his insides twisted. He couldn't tell if it was from panic or the way his sacrifice had altered himself. But he didn't care. He would assess his powers and his soul later, once Prue was healed.

Cyrus reached the healer's house, glancing once at the yellow flag whipping in the wind, before knocking firmly on the door.

A man with wild white hair and an equally unruly beard answered the door. Spectacles hung on a chain around his neck, and he quickly donned them to assess the situation.

"Bring her in, bring her in." He didn't even hesitate. Didn't even ask who Cyrus was.

A surge of respect swelled in Cyrus's chest as he hurried inside. Thank the gods this man was kind enough to inspect a complete stranger. The thought made his insides twist even more.

Stop that, he ordered himself, irritated at the array of emotions overwhelming him. *Now is not the time for feeling soft.*

The mortal realm was affecting him too strongly. He'd been here too long.

But there was hardly anything to be done about it now.

Cyrus carried Prue into the old man's home, dodging piles of books and clothes and various medical instruments strewn about. He had a disorderly appearance but moved with swift efficiency, as if the organized chaos was just how he operated.

"Over here." With quick work, the man cleared a large dining room table and draped a tablecloth over it before gesturing for Cyrus to lay Prue on top. He obeyed, resting her gingerly atop the table.

She was still unconscious. Her wounds had sealed, at least. But she should've woken by now. Something was wrong.

The man—Healer Barrow—bent over Prue, whispering nonsensically to himself as he did. Cyrus hovered behind him, resisting the urge to shout at the man to hurry up.

After a moment, the man paused and glanced over his shoulder at Cyrus. Suspicion prickled in his withered eyes. "What did you do?"

Cyrus blinked. "What?"

"She had bloodstains, but no wounds. And she reeks of death magic."

Cyrus went completely still. How did this mortal know of death magic?

At the wary aggression on Cyrus's face, Barrow barked out a laugh. "Sheath your blades, Dark Highness. I mean you no harm. But you don't tend to wounds—both mortal and not—for as long as I have without picking up a thing or two."

"You've seen death magic before?" Cyrus asked, his body still taut as if expecting a battle. Which was ridiculous, given the man's age. Even so, every fiber of his body quivered with unease.

"More than once," the man confirmed. "This woman smells the same."

“Then what’s wrong with her? My magic should have healed her.”

“It healed her on the outside. But inside, a storm still rages.”

“What does that *mean*?” Cyrus demanded, his patience thinning.

“It means something inside her has her trapped. And whatever it is, it’s reluctant to let her go.”

Ice filled Cyrus’s chest as he gazed at Prue’s limp form. What storm brewed inside her? What horrors kept her mind caged? Had this near-death experience altered her, just as it had altered Cyrus?

And if so, how could he get her back?

TRAPPED

PRUE

PRUE SAT ALONG THE SHORE, her feet buried in the sand as the tide washed over them again and again. Besides her, Mona leaned back on her elbows, lifting her face toward the warm sun.

"So, let me get this straight," Mona said, turning her head to crack open an eye at Prue. "You're married to this delicious hunk . . . and you still haven't made love to him yet?"

Prue whacked Mona's arm. "It's not that simple."

"Why not? You slept with Xandros without a problem."

Prue's face fell, her insides chilling. *Xandros.* Goddess, she hadn't allowed herself to think about him in months. "Yeah, and look where that got him." Her voice sounded hollow.

Mona touched her shoulder, and Prue relished the

feel of her sister, solid and warm, next to her. "His death wasn't your fault."

Prue shuddered. She didn't want to talk about this. "Regardless, that's the perfect reason for me to *not* go there with Cyrus. I've seen enough death and suffering. I don't want to be around it anymore, and being with someone like him pretty much guarantees death will be a regular occurrence."

Mona shook her head, smirking. "I'll never understand you, Prue. You've gone farther than I ever have with a man before, and somehow *you're* the one who's reluctant about it now? We must have swapped brains or something."

Prue snorted at the truth behind her words. This was very true. Mona always thought through everything. And then thought it through again, just be safe. She was overly cautious, anxious to a fault.

Whereas Prue was reckless and irresponsible.

Perhaps it would be better if they *did* switch brains. Maybe then Prue's decisions wouldn't keep getting people killed.

"Would it really be so bad if you had feelings for him?" Mona asked.

"*Yes*," Prue insisted.

"Why?"

"Because he's the devil. Because he belongs to another realm. Because I *tricked* him into binding himself to me. Because I brought him here against his will. Because he's power-hungry and murderous. Do I need to continue?"

Mona sighed, her expression turning somber. "You can't help who you love, Prue."

"I do *not* love him."

"Maybe you do, maybe you don't. But my point is, you can't force yourself to feel a certain way."

Prue bit her lip and looked away, though it pained her. Ever since she showed up on this beach with Mona, she'd wanted to drink in her sister every second, reminding herself she was really here. Even if Prue knew that, in a sense, none of this was real at all. Prue assumed she was dead. What other explanation was there?

But she was perfectly content with it.

"I can't afford to go down that road with him," Prue said at last. She would play along with Mona's game, using the present tense as if she had a world to go back to. It was fun to pretend she could just chat about boys with Mona without a care in the world.

"Why? Because of Xandros, or because of me?"

Prue flinched. That was one thing she didn't miss; Mona had an abrupt sort of frankness when she asked questions. She held nothing back. "I think . . . both. I gave Xandros my body, and he died. But I didn't love him." She finally met Mona's stare. "I *did* love you. I still do. Both losses still haunt me . . . for different reasons."

Mona nodded in understanding. She turned back

toward the rolling waves, her gaze turning distant. "I can't stay."

Prue blinked. "Why not?"

"Neither of us belongs here, Prue. You and I both know that."

Prue shook her head. "I don't—"

"Do me a favor," Mona said, her voice soft. "Don't hold back because of me, okay?" She took Prue's hand and squeezed. "If our roles were reversed, you'd want me to live, right? Instead of letting guilt consume me completely?"

A hard lump formed in Prue's throat, and she couldn't speak.

Mona stood, wiping sand from her dress.

"Where are you going?" Prue jumped to her feet, alarmed at the thought of parting from her sister.

"He's calling for me," Mona said, her eyes darkening. "If I delay, he'll come and fetch me himself. I can't risk him finding you."

"*Who*?"

"He won't tell me his name. Not until . . ." Her expression shuddered, and her face drained of color. "Shit. He's here."

Prue's heart thundered in her chest as a figure materialized behind Mona. He was tall and muscular, his broad shoulders spanning twice the width of Cyrus's, which was an impressive feat in itself. His black hair curled just past the nape of his neck, with a single streak of silver lining it. Small, dark horns protruded from his temples.

Prue knew without a doubt this was one of Cyrus's brothers. And she'd seen him before. He was the one from Prue's dream—the one who had snatched Mona, dragging her into the darkness. Prue's bones chilled from his very presence. His eyes, silver like Cyrus's, fixed on Mona with a cold, hungry look.

"It's time," he said, his voice a deep rumble.

Mona flinched, and Prue came forward, anger replacing her fear in a fierce protectiveness toward her sister. "She's not going anywhere."

The prince of Hell scoffed. "What will you do about it? You are between worlds, witch. You have no power here."

Prue's nostrils flared, though her chest quivered from the truth behind his words. *Between worlds.* Neither dead nor alive. She grabbed Mona's arms, fingernails digging in insistently. He would have to pry Mona free by force if he wanted to take her.

"Prue," Mona whispered, as if reading her sister's intent. "I can't stay. You know that."

Prue swallowed hard. Deep down, she *did* know this. During seances, the Mother of their coven always outlined the rules of communing between worlds. The spirits couldn't linger for very long or risk their souls being torn apart.

Part of her didn't want to believe that's what this

place was. She preferred to think she was dead, right alongside her sister. That they could spend an eternity together.

But, of course, that was too good to be true. Mona was already dead and belonged to the Underworld now. Prue was half-dead and belonged . . . where?

"Can't I go with you?" Prue asked.

The prince of Hell barked out a laugh. "You belong to my brother now, witch. And he never lets go of what's rightfully his."

"I belong to no one," Prue spat.

The prince only shot her a look of disdain, his nose wrinkling as if she smelled like horseshit.

Mona took Prue's hand, squeezing her fingers insistently. "You have to tell Cyrus." Her words were rushed. "Warn him. He has to know—"

"That's enough," the prince snarled, wrenching Mona away from Prue. "We're leaving now."

"Mona!" Prue shouted, but her sister's form was already fading, becoming more and more transparent.

"I love you, Prue! Please remember! And tell him—"

Prue's eyes flew open, and a slice of pain tore through her skull as if her brain had been ripped free. "Oh," she moaned, raising a hand to her temple. She stiffened when she noticed her hand was coated in blood. "Goddess above . . ."

"Prue!" A wooden chair groaned against the floor, and a man hurried over to her, his eyes wide with alarm.

Prue almost didn't recognize him—he looked so serious and anxious and . . . *human.*

But it was definitely him. Cyrus. Between the inky tattoos and the silver hair and the horns protruding from his head, Prue knew it was him, despite the foreign look of terror on his face.

"What—what happened?" Prue's tongue tasted like sawdust, and the splitting pain in her head persisted. She blinked blearily, taking in her surroundings. She was in a small, cramped kitchen and lying on a dining table, which did nothing for her massive headache. The area was cluttered and filled with books, papers, and all sorts of medical instruments.

"You fell on the mountain pass. I healed you, but . . ." Cyrus shook his head. "It wasn't enough. Something else had you trapped, so I brought you to a local healer."

Well, that explained the strange, cluttered house. But one word snagged on her mind: *trapped.* She blinked as a dozen images crossed her mind. A beach. The sand between her toes. Mona's smile. And a tall, black-haired figure.

Prue snatched Cyrus's arm, her eyes widening. "Cyrus. Your brother has Mona."

Cyrus stilled, his eyes searching hers for a moment as if trying to discern the truth in her gaze. Then, his expression darkened, and he morphed into the savage god Prue knew him to be. "Which one?" he growled.

"I don't know." Prue's mouth twisted as she struggled

to recall his face. But the memories in her mind were so foggy and sluggish. A side effect of being between worlds. But she was a witch, dammit, and she should be able to remember!

Understanding crept into Cyrus's eyes as if he knew why she struggled to recall details. He drew closer and asked, "Did he have short or long hair?"

"Long. But shorter than yours."

"Black hair? Or silver?"

"Mostly black. One streak of silver."

"Horns?"

"Yes, but they were small. And black."

Rage burned in his eyes, and his throat rumbled with a feral snarl. "Vasileios."

Prue's mouth went dry. "Who?"

"My oldest brother. The former heir to the throne of the Underworld. He's the one who has your sister."

TRUST

CYRUS

CYRUS COULDN'T THINK past the thunder roaring in his ears. Red crept into his vision as he thought of Vasileios threatening Prue.

And he had her sister.

Which meant Vasileios must have been planning this. In order to intercept a soul before it moved on, he would have had to wait for it, to ensnare it before it found passage to one of the rivers.

But how had he known? Mona had died before Prue even summoned Cyrus. So how did Vasileios know about the bond between Prue and Cyrus before it had even happened?

Cyrus barely registered Prue asking him questions, but he must have mumbled his responses because she didn't pester him for more information. Eventually, the wizened old healer appeared to check on Prue, inspecting her injuries and searching for any signs of fever or infection. Barrow, to his credit, didn't ask them any questions, but based on what he knew, Cyrus was certain the man was curious. When the healer deemed her healthy, he insisted on fixing them a meal. Borderline starving, Cyrus and Prue certainly didn't object, though they did assist him with the meal preparation and scrubbed the dishes for him afterward. The stew, while a bit bland, was surprisingly hearty and filled their empty stomachs.

"I'm happy to provide a room for you to spend the night," Barrow said as they donned their jackets and scarves.

"You've been far too generous already," Prue said with a soft smile. "We wish there was some way we could repay your kindness."

"You're here because of the spirits, aren't you?" Barrow asked.

Prue's smile fell, and she exchanged a worried look with Cyrus.

"You don't have to answer," Barrow went on. "But if that *is* why you're here, then sending those spirits home will be payment enough. Our village has been suffering these past few days. The people are terrified, and I can't tell you how many have shown up on my doorstep asking me to perform exorcisms." He choked out a wheezy laugh, but Prue and Cyrus didn't crack a smile.

"We'll do what we can," Cyrus said after a long moment. "I'm sorry for the trouble this has caused you."

He felt Prue's surprised gaze on his own, but he wouldn't meet her eyes. Instead, he grasped the healer's hand in his and shook it before they departed.

"That was kind of you," Prue muttered as they strode down the snowy path that led to the main road.

Cyrus snorted. "Don't sound so surprised. I *am* capable of being civil."

"Yes, that's the surprising part."

Cyrus scoffed in amusement and fell silent as they trudged through snow and mud. He kept glancing at Prue to ensure her steps were steady, but she seemed to carry herself just fine.

"You were quiet today," Prue remarked, meeting his gaze with concern. "Is everything all right?"

No, Cyrus wanted to say. *You almost died and my brother is after us, and the most frightening part of all is how much your accident almost broke me. And I don't even know why.*

But he couldn't say any of that, so instead, he shrugged vaguely.

"Don't do that," Prue said. "It was one thing when our quest only involved my sister. But now your brother is involved. I need you to be honest with me."

Cyrus laughed dryly. "I have no choice but to be honest with you."

She tugged on his shoulder, forcing him to stop and

look at her. "You know what I mean. I'm asking you to open up to me. I haven't taken your magic away yet. Because right now, I trust you. We'll *both* have to trust each other if we want to successfully reach the Underworld and bring back my sister. I don't know anything about your brother. I want to be prepared."

Cyrus heaved a sigh and clenched his fingers into fists at his sides. It was one thing to be bound to this witch. It was another thing entirely to lay out his messy past with his brothers. He had cared for a witch before, and she had used him. Betrayed him.

Would Prue do the same? How much did he really know about her?

But she did have a point . . . She *hadn't* taken his magic away. He'd thought she'd just forgotten. But here she was, fully aware of how powerful he was, and she made no move to stop him.

"How about a trade?" Cyrus asked. "For each question you answer, I will answer one as well."

Prue arched an eyebrow. "You really think *another* bargain between us is the best idea?"

"This one won't be sealed in blood." Cyrus shot her a wolfish grin.

Prue huffed in exasperation as they both fell into step together, weaving down the main road toward the palace turrets that pierced through the clouds. In the sky, above the towering castle, floated several ghosts, reminding them of their mission. "Very well. Ask your question."

"What happened while you were unconscious?" Cyrus asked.

Prue's eyes darkened briefly before sorrow took over. With a shuddering breath, she said, "I was with Mona. Between worlds."

Between worlds. Cyrus knew a space existed between life and death, but souls did not reside there for very long. He'd never actually been there before.

But Vasileios had.

Before Cyrus could ask a follow-up question, Prue asked, "What happened between you and Vasileios?"

"He was the heir to my father's throne. When I gained my powers, I took the crown from him by force."

Prue's eyebrows lifted. "Well, that would certainly be reason enough to want revenge, wouldn't it?"

"It would indeed." Cyrus glanced at her. "What is Mona like?"

A mixture of sadness and affection filled her face. "Bookish. She loved to study and find new spells. She was clever and imaginative with her magic. It was better than mine, and Mama always loved her more because of it. I think it's because she saw more of herself in Mona than in me."

"So Mona was powerful? Like you and your mother?"

"Oh, yes. She always had a stronger affinity than mine, and she was constantly seeking for ways to grow and improve. But her curiosity wasn't always a good thing. It prompted her to—" She faltered, her face paling slightly.

"What?" Cyrus urged.

Prue's breath trembled as she inhaled, her gaze fixed toward the road. "I believe . . . that requires another question." She smirked at him, but it lacked her usual snark.

Cyrus chuckled. "As you say."

"What is Vasileios like?" Prue asked.

"He's strong and clever. Father favored him because he possessed all the qualities of a great ruler. Power. Wisdom. Confidence. He wasn't obnoxious with his strength like Marcellus or sly and sneaky like Leonidas. But he anticipated threats before they came, and he was strong enough to keep the souls within the river Styx." Cyrus shook his head, grimacing at his own lack of foresight. "He was quiet and unassuming, and I never gave him much thought. I was so focused on my own bitter feelings about his birthright that I didn't really see him for who he was. But now I understand he was always crafting a careful plan. He's more cunning than I gave him credit for."

Prue was silent for a moment, her gaze distant as she considered his words. "Mona and I were meant to converge our magic. It was foretold that the Gemini twins, with the power of Janus, would join together, leaving one twin dead and the other fully empowered. Our coven—our *mother*"—she spat the word like a filthy curse—"lied to us our whole lives, withholding this information from us until right before our powers were supposed to converge."

"Why would they keep that from you?"

"Because we would've fought it if we'd known! But that's no excuse. Mama should have told us from the start. She's powerful; together, we could've found a way around it, I'm certain. We could've prevented—" She broke off, her eyes moist as she gritted her teeth in obvious frustration.

Cyrus stilled as he watched her. "And what happened?"

"We refused. We tried to find another way. We discovered the Book of Eyes, and . . ." She took a shuddering breath. "It was Mona's idea to open it."

Cyrus stiffened. "What?"

"She thought it was a grimoire that could provide us with new spells. A new way to undo the prophecy of Janus's powers. We cast a spell together, and instead of saving us from that fate, it unlocked the gate to your world."

Cyrus grasped her arm, stopping them both. His chest roared with terror. "Prue. Did Mona open it with her blood?"

Prue nodded, her lips trembling. "We both did."

"Shit." Cyrus ran a hand through his hair and closed his eyes. "Then you are *both* bound to the Underworld."

Prue sucked in a breath. “What exactly does that mean?”

“For you, not much, since you are now bound specifically to me. But for Mona . . . Gods, it all makes sense now. Of course Vasileios would find her right away.”

“Cyrus, you aren’t making any sense! I thought the Book of Eyes was bound to *you*. Doesn’t that mean *you* and Mona are connected?”

“Not necessarily. Blood can be manipulated in different ways and for different kinds of magic. If the spell you cast unlocked the gate to the Underworld, then Mona’s blood could’ve been used to bind herself to any one of my brothers.”

Prue’s face drained of color. “I—No, Cyrus, she can’t—”

Cyrus lifted a hand, his ears prickling. In the distance, a horse whinnied and the sound of wheels on the ground made him straighten in alarm. “Someone’s coming.”

He grabbed Prue’s arm and dragged her off the road, their boots slipping on the snow as they hurried to the shelter of the trees. Just before hiding behind a thick oak tree, Prue waved her hand and whispered, “*Abscondo*.”

The roots from under the earth shifted, and tufts of snow drifted over their footprints, masking their trail from view.

Cyrus lifted his eyebrows, impressed. Prue just

shrugged a shoulder, though a satisfied smile tugged at her lips. "My magic has its uses."

They both ducked behind the tree, pressed up against each other to stay fully out of sight. Though the tree trunk itself was massive and thick, it felt far too small for the both of them. Cyrus had her pinned up against the bark, his face inches from hers, her breath tickling his face. Despite the layers of clothing between them, the curves and shape of her body molded against his, tucked so perfectly like pieces of a puzzle. He felt her rapid heartbeat from within her chest. Her breasts rose and fell against his abdomen, betraying her fear. But when Cyrus glanced down, he found her eyes dark with need and hunger. Not a trace of terror on her face. Her cheeks were flushed, her lips slightly parted. She held his gaze, unabashed.

Cyrus's fingers seemed to move of their own accord, lifting to stroke her throat, then to dip under her scarf where a sliver of her collarbone was exposed. She shuddered, her eyes closing as a look of pleasure crossed her face.

What he wouldn't give to be able to incite that same pleasure in other more sensitive areas . . . To hear her moan and cry out with delight and rapture. His own skin heated at the thought, and his arousal pressed against her. But instead of mocking him, as she had last time, she leaned into him, grinding her hips against him, the friction making him go mad with desire.

"Over here!" called a voice.

Cyrus snapped out of his intoxicating fog, realizing he hadn't heard the wagon approach because he'd been so consumed by Prue. She was like a poison to him, weakening him when he needed to be alert. He turned his head away from her, sliding sideways so their bodies weren't flush against each other any longer. He ignored the absence of her heat against him and the way his body yearned for hers.

She was a weakness he couldn't afford.

Instead, his eyes closed and his ears strained to pick up the noises of the newcomers. Several pairs of boots clomped in the snow. At least half a dozen. Metal rattled, indicating they were either armed or wore armor. Or both.

"He said they would be well hidden," remarked another man. "Stay alert."

He who? Cyrus wondered. They couldn't possibly be looking for Cyrus and Prue . . . could they?

The footsteps continued. At one point, they drew close enough for Cyrus to hold his breath. Prue went completely stiff next to him as they waited . . .

But then the steps withdrew, and Cyrus exhaled slowly.

"We need the witch dust," said a third man.

Prue sucked in a breath, her face draining of color. Her horrified gaze met Cyrus's. *They have witch dust.*

How?

Terror filled Prue's eyes, conveying an unspoken question: *What do we do?*

Cyrus set his jaw and gave her a fearsome look in response. *We fight.*

His fingers curled into fists, and Prue's hand went to the pomegranate necklace at her throat. Something shimmered in the air close by, and the familiar gold sparks of witch dust floated into view.

Cyrus looked at Prue again, his eyes widening expectantly. *Get ready.*

"This way," said the third man.

Several sets of footsteps drew nearer, the crunching snow growing louder and louder. Anticipation hummed in Cyrus's ears, a persistent buzzing that made his blood pulse with power.

When the first soldier came into view, Cyrus sprang into action.

EMPIRE

PRUE

TIME SEEMED to slow in that split second when Cyrus attacked. And as he moved, only one thing occupied Prue's mind.

The god of the dead was horrifyingly beautiful. And she was absolutely mesmerized by him.

Despite the soldiers surrounding them, she couldn't look away from Cyrus and his jets of black flame. Transfixed, she gaped as he swept forward, a blur of silver hair and black mist. A soldier raised his sword, but Cyrus darted under the man's swing, sending a slice of flame straight into the soldier's chest. The rippling black seemed to pierce *through* the man's armor and paralyze him entirely. He fell, and Prue wasn't even sure if he was dead or not. Three other soldiers lunged for Cyrus, clearly identifying him as the bigger threat, but Cyrus danced out of reach, his body twisting and turning with all the grace of the most lithe of dancers.

Prue jerked her gaze away from Cyrus as the remaining soldiers came for her. Alarm jolted through her, and she mentally cursed herself for her hesitation. Cyrus's powerful movements had been so distracting . . . She flexed her fingers, and her trusty vines sprang from the earth, winding through the snow and tugging at the closest soldier's legs. He grunted, jerking his feet and snapping several vines, but more ivy climbed up his leg, rooting him to the ground. Another man hacked at the vines with his sword.

But the ivy was only slowing them down, not stopping them. Gritting her teeth, Prue sent an onslaught of magic, her third eye winking open. She suppressed the shudder that usually accompanied that sensation, the sickness and disgust at the thought of using Mona's power for herself.

Not now, she told herself. *If there's a time to use it, it's here and now. This is for Mona, not me.*

But the revulsion had been so ingrained in her since Mona's death that it was hard to shake.

Plus, she didn't know what these men wanted with her and Cyrus. Did they want to kill or capture? And *why* were they after them?

If only she knew the answers to these questions, then she could make a decision. But her spinning thoughts wouldn't solidify, and the only thing blaring into her mind was pure panic.

Focus! she roared at herself. She shot a glance at Cyrus, who battled several soldiers at once. Judging by the way the men swung their swords without restraint, she knew they aimed to kill.

She would have to do the same.

Sweat pooled on her neck and back as she urged the more deadly plants to rise up from the ground. Hemlock, nightshade, oleander . . . She felt the roots climbing and spreading, the leaves blooming along the vines. The soldiers, assuming they were just more Algerian ivy, kept ripping off the vines, not noticing the different shape and texture of the leaves.

And then, the poisonous plants reached skin, winding and twisting, forcing their way into the soldiers' mouths. Several men started retching and gasping, arms flailing as they tried to fling the ivy away from them. But even as they snapped the vines and continued their assault, they couldn't escape the deadly effects of the poison that had already entered their bodies.

The nearest soldier screamed as the toxicity claimed him. He fell to his knees and slumped over, unmoving.

His companion stiffened, paling at the sight of his dead friend. "It's poisonous! It's—" His words were cut off with a choked gagging sound as the plant slithered between his lips and plunged down his throat. Foam spread from his mouth, and his body jerked and twitched before falling over, dead.

The other two soldiers stiffened, now tugging at the vines with more urgency. Prue offered a cruel smile, knowing she'd won. Her pesky vines had grounded them, holding them in place while the poison did its job.

Perhaps her ivy wasn't so bad after all.

Something grabbed at her from behind. Yelping, Prue stiffened and tried to move, to raise her hands to strike down her assailant. But the soldier pinned her arms behind her with one hand and grabbed her throat with the other.

Shit. Prue hadn't realized one of the soldiers had peeled away from the others. Already, his gloved fingers put pressure on her throat, making each breath strain.

"Come quietly," the man said in a gruff voice, "or die, *witch*."

A sudden burst of ice filled Prue's chest, and she gasped from the intensity of it. But it wasn't *her* magic.

It was Cyrus's.

Then, Cyrus was there, appearing out of nowhere just behind the soldier. Though Prue couldn't see him, she *felt* that dark, powerful presence taking up space behind her.

"Don't. Touch. Her." Cyrus's voice was a snarl, so venomous and full of hatred that it reminded Prue of their first meeting in the crypt.

Only this time, his fury wasn't directed at her.

The soldier's hands loosened ever so slightly, and Prue took advantage of his lapse in concentration. On instinct, she ducked down, just as a horrible squelching sound echoed behind her. Thick, warm blood sprayed along the snow in front of her, and she winced as flecks showered down on her head.

Panting, Prue stood up slowly, once she was certain the man wouldn't grab her again. When she shifted, facing where the man had once been, her stomach turned over.

The soldier's body lay in the snow, his head completely severed. Prue's eyes grew wide, and she couldn't look away from it. Only belatedly did she realize Cyrus was speaking to her.

"*Prudence*. Are you hurt?"

Prue blinked, just now noticing the blood dribbling down her face. "I—No, I'm not hurt." Her gaze roved over the snowy expanse before them, which was now soaked with blood. All around them, the dismembered remains of the soldiers lay scattered like forgotten sacks of raw meat.

"Are you—Did you—" Prue couldn't speak between the panic still racing in her chest and the breaths that just would not come. "Did you kill him with your *hands*?" She felt lightheaded, and a distant part of her registered she was close to burning out. She had never used so much magic before.

Cyrus said nothing, but the darkness in his eyes and the blood coating his hands said enough.

Yes. This god was powerful enough to decapitate a man with his bare hands.

A howl echoed through the night, and Prue's head shot up as she noticed the ghosts in the sky. Slowly, the spirits floated nearer, closing in on Prue and Cyrus.

"Shit," Prue whispered. "They're drawn to the magic."

Hoofbeats thundered nearby, and Cyrus swore. "Come on." He took Prue's hand and dragged her deeper into the woods. The horses advanced, a cacophony of clomping. It sounded like an entire army was after them.

Each step sent rippling waves of dizziness and nausea through Prue. She wouldn't last much longer. She wanted to scream. Why were these soldiers chasing after them? Didn't they understand that Prue and Cyrus were trying to put a *stop* to the ghosts haunting the city?

The woods opened up to a narrow road that snaked between snow-capped houses. As Prue and Cyrus hurried forward, they stopped short at the sight of three horsemen waiting for them at the edge of the road. Cyrus backed away, glancing over his shoulder to find two more trailing them through the woods.

They were cornered.

Cyrus's hand was warm in Prue's grasp. He squeezed her fingers as if to reassure her. She sucked in a breath, ready for the onslaught of his power once more . . .

Then, more hoofbeats thumped along the road. Prue's eyes widened as dozens of soldiers atop horses rode toward them. More and more horsemen poured out from the main road, and Prue lost count, but there were more than *fifty* of them.

Beside her, Cyrus deflated. Even he couldn't handle that many assailants, and Prue's magic was spent.

"Witch. Demon." The soldier in front motioned to them both. "Come with us. The emperor has orders for you to be brought to the palace."

What does the emperor want with us? Prue thought in bewilderment.

Fury rippled off Cyrus, and Prue wouldn't have been surprised if he launched an offensive, regardless of the odds. But, after shooting a nervous glance at Prue, he slowly lifted his hands in surrender. His face revealed the full force of his dark rage, contradicting the acquiescence he demonstrated.

But in that moment, Prue knew he was giving up . . . for her. Her chest tightened at the thought.

It's just because of your bond, she told herself. *If something happens to you, it could affect him, too.*

She swayed slightly, and then Cyrus was there, his hands on her shoulders, grounding her in place. In ordinary circumstances, she would've snapped at him, insisting she could handle herself. But she was too weak to argue.

And the truth was, she *couldn't* handle herself. Not right now. She had never felt so weak in all her life.

"Take my magic back," Cyrus murmured in her ear.

"Why?" Prue's voice wasn't more than a groggy mumble.

"You need the strength."

Prue tried to shake her head, but her body wouldn't move. "You need it more."

Cyrus's hands on her shoulders tightened. "Please, Prue. At this rate, you'll faint before we even reach the palace."

Prue closed her eyes. She wanted to disagree, but she didn't even have the strength for that. After a moment, she whispered, "I take your magic back."

For one second, she thought it wouldn't work. Perhaps she had to put more vigor in her voice or summon more energy. But, to her amazement, the fire swelled in her chest, making her straighten slightly. She'd never noticed a significant presence from Cyrus's magic except for that first time down in the crypt. But now, she felt it. A rising inside her, like the empty space was being filled with something else. Something *colder*. She took a deep breath, and pinpricks of ice rose up her throat. She winced, but the dull throbbing in her limbs receded slightly. To her relief, she was able to walk without Cyrus's help.

She glanced at him, and he nodded, his face solemn. "Thank you," she breathed.

He only inclined his head, his eyes roving over the soldiers surrounding them. Prue knew he was assessing the threat, his quick mind calculating a way out. Perhaps if Prue had a full night's sleep, she could be more useful. She knew Cyrus could get out on his own if he had his magic. So, why didn't he?

Then, she remembered the pomegranate tea Polina had forced him to drink. *It will prevent you from harming or abandoning Prudence.*

Cyrus couldn't leave Prue. Not until they'd reached their destination.

Prue glanced up at the sky, wondering if the approaching ghosts would provide enough distraction for her and Cyrus to escape. But the pearly white forms were retreating, returning to their position above the castle turrets.

Prue frowned. Why were they retreating? Could they sense that Prue was too weak? That her magic wouldn't provide any fuel for them?

Or perhaps they were drawn to something else. Something lurking in the castle.

The horsemen made them trudge behind them, with several at their backs to ensure they didn't flee. Thankfully, the men didn't chain or tie them up, though Prue had a sense it was because they knew magic could easily get them out. Which brought her back to her original question: how did they know about Prue and Cyrus? And about magic? Some villages, like Krenia, were open about magic because they were so small and it was impossible to keep secrets. But as a whole, the Realm of Gaia was quite secretive about magic and the supernatural.

So, how did these Thanassian soldiers know? How did they obtain witch dust? The only thing Prue could think of was that there must be a witch among their court, searching for them.

But *why*?

Her frustration mounted, and she gritted her teeth. Each step sent a jolt of icy pain through her body. She'd been numb before, so close to unconsciousness that she'd felt nothing. Now she felt it all. The biting wind. The snow crunching against her boots. The frigid air chilling her entire body.

This didn't feel like an improvement. Despite her knowing full well that collapsing on one of the soldiers wouldn't have been a wise idea, either.

Gradually, the mighty turrets of the palace drew nearer, and Prue had to crane her neck to take in the full view. The towers pierced the sky like jagged knives, and the image made Prue want to shudder. This didn't look like the fairy tale castles she'd read about as a child.

This looked more like a prison.

She shot a glance at Cyrus, who glared up at the castle with all the might of his fury, as if he could send it crumbling with a look. Prue wouldn't be surprised if he *could.*

She couldn't shake the image of that man's head tumbling from his body . . . And he had done that with his *hands*. What else was he capable of?

A loud, metallic grating sound split the air as the portcullis was raised for them. Prue followed the soldiers as they emerged into a courtyard within the castle. The heavy metal gate slammed shut behind them, and Prue flinched.

They were sealed inside.

Prue expected to be led straight to the dungeon or prison cells or wherever they kept their enemies. But instead, the soldiers dismounted their horses, sending them off to stable hands, and led Prue and Cyrus up a narrow set of steps. Heavy oak doors were thrown open, and Prue exhaled in relief as warmth surrounded her, a blissful reprieve from the chill outside. Torches lined the hallway, along with elaborate paintings of mountain landscapes. Prue recognized the Emdale Mountains in several of them, and her insides wriggled nervously at the reminder of what she'd shared with Cyrus in that cave the night before. Goddess, that felt like ages ago . . .

The soldiers escorted them down the hallway until they reached another set of double doors, this one flanked by four men wearing identical blue jackets as the men with Prue. The soldiers nodded at each other before the doors swung open. Prue held her breath as she followed the line of men inside.

They stepped into a massive throne room. Already, a

crowd stood before them, parted to form a small aisle before the two thrones atop a small dais. In one throne stood a figure Prue recognized immediately. Cyrus's brother, Vaileios. He smirked at them, a gold crown gleaming atop his black hair.

Well, that explained a lot.

But as her gaze shifted to the woman standing beside him, all thoughts fled from her mind. Her body went still as ice crept into her veins, freezing her completely. Someone nudged her in the back to urge her forward, but she couldn't move even if she wanted to. All she saw —all she *felt*—was the sheer impossibility of the woman standing alongside Vasileios.

It was Mona.

CHALLENGE

CYRUS

CYRUS'S CHEST swelled with the absence of his power, a cold emptiness that slithered through him at the sight of his brother. And that crown atop his head . . .

Rage bled through Cyrus's vision. With a snarl, he strode forward, intent on ripping Vasileios's head off. But in a flash, several soldiers stepped in front of him, blocking his path.

Vasileios laughed. "What will you do, brother? You have no magic."

"I don't need magic to tear out your throat," Cyrus growled.

Vasileios's eyes glinted. "With what weapons? For once in your pitiful existence, learn to shut your mouth and bow to someone else's authority, Cyrus."

Cyrus's nostrils flared. Part of him yearned to lunge at his older brother, regardless of the mass of soldiers standing between them. He didn't care if they gutted him, if they bled him dry. As long as he had his hands around Vasileios's throat.

But something pulled his gaze from the two thrones: Prue. Slowly, his eyes shifted to her, finding her face bone-white, her wide eyes fixed on the girl standing beside Vasileios.

Cyrus's heart dropped to his stomach. *Oh, gods, no . . .* Following Prue's gaze, he scrutinized the young woman with the matching gold crown. She stood, poised and erect, the perfect picture of elegance and grace. Her wavy black hair was styled in an elaborate knot, her sweeping purple gown complimenting her dark bronze skin. Her eyes were a luminescent light green, standing out starkly against her dark skin and hair. Though her skin was darker and her eyes a different shade, her nose and mouth were the same shape as Prue's. They shared the same defiant chin, the same high cheekbones.

This was Mona. Prue's sister.

Mona stared down at them with cold apathy, her expression void of any emotion. It was bizarre for Cyrus to gaze upon this face—almost a mirror image of the one he knew so well—without any semblance of humor or anger.

She was like a statue, rigid and merciless.

Cyrus's eyes cut to Vasileios, who looked quite pleased with himself. In a low voice, Cyrus uttered a single word: "How." He bit it out like a demand rather than a question.

"Same as you, brother," Vasileios said. "I bound myself to this witch . . . through marriage."

"No!" The word was strangled, like it was wrenched from Prue's throat by force. She staggered forward, her face stricken with horror. Around them, the soldiers shifted, clearly uneasy with her movements.

Cyrus needed to gain control of the situation. Now. Prue was in no shape to play Vasileios's game, so he had to play for the two of them. He *had* to.

Bury everything, he told himself, schooling his features into something neutral and unfeeling. *Bury it so far deep that it can't rise again.* Down, down, down he shoved his anger and his shock until it sank like a heavy weight at the bottom of his chest, leaving nothing but a hollow emptiness in its wake. With a deep breath, he fixed his gaze on his brother once more.

"How?" he asked again, his voice more level now. "Mona died. She sealed her fate with blood, bound to the Book of Eyes."

Beside him, Prue flinched, but Cyrus ignored her. *Keep it buried. Keep it all buried.*

"Ah, yes, but *many* mortals died that day, did they not?" Vasileios's gaze slid to Prue, a hungry glint gleaming in his silver eyes.

Something roared in Cyrus's chest as his brother stared openly at Prue, at his *wife*, but with all his strength, he shoved those emotions down. *Bury everything,* he reminded himself. *It cannot resurface. Not now.*

"Perhaps if you had been more attentive to the rivers, you would have noticed," Vasileios went on. "Another mortal perished at the same time Pomona did. A lowly villager. But I saw Pomona's soul for what it was: a rare treasure indeed. I caught the pair of souls just before they moved on . . . and I swapped them. The villager's soul paid the price to the Book of Eyes, and Pomona's was freed. It was as if she suffered only a mortal death. And, for us gods, a mortal death is easy to circumvent."

"You swapped the souls?" Cyrus repeated slowly. He shook his head. "That's impossible."

"It's not," Vasileios snapped, his eyes flaring. His expression cleared, but not before Cyrus caught that familiar echo of indignation, of anger and resentment. In that moment, Cyrus saw himself: someone desperate to prove himself worthy and capable, frustrated by everyone underestimating him.

It was alarming seeing such emotions in Vasileios, the former heir, the oldest prince of Hell, beloved by Aidoneus.

The thought sent a strange sense of calmness washing over Cyrus, and he found himself smirking. "Does Father know?"

The stiffness in Vasileios's jaw was answer enough. Aidoneus did *not* know. How interesting . . .

Prue inhaled a shuddering breath. Cyrus chanced a

glance her way and found tears streaming down her face.

Before Vasileios could notice, Cyrus pulled his brother's attention back to himself. "And here I was, under the impression you and Father were conspiring against me. I'm sure he'd be very interested to know you have your own agenda." Cyrus spread his arms, gesturing to the soldiers at large. "You've amassed yourself a mortal army! I must say I'm impressed."

"You'd be surprised what a well-placed glamour can do," Vasileios said. "One spark of my magic—combined with Pomona's, of course—and this whole kingdom now believes me to be its rightful ruler."

Coldness seeped into Cyrus's chest at the implication. Gods, the sheer power that spell must've required . . . Uncertainty crept into his thoughts. He'd doubted Vasileios's words before, but could it be true? Could Mona truly be alive . . . and bound to Vasileios?

He shot a quick glance at Mona, but the witch's face was as blank as before. Completely expressionless. She looked more like a porcelain doll than anything alive.

The sight of her like this made Cyrus's skin prickle. Something was very . . . *off* about her.

"What need have you of a mortal kingdom?" Cyrus asked, though his mind was spinning with thoughts. *If Vasileios has Mona's magic, how can I overpower him? What is the state of the Underworld? If he's here, does that mean it's been destroyed?*

Vasileios rose from his throne, his cape sweeping behind him as he descended the dais to stand in front of Cyrus. Cyrus's fingers itched to claw at him, to strike him while he was so near, but he balled his hands into fists to contain his rage.

"Consider this my challenge to you, brother," Vasileios said softly. "I challenge you for the throne to the Underworld. If you do not surrender, then I will make my home *here* and wage war on your precious mortal realm."

Cyrus remained perfectly still, his mind spinning as he processed this. How was he supposed to reach the gate to the Underworld with Vasileios and an army of soldiers standing in his way? He had to think fast. "What makes you think I would care if you destroyed this realm?"

Vasileios snorted, shaking his head in amusement. "You cannot fool me, Cyrus. I know you are bound to this realm, just as you are bound to this witch." He gestured to Prue, and Cyrus's chest burned hot once more. Thankfully, Vasileios seemed uninterested with Prue, because he turned back to face his brother. A small crease formed between his eyebrows. "In fact, I'm rather puzzled as to *why* you haven't completed the bond. Is she not to your liking?"

Vasileios glanced at Prue again, his gaze calculating as it roved up and down her body. Slowly.

"Stop it," Cyrus barked, stepping closer to his brother.

Vasileios's eyes glinted, and Cyrus knew he'd shown his hand. *Shit.* "Don't tell me you've developed feelings for her . . ." Vasileios chuckled. "I would've thought you'd learned after last time. How long before this one betrays you, too?" He leaned closer to whisper conspiratorially, "Just take her and be done with it. You can dispose of her afterward."

Cyrus's restraint snapped. With a roar of fury, he lunged, swinging his fist into Vasileios's jaw, then his gut. The gold crown crashed to the floor, the sound reverberating off the walls. Cyrus wrapped his hands around his brother's throat, his grip tightening until Vasileios's face turned red, then purple.

An explosion of black magic slammed into Cyrus's chest, sending him flying backward. He tumbled to the floor and swung around, easily righting himself to charge at Vasileios again.

"Stop him," Vasileios said hoarsely, rubbing at his throat.

Six soldiers formed a wall between Vasileios and Cyrus, but Cyrus was undeterred. He elbowed one in the face, then threw his weight into another, knocking him down. Several arms grabbed him, pinning him in place. Though Cyrus thrashed, his movements were no match for the six armed men keeping him down.

"You really are an animal, aren't you?" Vasileios

asked, though his tone lacked the usual venom. "This place has turned you feral. Father would be so disappointed."

"Mona," Prue croaked.

Cyrus sucked in a breath, glancing over at her. She still stared at Mona as if her mind had finally registered who stood in front of her. As if the skirmish with Cyrus and his brother hadn't even happened.

Prue took a tiny step forward, her face pleading. "Mona, is—is it really you?"

Mona blinked slowly. "It is." Her voice was hollow and empty.

Prue inhaled a shaky breath, and Cyrus had no doubt the sound of her sister's voice was undoing her completely. "Why? Why would you do this?"

Mona's gaze slid to Vasileios, and something flickered in her eyes, something Cyrus couldn't place. But it was gone before he could scrutinize it. "I don't expect you to understand, sister."

Prue stiffened, her eyes narrowing ever so slightly. And Cyrus, who knew her well enough to discern her expressions, wondered what she'd just discovered.

"So, what, you'll kill us?" Cyrus asked loudly. He hadn't missed the shrewd gleam in his brother's eyes as he'd watched the sisters' exchange. Vasileios might have been an arrogant ass, but he was also clever.

Keep him distracted, Cyrus told himself. *Keep his attention off Prue.*

"As delightful as that would be, I need you in the Underworld to pass the crown to me," Vasileios said. "The transition must be made in that realm. Not here."

"You're assuming I'm agreeing to hand it over."

Vasileios's mouth curved into a cruel smile. "You will." He snapped his fingers, then gestured to Prue.

Two soldiers drew forward, pinning her arms to her sides. Prue yelped in alarm, glancing around in horror. "Get your hands off me!" That familiar fire blazed in her eyes, and she struggled, but her magic was still drained. She couldn't fight them off.

"Surrender the crown," Vasileios said, "or she—and every other mortal in this pitiful realm—will die."

IMPOSTER

PRUE

PRUE ALLOWED the soldiers to cart her off to the dungeons. She let them toss her in unceremoniously and didn't even flinch when they slammed the cell shut, leaving her to rot in the dank and moldy prison.

She let it all happen because she knew one thing for certain: the woman in that throne room was not Mona.

And as bizarre as it was, this knowledge sent a spark of hope burning in her chest. Prue clung to this hope with all her strength, knowing it was the only thing keeping her afloat.

Mona's not really here. She's not trapped in a marriage with Vasileios. He didn't force her to consummate. She repeated the words in her mind over and over, and with each repetition, the knots in her chest eased slightly.

Vasileios had given Cyrus one day to think over his proposal. But Prue wouldn't be surprised if the oldest prince of Hell came for her sooner. She hadn't liked the hungry gleam in his eye . . .

Vasileios was a monster. She could see it all over his slimy expression, the smugness of his cruel face. How had she ever been repulsed by Cyrus when his brother was ten times worse?

Prue had been lying when she'd called Cyrus a vile monster in that cave. She wasn't sure when—perhaps during the carriage ride—but at some point, she had stopped thinking of Cyrus as a monster. Compared to Vasileios, he was . . .

No. Prue slammed down the thought before it could form. Even if she weren't in a dire situation, it was too dangerous to think of Cyrus as anything but a prince of Hell bound to her by force.

Nothing more. She couldn't afford to assess her feelings toward him.

Even if he *had* fought for her in the throne room earlier . . . The memory sent a tingle of heat coursing through her.

But no, she needed to focus on Mona. If that *wasn't* her sister, then who was it? And how had she possessed Mona's body? She thought of the death shadows that had attacked Krenia when the Book of Eyes was opened the first time. The victims had been momentarily possessed, their eyes turning black, just before they died.

But Mona's eyes had been clear. Startlingly so. This

was different. And Prue was certain Vasileios was behind it.

Prue knew nothing about death magic or the Underworld or the concept of *swapping souls,* which apparently had shocked Cyrus, too. She didn't even allow herself to think of *who* he had swapped souls with—if it was a villager, it was probably someone she knew, and the thought made her feel ill.

But she *did* know Cyrus. And this particular problem required his magic.

She needed that dark power, and she needed Mona. The *real* Mona.

For several minutes, Prue paced the length of her tiny cell, taking deep breaths and mentally walking through what she had to do. She didn't have spell ingredients, but she *did* have her blood, and right now, that was plenty. Her limbs still weighed heavily from the taxing ordeal in the woods earlier, but she would have to push it aside. As much as she wanted to collapse and rest, time was of the essence.

She had to do this now.

"Goddess above, grant me power," she whispered. Her skin prickled with awareness, and her third eye slid open. Prue suppressed a shudder. She had never liked the third eye. It felt . . . strange. Foreign. Like an extra body part she didn't want.

It opened so much more easily than she'd expected. Usually, the magic in the air had to be quite potent to awaken her witch senses. But perhaps her powers were still present from all the magic she'd summoned in the woods with the soldiers.

Or perhaps it was already awakened from how much power thrummed through the palace. She thought of the ghosts swirling above the castle and knew the place must have been warded somehow to keep the spirits out.

With her third eye open, Prue could feel the power reverberating off her bones and buzzing in her chest. Goddess, it was everywhere, this magic. Every breath, every blink . . . The energy surged through her, sweeping over her like a tidal wave.

Prue inhaled a shuddering breath, her eyes stinging from the intensity of it. The power in the air was so thick she could hardly breathe. In one instant, she sensed darkness, a sticky sludge like molasses. And in another, she sensed the light, flowery scent of Mona's pure earth magic.

Mona's magic. It was *here*.

Now Prue's eyes were burning for a different reason. She hadn't smelled her sister's magic in so long . . . It brought on a burst of memories and trauma. Prue shut her eyes, groaning from the force of it all.

It's not really Mona, she reminded herself. *It isn't. It can't be.* But a sliver of doubt worked its way into her thoughts. How could this imposter have Mona's magical scent? Her aura?

Prue gritted her teeth and shook her head. She would

get all the answers she needed once she summoned Mona's spirit. Her eyes flew open, and she scanned the rocky ground of her prison cell. Her eyes landed on a pile of broken pebbles at her feet. She crouched and sifted through them before finding a jagged edge, almost like a spearhead.

Prue pressed the sharp edge into her palm until a bead of blood welled from the wound. She let it fall to the ground, and it sizzled when it met the earth. "I invoke the death magic of Osiris, god of the Underworld." Her voice was low and even and didn't sound like herself at all.

Prue's fingers curled into a fist, her nails digging into the wound, widening it as more droplets of blood fell. An ethereal gust of wind whipped at her hair, and that horrifying ice-cold power swelled in her chest. Cyrus's power.

As blood ran down her hand, Prue whispered, "Pomona Donati, I summon thee."

The wind continued to lash at her, fierce and merciless, as the cold hardened to ice in her chest, stealing her breath.

Then, a figure materialized outside her cell door. Prue watched, transfixed, as it took shape. At first, it was pearly white and slightly transparent, nothing more than an ambiguous shape hovering in the air. It looked so similar to the ghosts outside that a spike of fear bolted through Prue's chest. Then, wavy hair formed, along with a skirt Prue knew so well—the same skirt Mona had been wearing when she'd died. Gradually, her twin's face came into view: large eyes, full lips, strong chin . . . Prue couldn't make out colors with this ghostly form, but she could see the luminescent eyes peering at her. In this form, they looked like silver orbs, and it reminded Prue so much of Cyrus that she had to drop her gaze.

"Prue," Mona whispered, her voice echoing slightly. "What—what have you done?"

"I had to summon you," Prue said, her tone pleading. "Do you know what's happened?"

"Of course I know." Mona's voice was harsh, reminiscent of the days when Prue made a foolish mistake that could've been solved by simply opening the right book. Not much had changed, even in death. "How could you summon me? I can't be here, not when that *thing* is so close by, parading as me!"

Prue's heart lurched at her words. "What the hell is going on, Mona? Who *is* that?" She gestured vaguely to the ceiling, to where she thought the throne room would be. "And how did Vasileios get your body?"

"I don't have time to explain it all to you."

"Then *try*," Prue bit out. "I need some answers. In case you can't tell, I'm in a *dungeon*."

Mona glanced around as if she had indeed failed to notice this. She huffed a breath—which, in that moment, Prue found to be quite amusing, given that she didn't *need* air—and said, "All right, I'll try to sum it up as quickly as I can. When I died, my soul was separated from my body, which I'm told is the normal situation for those about to enter the rivers of Hell. Vasileios snatched me before I could fully transition, though, and claimed me for himself. However, he only has one half of me—my body. Until he merges it with my spirit, he cannot fully access my magic."

Relief and shock mingled in Prue's chest.

Mona could easily read her expression because she snapped, "Don't look so relieved. All Vasileios has to do is bring that imposter down here. If we physically occupy the same space, we'll merge, and he'll have full access to my powers."

Prue barely contained a shudder. "But . . . I can *smell* your magic here, Mona. How?"

"It's my essence. Part of it lingers with my body, but it's only an echo of my true power. I . . . was told that magic resides with the soul, not the body."

Prue's eyes narrowed. She hadn't missed the catch in Mona's voice. "Told . . . by whom?"

Mona's form rippled slightly. "It doesn't matter. I can't explain it all right now."

"Mona, who have you been talking to?" Alarm quivered in Prue's thoughts as she imagined Cyrus's other horrible brothers and how they might be manipulating her.

"Prue, *focus*!" Mona snapped, sounding so much like

her usual self that Prue almost laughed. "Remember that rune I taught you during Samhain last year?"

Prue wracked her brain as she tried to recall. "The one to dislodge a person's spirit?" She shuddered. "Goddess, Mona, do you want me to do that to fake-Mona?"

"No, no, she doesn't have a spirit *to* dislodge. I'm suggesting you paint the rune in your blood . . . right there." Mona lifted a wispy hand, gesturing to the ground just beneath her. Within reaching distance, if Prue stretched her arm through the bars of her cell.

Prue frowned, her mind working furiously. Then, comprehension dawned. "Oh. I see." She grinned wickedly at her sister. "That's quite clever, Mona."

"I know." Mona sounded so pleased with herself that Prue actually did laugh this time. Mona's spirit flickered like the dying light of a candle, and Prue's smile faded.

"I have to go now," Mona said, her voice far away. "If I'm here too long, he'll sense me."

"Mona." Prue stumbled forward subconsciously, even knowing she couldn't touch her sister. She couldn't just let her leave.

"I'll see you soon," Mona said. "I swear it, Prue."

And then she was gone.

BLOOD

CYRUS

CYRUS STARED STONILY at the decanter in his brother's hand as Vasileios poured the amber liquid into a chalice.

"Drink," Vasileios ordered. "It doesn't do much for our immortal forms, but it helps."

Cyrus merely glared up at him. They were in an ornate guest suite as big as the throne room with an enormous bed topped with plush pillows on one end and a chaise sofa and table on the other. Behind the sitting area was a series of luxurious bathing chambers.

It would've felt extravagant, were it not for the circumstances.

Cyrus sat on the chaise, only to keep himself from pacing. Vasileios stood over him, still holding the chalice.

Instead of accepting it, Cyrus bit out, "Where is Prue."

Vasileios sighed and sat opposite Cyrus, drinking out of the chalice. "She's safe."

"Liar."

"It doesn't need to be this way, Cyrus. The crown was always mine to begin with. Simply give it back, and I can put you in a comfortable position. Take my place here. An empire at your disposal. An entire palace for yourself!" He spread one arm to indicate the vastness of the suite. "You can even keep your little witch here to be your empress."

Cyrus's scowl deepened.

"Or you can execute her," Vasileios added with a shrug. "I honestly can't understand you two. One minute it seems like you'll slaughter an entire army to save her, the next it looks like you want to wring her neck."

Cyrus couldn't help but lift his eyebrows at that. Vasileios had a point there.

"Is the Underworld really that important to you?" Vasileios went on, taking another sip.

"It's my home," Cyrus said incredulously. "The only place where I ever *meant* something."

"Not anymore. Take my deal, and you'll be an emperor."

Cyrus leaned forward, bracing his arms against his legs. "Do you even feel them? The souls?"

Vasileios stilled, and something unreadable stirred in

his eyes. After a moment, he said, "I'm not sure what you mean."

"Well, I do. I feel them constantly. I am connected to that realm, brother. Even when I'm here. Even when I don't want to be. I am *bound* to protect those souls. As much as I despise that connection, it is there."

"Correct me if I'm wrong, but I was under the impression you were connected to the mortal realm, and *that* was the bond you despised."

Cyrus closed his eyes for a moment. Gods, he was right. When Cyrus had the right to the throne of the Underworld, he could only complain about his tether to the mortal realm. And now that he was in the mortal realm, he complained about being drawn to the Underworld.

He was never content to be where he was.

That sounded like something Evander would say.

For the briefest moment, Cyrus's thoughts turned to his kindest brother, wondering how he fared in the Underworld. With Vasileios here, did that make things better or worse in the Underworld? What were Aidoneus and Marcellus doing? Was Evander safe?

Cyrus had never let himself worry about Evander before. It had been too dangerous a thought, far too close to affection and weakness for his liking. But now, he let those thoughts roam free.

"What will happen to . . . the rest of our brothers if I agree to your terms?" Cyrus asked. He wasn't entertaining the idea; he knew Vasileios to be crafty and didn't for one moment trust he would honor his side of the agreement. But he *was* curious as to where he stood regarding their brothers.

Vasileios's expression went rigid for one brief moment before he said smoothly, "They will be treated with respect. I don't plan to repeat the mistakes we made with you, Cyrus. We share blood. And that should stand for something."

Shared blood. Cyrus wanted to scoff at the notion. Blood meant nothing to Vasileios. It didn't matter to him before, and it certainly didn't now.

This was a test, and Vasileios failed. Cyrus was never intending to consider this agreement. He just wanted to know how forthcoming his brother would be about his plans.

It was clear Vasileios would reveal nothing.

Now, it was time for Cyrus to plant his own seeds of deception. "I'm assuming Aidoneus will have Styx, then?"

Vasileios's eyes flashed. "What? Of course not. Styx belongs to me." His voice was harsh, like shards of glass.

Cyrus dropped his gaze, trying to adopt a conflicted expression. "Oh, right. I just thought . . . Never mind."

"What? What did you hear?" Panic laced Vasileios's voice.

"When Aidoneus was poisoning Acheron," Cyrus said, allowing a bit of venom into his voice that he didn't have to force, "he mentioned he longed to have control over Styx once more. That it had been too long."

Vasileios's jaw twitched. After a moment, he said, "You're lying."

Cyrus lifted his hands, palms out, in a sign of surrender. "Must have been my mistake. Surely Aidoneus wouldn't resume his duties after everything that's happened. It's a ridiculous notion."

Cyrus leaned back against the chaise, draping one arm behind his head in the picture of ease. Across from him, he could feel Vasileios's rage and confusion rippling.

With a bit too much force, Vasileios slammed the chalice down on the table and stood, adjusting his tunic. "Right. Well. I'm sure you'll be comfortable here. I'll give you a moment to consider my bargain. When I return, I expect an answer. Otherwise, your little witch is the first to die."

Cyrus merely lifted his eyebrows. "What ever happened to providing me with a comfortable situation? Threats don't seem entirely hospitable."

Vasileios offered a cold smile. "That's only after you accept our bargain. Consider this"—he gestured to the suite at large—"a show of good faith. But the gesture ends in one hour. After that, your arrangements will be far less pleasant while you consider my offer." With that, he slammed the doors shut.

In a flash, Cyrus was on his feet, his ear pressed to

the door. Once Vasileios's footsteps faded, Cyrus jiggled the handles. Locked. Of course.

Cursing, Cyrus scanned the vast room, looking for some kind of weapon. Naturally, Vasileios removed anything remotely sharp. But as Cyrus glanced around with more focus, his eyes snagged on the glistening jewels and gems from a vanity table nearby. Frowning, he drew nearer and realized it was jewelry. This must have been a woman's suite. Cyrus pulled open a drawer only to find piles of necklaces, earrings, bracelets, pendants, and broaches. He uttered a bewildered chuckle before pocketing several of them, knowing he could use them as currency once he got out of here.

Vasileios either must have been foolish or incredibly smug to leave these lying around. In fact, Cyrus wouldn't have been surprised if his brother had done it on purpose to gloat about his abundant wealth.

What an idiot.

When Cyrus's pockets were heavy with jewels, he inspected the room once more, hoping to find a tool he could use to pry open the door. His eyes fell on the poker resting by the fireplace. He strode toward it and slid the sharp metal tip into the door's lock, trying to jiggle it free.

Soft footsteps sounded on the other side. Cyrus suddenly went still, his hands slick with sweat as he gripped the fire poker. The footsteps stopped just on the other side of the door. Then, a soft voice whispered, "*Recludo.*"

Uncertain if it was Prue or Mona, Cyrus drew back, raising the poker, prepared to strike if he had to . . .

Only to find Prue, her garments filthy and covered in blood. Her entire left arm was stained crimson, and Cyrus's jaw dropped at the sight of her.

"Gods, Prue! What the hell happened to you?" Slowly, Cyrus lowered his poker, though he didn't release it. His entire body was still on edge, prepared to fight off a threat.

Prue stared at him, then shifted her gaze to the room. Her eyes narrowed. "You sure seem to be suffering right now."

Cyrus groaned. "It's just Vasileios trying to bribe me." He stepped closer to Prue, scanning her for injuries. "Are you all right? Did they hurt you?" His words were a growl as he pictured the soldiers Vasileios had control over. If one of them had harmed her . . .

"No, no, I did this to myself," Prue said absently. "You know, for magic." When he continued to watch her in confusion, she said quickly, "I'll tell you later. What's more important is, that's not really Mona out there."

Cyrus straightened. Well, *this* was interesting.

In a hasty murmur, Prue filled him in on everything her sister's spirit had conveyed to her. In spite of it all, Cyrus found himself grinning.

"All of it was a lie," he said with a laugh. "Vasileios,

he's absolutely bluffing. Gods, the irony of it all. He was taunting *me* for not sealing our bond, when all along, he's created himself a false bride!"

"It's not completely false," Prue whispered. "As soon as he binds her body with her soul, he'll have her." Worry flared in her expression.

"He won't," Cyrus said at once. "Her soul is bound to the Underworld. In order to access it, he has to . . . Ah. I understand now."

"What?"

"He has to possess full control of the realm to do as he pleases with the souls. As of right now, he only has authority over the realm I assigned him to."

"That's why he wants your throne. For Mona's soul."

"Yes."

Prue shook her head. "But *why*? What's so important about my sister? Won't any witch suffice? Can't he just marry into another powerful coven?"

"You and your sister aren't just any witches, Prue. You're twins blessed by the Triple Goddess. Do you know how rare that is?"

Prue's jaw went slack, her gaze unfocused as she stared at the floor. After a moment, she whispered, "Janus, the Doorkeeper of the Heavens, imbued the two faces of his power into the souls of mortal witches. Two halves of the same whole. Two twins of the same bloodline. If one twin dies, Janus's spell would be undone, and the twin powers would merge together into one being and one soul."

Cyrus frowned. "What is that?"

"It's from my family grimoire. The legend of Janus. The prophecy I told you about before. We were told since birth that our powers were special because of our bond as twin witches. But one of us had to die for the power convergence to occur. And Mona *did* die. Or so we thought. With Mona not technically 'dead,' then . . ."

"You haven't converged yet," Cyrus said slowly. Then, he blinked, having just realized something. "Vasileios sent the assassin after you. In Voula City."

Prue nodded as if she'd just realized this as well. "If I die, that leaves Mona free to absorb my powers."

Cyrus cocked his head at her, considering. "You've been holding back for nothing, Prue."

"What do you mean?"

"You've held back because you believed you'd stolen Mona's magic. But you haven't. Everything you've done has been *you*."

Prue's eyes widened at his words, and Cyrus saw the comprehension dawn on her. All those powerful spells she'd cast had been on her own merit.

She shook her head. "No. No, it isn't possible. There's no way . . ." She faltered and bit her lip, conflict warring in her expression.

Footsteps echoed nearby, and Prue inhaled sharply. In an instant, Cyrus snatched her arm, shoving her behind him as a soldier entered the room. His eyes flicked from Cyrus to Prue. He gasped, but before he could shout for aid, Cyrus shoved the tip of the poker into the man's throat.

Prue yelped as the soldier crumpled to the floor, blood pooling from the gash in his throat.

"Goddess, Cyrus! You didn't have to do that." Prue shot a horrified look at him. "He's innocent. Your brother is controlling him!"

Cyrus stared coldly at the man, who was choking on his own blood. "Would you have preferred I let him live and sound the alarm? It was either him . . . or us." He leveled a sharp look at Prue, whose face had drained of color. Judgment emanated from her gaze, along with disgust and loathing and shock.

He was a monster. She said as much to him in the cave. And for a moment, it seemed she'd forgotten.

Good, he thought with savage satisfaction. *She needs to be reminded.*

And so do I.

"Come on." Cyrus strode forward, not bothering to glance back to ensure she followed. "Let's get out of this shithole."

GAMES
PRUE

PRUE WAS FADING. All the magic she'd used, with no rest or food . . . She was lucky she wasn't unconscious.

But it was only a matter of time.

Cyrus seemed to sense how weak she was. He guided her by the elbow, half hauling her as they raced down the staircase toward the servants' quarters. Cyrus insisted his brother wouldn't frequent this side of the castle.

"He'll be quite busy right now anyway," Prue said, her voice a bit raspy.

"Why?" Cyrus asked. "What did you do?"

"I painted a rune on the ground, then summoned a dozen guards to my cell. My magic dislodged their souls from their bodies."

Cyrus halted, jerking her to a stop with his surprise.

"You—What?" A slow smile spread across his face. "That's delightfully wicked, Prue."

She really shouldn't feel pleased by his pride. He'd just murdered an innocent man in front of her. Even so, she couldn't stop the warmth from spreading through her chest as she smiled back. "To be fair, it was Mona's idea."

When they reached the servants' hall, they paused and listened, waiting to see if any soldiers pursued them. But all that met Prue's ears were the bustling sounds of staff working in the kitchens. She and Cyrus crept onward, sneaking down the narrow hallway. All it would take was one servant to shout in alarm, and a whole squadron of soldiers would come running.

"Shit," Cyrus hissed as hurried footsteps drew nearer. Without preamble, he snatched Prue's wrist and dragged her into a closet, easing the door shut behind them.

Prue's heart thundered in her ears as darkness swallowed them. The space was cramped and smelled of mildew. Cyrus's chest was pressed up against her, the tiny space far too small for one person, let alone two. His arms were around her, his cedar-and-ash scent enveloping her. Prue closed her eyes, trying not to focus on the heat of him, the strength of his arms, the muscles of his chest as her fingertips drifted across his shirt . . .

The footsteps rushed past them, shoes clacking as if someone was in a hurry. Prue's breath caught in her throat as she realized she'd fisted the fabric of Cyrus's tunic. Slowly, she released him, but he didn't move. She could still feel his breath against her, the rise and fall of his chest. She tried to look up, to meet his gaze, but it was too dark. Her nose brushed his, and she went perfectly still, realizing how close their faces were. All she had to do was angle her head slightly, and their lips would meet.

Light spilled into the small space as Cyrus opened the door and backed away from her. Startled, Prue blinked against the brightness, trying to steady her racing heart. She looked at Cyrus, whose silver eyes were wild and blazing, but she couldn't read the emotion there. Was it anger? Fear? Had she upset him by being so close?

"Come on," he said quietly, helping her out of the closet. Without another word, they darted down the hallway and burst out the back door.

Prue expected a mass of soldiers to be waiting for them, but to her surprise, the snowy expanse before them was completely empty. Flurries swirled around her, and she swayed as the chilled air made her head spin.

"Prue." Cyrus's arms were around her again, but this time, she was too consumed by darkness to notice. With a groan, she slumped over and lost consciousness.

A LIGHT JOSTLING AWOKE HER. The ground beneath her rocked with a rhythmic movement, and her eyes slowly opened.

Darkness surrounded her, and Prue squinted as her eyes adjusted. A hand brushed her arm, and she stiffened.

"Shh," said the voice. "Easy. It's me."

Cyrus. Thank the Goddess. Prue deflated and tried to sit up, but Cyrus grasped her shoulders to keep her down.

"We're in the back of a merchant's wagon," Cyrus whispered. "I paid him to smuggle us out of the city."

Prue stared at him. "With what money?"

A dastardly smile spread across his face. "I may have pocketed some expensive jewels in that luxurious suite my brother put me in."

Prue's eyebrows lifted, and she huffed a laugh. "I can't believe he left those lying around."

"Vasileios wanted to gloat. Besides, he never cared for mortal wealth."

"And yet he's seized a kingdom for himself."

Cyrus's expression darkened. "That was for me. To taunt me."

"Why?"

Cyrus didn't answer for a moment. Then, he took a breath and said, "When I was last in this realm, I was manipulated and deceived. Almost everyone I came across tried to kill me. Vasileios knows how despised I was in this realm and in the Underworld. He thinks he can lure me with the promise of being a beloved king, respected and admired and feared."

"Does that not appeal to you?"

She felt his silvery eyes on her and resisted the urge to drop her gaze. "No." His voice was solemn. "Because it wouldn't be real."

The emotion in his eyes intensified, and her breath hitched. As she stared at him, she felt herself falling into their depths, down, down, down until she couldn't see anything else anymore.

But she didn't mind. She *wanted* to fall.

The wagon lurched to a stop, and Prue almost fell forward, but Cyrus held her again, his arms reaching for her as if it were pure instinct to protect her. She tried not to dwell on how good it felt to be touched by him, how easy it was to fall into him.

Goddess, Prue, get ahold of yourself.

She was just groggy from the sleep. That was all. Shaking off her bleary thoughts, she followed Cyrus out the back of the wagon.

The merchant was a portly fellow with orange hair and a thick mustache. He grumbled something about "unnecessary risks" as Prue and Cyrus climbed out. Cyrus withdrew a shining emerald broach from his pocket and handed it to the merchant, and the man's discontent vanished. He bowed to them both before hopping on his wagon and disappearing down the winding road.

A chilled wind whipped at them, swirling Prue's hair and skirts around her as if she were in a tornado. She tucked her wayward curls behind her ears as she surveyed their surroundings. Behind them, the castle turrets pierced the sky, still surrounded by ghosts, but the scene felt much less foreboding from a distance. They stood on a narrow road with vast, snowy fields on either side. Behind them was the massive city they'd left behind, where Vasileios was no doubt trying to find them. And ahead of them rested a tiny hamlet with small dwellings clustered together, reminding Prue so much of Krenia that her heart twisted in her chest.

"That's Faidon," Cyrus said quietly.

Prue sucked in a breath. *Faidon.* The gate to the Underworld was somewhere in that village. Just beyond were the peaks of the Astir Mountains, just barely visible through the snow drifting in the air.

"If we walk fast, we can make it there by dusk," Cyrus continued.

Prue glanced upward toward the sky, but between the murky gray clouds and the swirling flurries around her, it was impossible to see the sun. Still, she trusted Cyrus's assessment. She'd been unconscious, after all. Had she really slept almost the entire day?

"Are you well?" he asked. If Prue didn't know any better, she would say he sounded concerned.

"Yes," Prue said at once, before fully evaluating her needs. She was ravenous, and her limbs were weary, but she no longer felt dizzy or deliriously weak. She was too nervous to check her store of magic to see if it was replenished—between her general reluctance to use magic and Cyrus's insistence that she didn't acquire any of Mona's magic, casting a spell was the last thing Prue wanted to do right now.

She nodded at Cyrus and strode forward, eager to reach their destination and put this journey behind her.

Mona's imposter changed nothing. According to Cyrus, her soul was still stuck in the Underworld somewhere. And Prue was confident she'd be able to find it and reunite it with her sister's body.

She could still do this.

By the time they reached the village, the sun had set. A few lampposts bathed the snow-capped square in soft light. The streets were silent and still. Prue knew if they were in Voula City, the town would be bustling, but in this quiet little hamlet, everyone had turned in already.

It didn't take them long to find an inn. Cyrus slowed behind her, and Prue knew he was recalling his last time here. How much had the village changed since then? How many years had it been?

She didn't dare ask. Even if she did, she knew he wouldn't say. They were still strangers to each other, after all. No matter how much Prue felt like she knew him to his core.

He was not her friend. And he never would be.

The thought made her feel strangely hollow inside, but she shoved the feeling away.

So close, she told herself. *So close to getting Mona back. Just find the gate, cross over, and locate her soul. That's all that matters.*

Prue led him inside the cozy inn at the end of the lane, relishing in the warmth that soothed her numb fingers and toes upon entering. A small bell signaled their arrival, and a frail old woman with spectacles hurried forward to greet them.

"Welcome, travelers!" she said with a jovial smile, taking their hats and scarves.

"Thank you," Prue said. "My husband and I would like a room for the night."

"Of course!" The woman beamed, her brows furrowing as she took in Cyrus's strange tattoos and hair, but she quickly masked her alarm. "Give me one moment and I'll fetch your key." After draping their hats and scarves over the coat rack, she bustled away.

Cyrus nudged Prue's shoulder. "You didn't flinch that time. When you told her we were married."

"The lie gets easier to tell every time." Prue wouldn't meet his gaze.

"It's not a lie."

"It is to me."

She felt his gaze on her, pinning her in place. Her

pulse thrummed from the intensity of it, but she refused to look at him.

The woman soon returned with a large, brass key, informing them it unlocked room seventeen. Prue and Cyrus thanked her before climbing the stairs.

Once they entered the room, the first thing Prue did was relieve herself in the chamber pot, not even caring that Cyrus witnessed it. She'd suppressed the need all day and couldn't hold it in any longer. Cyrus paid a servant to bring a meal up for them, and Prue didn't object; she was practically starving. In just a few minutes, the staff brought up a roast chicken, spiced vegetables, half a loaf of bread, and a bottle of wine. Prue's mouth watered at the sight, but as soon as the servants disappeared, she forced herself to confront Cyrus.

No more avoiding the subject.

She squared her shoulders and said firmly. "We need to have sex."

Cyrus, who had been sniffing the food before them, suddenly went still. After a moment, he looked at her with an arched eyebrow. "I beg your pardon?"

"The confrontation with your brother proved we can't afford to wait any longer. We need to consummate this marriage to make us both more powerful. If he finds us—"

"He won't."

"If he *does*, I don't want to be outmatched again. Do you?"

Cyrus's nostrils flared, his silver eyes flashing.

Prue crossed her arms, challenging him with a stare. "Unless there's some other reason you don't want to?"

Cyrus's gaze darkened. "Like what?"

Prue snorted. "Well, I'm not a demon. Maybe I'm not fit to your taste."

Cyrus scowled. "I would prefer a demon."

Prue tried to ignore the ache in her chest at hearing those words. "Are you serious? The lack of tail and forked tongue is off-putting to you?"

"So, you would really let me make love you? Me, a prince of Hell?"

Prue nodded. "It would mean nothing, Cyrus."

"Is that so?"

"Yes."

He scoffed. "And you assume I would be so willing? Do you honestly think I'd sully myself with the likes of witches?" He spat the last word.

Prue barely concealed her flinch. She forced herself to laugh. "Witches? Really? *That's* where you draw the line? Not pus-filled three-headed clawed creatures from Hell?" She raised her eyebrows. "I don't believe you."

Cyrus drew closer to her, and it took all her will power not to melt away into the wall behind her. She lifted her chin at his approach.

"So you're ready . . . right here, right now?" His voice was a low murmur that made her skin grow hot.

"Yes." Damn her trembling voice . . .

He took another step until they were only a breath apart. Prue felt the way his chest rose and fell so close to hers. Her heart thundered loudly, and it was a wonder he didn't comment on it. Surely the entire inn could hear it.

"And it would mean nothing?"

"Nothing at all," she whispered.

Cyrus cocked his head at her, his eyes glittering like a predator sizing up his prey. Then, with a smirk, he echoed her words. "I don't believe you."

"If this is about what happened in the cave . . ." Prue began.

Now it was Cyrus's turn to laugh. "You think that meant something to me? It was release and nothing more. We both needed to unwind and stay warm. That was all." The coldness of his gaze left no room for argument.

Prue's heart twisted painfully. *He can't lie,* she reminded herself.

Of course he'd only been toying with her in the cave. He'd only wanted to best her, to triumph in granting her pleasure when she insisted he couldn't.

It was nothing more than a game to him.

Something inside her shattered at the thought, but she clung to her composure as if it were her only lifeline.

Though her chest felt like it was crumbling, she somehow managed to shrug and frown at the same time. "Good. Then, this won't mean anything to you either." She started unbuttoning her dress.

Cyrus stilled. "What are you doing?"

"Tell me why we shouldn't," she challenged, "and I'll stop."

A muscle feathered in his jaw, but he said nothing.

When her dress was fully unbuttoned, revealing her shift underneath, she looked at him with raised eyebrows, praying he couldn't sense the heat rising in her cheeks. "Well?"

Please say no.

Please say yes.

Please do nothing at all.

Please just disappear entirely.

Prue wasn't sure what she wanted. She wanted everything and nothing. Her mind was a mass of muddled thoughts she couldn't sift through.

Cyrus closed the gap between them until his chest was flush against hers. She was aware of every breath she took, of the way her breasts rose against him. By the way his eyes turned molten, she knew he was, too.

Prue wasn't sure what possessed her to do it, but she couldn't stop herself. Perhaps it was mere curiosity. Or perhaps, subconsciously, she was trying to find a way out of this situation. She lifted a hand and stroked a finger along the length of one of his horns. It was cool to the touch, and much rougher than she'd anticipated.

At her touch, Cyrus went perfectly still, and then a tremor swept through him. The motion rippled across his body so violently that Prue jerked her hand back.

"Did I hurt you?" she asked, though she wasn't sure why she cared.

"No." His voice was strained. "It's just . . . very sensitive."

Heat blossomed in Prue's chest. Well, now she couldn't resist. She lifted her hand again, and he didn't stop her. This time, she trailed her finger from the edge of his horn all the way to where it protruded from his temple, unable to shake the idea of stroking another lengthy part of his body in the same manner.

A growl built up in Cyrus's throat, and in a flash, he had her pinned up against the wall, the sconce rattling from the impact. Prue gasped as his hips ground into hers and she felt exactly *how* her touch had affected him. His arousal pressed into her, firm and deliciously hard.

Oh, Goddess . . .

Cyrus leaned in, his breath tickling her ear as he hissed, "The last one to touch me there lost their life for it."

Prue's eyes closed, her body succumbing to heat and desire. Her voice was raspy as she asked, "Who?"

"A demon lover. She was curious. Playful. Too explorative for my liking."

"And me?" Prue breathed. "What will you do to me for it?"

A low, feral sound rumbled in his throat, somewhere between a growl and a snarl. It made Prue's toes curl.

"I will do all manner of despicable things to you," Cyrus promised, his nose gliding up and down her throat and jaw, his breath sending shivers along her body.

Prue arched into him, rubbing against the hardness in his trousers. *Please,* she thought. But she wouldn't give him the pleasure of begging. Not again.

She needed to take control of this situation. Fast. Before he undid her completely.

In a moment of panic and weakness, her hand snaked forward, plunging into his trousers until she grasped him firmly.

He stiffened, his body going rigid. But his cock throbbed under her touch.

"Shit," he groaned. His hands slammed against the wall behind her as he made a pained sound. But he thrust against her, his body clearly demanding more. Prue squeezed, then ran her hand up and down with deliberate slowness.

"*Shit*, Prue." His words sounded like a plea.

There we go. A triumphant smile lit her face.

And then he lowered his head, his teeth scraping against her neck. Her breath hitched as tingles shot through her body. Heat pounded in her core, and she couldn't stifle the sigh of longing that swept over her.

Goddess, this is agony. Pure agony. She wished he would get on with it. But at the same time, she wanted him to slow down.

His mouth traveled lower. And lower. With one hand, he tugged her shift to the side, cupping her breast and running his thumb over her nipple. She moaned, throwing her head back. His fingers continued working, fondling her breast, until his mouth joined in. His tongue skirted over her nipple, and he closed his mouth over it, sucking and teasing. Then, his teeth grazed her, the sensation hard and soft all at once.

"Goddess above," she whispered, her insides churning with liquid fire.

Cyrus's hands found the edges of her skirts before hiking them up. She wrapped her legs around his middle, grinding against him. Moisture pooled in her core as she urged him onward, tugging at his cock to pull it free.

"No. Stop, stop. Please." Cyrus rested his forehead against hers, gasping for breath. "I can't, Prue. I can't."

"Why—why not?" Her words were nothing more than a rasp.

He drew back to look at her with haunted eyes. "Because if we do this, you'll be bound to me for all eternity."

SEALED

CYRUS

GODS, this witch would be the death of him. He was certain of it.

As much as his body cried out for her, as much as the fierce intensity of the moment set fire roaring in his blood, he refused to do this to her.

When their journey first began, he told himself he wouldn't take her by force. Then, he told himself it was merely a game, to see how long she could last.

But now, when she all but begged him to take her, he couldn't deny it any longer.

He cared for her. So much that he couldn't sacrifice her for more power.

"What?" Prue asked faintly. Her ragged panting was driving Cyrus mad.

He stepped away, letting her legs drop. He had to put distance between them. *Now.*

He shut his eyes, trying to blot out the image of her breasts rising and falling, of the swell of her cleavage from beneath her shift. Gods, that perfect body . . .

"Once . . . we are sealed," Cyrus said, "the bond is permanent. I am a *god*, Prue. And there is a reason gods do not marry. It is as good as a prison sentence. For all eternity." Slowly, he opened his eyes, forcing himself to meet the horrified look on her face. "I can't—I can't condemn you to that fate."

Her mouth opened and closed. At long last, her brows knitted together, and anger flashed in her eyes. "I'm prepared to give up *everything*, Cyrus. What part of that do you not understand? Even if it means an eternity with you, I will do it to bring back Mona."

"But that's just it," Cyrus said. "I don't know if this *will* bring her back. You may be chaining yourself to me for nothing."

Wariness crept into her expression. "What do you mean? Why wouldn't this work?"

"If Vasileios couldn't find her soul, I'm not sure I'd be able to."

"But you said the ruler of the Underworld has dominion over all souls. That's why he wants the crown."

"Yes, but I've *never* encountered a soul split from a body before. Not in the Underworld. I don't know if it *can* be rectified. If he ripped her apart by force . . ."

Prue flinched, and Cyrus instantly regretted his

words. Slowly, she sagged backward against the wall, her expression dejected. “So . . . you’re saying there’s nothing we can do.”

“I’m saying there’s no way to know for sure. I was hoping that once we reached the gate, I would be able to find out for myself. Before you sealed this bargain with me.”

Her eyes burned with renewed intensity. “Were you ever planning on telling me about this *permanent* bond?”

Cyrus couldn’t hide the truth from her. Not when he’d already laid everything at her feet. “No.”

“So your original plan was to take my body when it suited you, granting you the power you wanted.” The words were more of an accusation than a question.

“Yes.”

“When? When did you change your mind?”

Cyrus opened his mouth to respond, then reconsidered. “In a way, I made up my mind just now. But I’ve had my doubts for a few days now. It’s why I kept pushing you away. Kept avoiding it.”

“You said you would prefer a demon.” Prue’s eyes flashed with indignation and something akin to . . . hurt.

Cyrus winced. “That wasn’t a lie. But the truth is, I would’ve preferred bedding a demon because at least you would still be free.”

Prue blinked at him, clearly stunned. “So that night in the cave . . .”

Cyrus shut his eyes again as the sounds of her moaning in pleasure rose to his mind. "It was a moment of weakness. And it shouldn't have happened. Because it proved just how much I wanted you. Just how much I care for you."

She was so still, so silent, that he didn't dare open his eyes. He couldn't look at her—couldn't bear to see the pity in her eyes, or worse: the loathing. She should be disgusted with his confession.

After a moment, she whispered, "You really do like playing games, don't you?"

Cyrus's eyes flew open. She stared at him with accusation in her gaze, her eyes pooling with moisture.

"Prue—"

"If you truly care for me, as you say, then prove it," she challenged. A tear trickled down her cheek, but her conviction didn't waver. "Tell me what happened when you first came here. What *really* happened."

Cyrus pressed his lips together. "No."

Prue huffed a cold laugh and raised her hands. "I knew it." She adjusted her dress to cover herself before buttoning it again. When she was fully clothed again, she shoved past him, her shoulder hitting his chest in the process. Without looking at him, she drew a chair up to the tray of food and started eating.

For a long, agonizing moment, Cyrus only watched her. The careful way she cut into the meat, the grace with which she chewed her food. Even though she was probably famished, she still dined like a queen.

How had Cyrus ever thought of her as a filthy commoner? When he'd first seen her village, he'd wrinkled his nose in disgust. She'd spent her whole life there, and yet here she was, showing more elegance than he ever could.

"Quit staring at me and eat," she snapped without looking up. "You must be hungry, too."

Cyrus deflated and sank into the chair opposite her. The food smelled delicious, but he had no appetite. Even so, she was right; tomorrow, they would find the gate, and they both needed as much strength as possible. With a sigh, he loaded meat and potatoes onto his plate and took a few bites. The food tasted like ash in his mouth, but he knew it would help strengthen his body.

He couldn't shake the betrayed look on Prue's face from his mind. She'd thought he was toying with her. Again.

And why shouldn't she? He'd never been earnest with her. Sure, he couldn't lie to her, but that didn't mean he'd opened up or revealed anything sincere with her. He'd never given her a reason to take him seriously.

Cyrus set down his fork and said softly, "I met a witch."

Prue stilled, frozen mid-chew. After a moment, she swallowed and asked, "Here?"

Cyrus nodded. "Her name was Jade. I was under the impression she had summoned me to help banish a wayward spirit in the village. But it turned out, she escaped from Tartarus and used me to find the Book of Eyes."

Prue sucked in a sharp breath, her eyes widening slightly. "Did—did you love her?"

Cyrus offered a hollow laugh. "I don't even know what love is, Prue. I can't answer that. But I did care for her. Deeply."

"What happened to her?"

"She betrayed me. She was willing to sacrifice me to the Book of Eyes in order to absorb its power." Emotion churned in Cyrus's chest as these long-buried memories rose to the surface. But he forced himself to remain composed. To keep his voice level. "I overpowered her and . . . destroyed her. I gave up my soul to bind myself to the book and return to the Underworld, along with the souls she unleashed."

Prue was silent for a long moment. Cyrus felt her gaze on him, but he knew if he looked at her, it would undo him completely. And he was already on the brink of collapsing. The raw, festering wounds inside him throbbed and ached, pulsing with a rhythm that echoed in every bone of his body.

This was why he hated humans. This was why he hated the mortal realm. It made him *feel*. And those feelings made him weak.

"Destroyed," Prue repeated at last. "What does that mean, exactly?"

"It means I burned her from existence. She is . . . no more."

Prue fell silent, but he could sense the horror rippling off her. Once again, he was forced to remind her that he was a monster. How could she keep forgetting?

The thought fueled his anger, and he clung to it, eager for an emotion that empowered him instead of weakened him. Baring his teeth, he leaned over the table toward her. "This is who you married. This is what you're binding yourself to, Prue. A beast. A monster. A killer. Is that what you want? An eternity of that? Because I won't stop. I won't *change* for you. Don't delude yourself into thinking otherwise."

Her breath shuddered, and this time, Cyrus forced himself to meet her gaze. To face the truth in her eyes. Once he did, he could finally put all this behind him. He was ready.

But when he looked at her, his whole body seemed to freeze over. His breath stilled. His mind halted. He was drowning in the depths of her lavender eyes.

She wasn't looking at him in revulsion or terror, disbelief or anger. She was looking at him with sympathy and affection, her eyes shining. Her mouth was a soft curve, her lips parting slightly. Her cheeks were pink, her eyebrows lifted in concern.

This was almost worse. Because it made all his pent-up emotions come roiling to the surface once more. Heat stung his eyes, and he gritted his teeth.

Why am I so weak? He wanted to scream, to smash furniture, to punch holes in the wall. He couldn't stand this. Any of it.

"That's why you hate witches so much," Prue said quietly. "Because of what she did to you."

Cyrus's nostrils flared, his teeth grinding so hard that his head throbbed. He couldn't answer.

Prue leaned forward and grasped his hand on the table. It took all his restraint not to jerk away from her, to flip the table over in his rage.

"You've already changed, Cyrus," she whispered, her thumb stroking over his knuckles. "I've seen it. You despised me when we first met. And now, you claim to care for me. You shared your secrets with me. How can you say you are incapable of change?"

Cyrus closed his eyes against the hope in her voice. "I don't *want* to change, Prue." His words were barely audible, but he knew she could hear them. "You can't hold on to that hope."

"I can do whatever I damn well please," she snapped.

In spite of the situation, Cyrus snorted. *There* was that fire-breathing witch he knew so well.

The chair creaked, and Cyrus stiffened as Prue rose and stepped around the table to stand before him.

"I'm not Jade," she said softly. "I bound myself to you by blood. I won't betray you, Cyrus. And I'll prove it to you." She approached him, swinging her legs until she sat atop him, straddling him.

Cyrus was still completely rigid, unable to move. "Prue—"

"You say you won't condemn me to this fate," she murmured, her breath tickling his face. "But I'll condemn myself. It's *my choice.* And I choose you."

She leaned closer until her nose brushed his. His breath hitched.

"What do you choose?" she whispered.

Mere days ago, he would've easily said *power.* He always chose power. Because he never wanted to feel weak again. But this weakness, with Prue, was different. It was a weakness that made him stronger, a vulnerability that made him fuller. To be with her was to be empowered in a different way; a way he didn't think himself capable of feeling.

Prue's lips brushed against his cheek, the softest of touches. Then, her mouth trailed down his jaw to his throat, and she pressed a kiss there as well. Cyrus's whole body went alert at her touch, and he knew she felt it too, because she pressed more incessantly against him. He groaned.

Prue's mouth was at his ear. "Tell me." A command. How could he refuse?

The words were practically ripped from him by force. "I choose you, Prue."

She drew back to look at him more fully. Her fingers

brushed silver strands of hair from his eyes. For one wild moment, he thought she would touch his horns again—hell, he even wanted her to. But instead, her fingers trailed down his face, halting at the tattoos etched on his skin. She frowned.

"This one's new." Her hand pushed his shirt aside, exposing the left side of his collarbone where fresh ink spread, creeping toward his neck. It was the only portion of his left side that was tattooed.

Cyrus nodded, swallowing hard. "When I saved you. On the mountain."

Prue looked at him in confusion. "What?"

"That particular kind of magic requires . . . a payment. A part of my soul. It was the only thing I could offer." He looked at her, almost pleading with her to understand. He couldn't crack himself open again. His heart wouldn't survive it.

Prue's lips parted in surprise. "You—you did that? For me?"

He said nothing. He simply met her gaze, forcing the intensity of his feelings into that one look. *For you, Prue. Always.*

Time seemed suspended between them, as if the whole world had frozen for this moment. For them.

Then, her mouth was on his.

At first, he held perfectly still, just to experience the sensation. Her lips were soft and smooth, and a faint, minty taste lingered on her tongue, mingled with the spices and seasoning from the meal they'd shared. She was moist and warm and soft and perfect. And Cyrus could hold back no longer.

His body responded in kind. His mouth captured hers again and again, claiming her. His hands fell to her waist, holding her against him as their lips grew more insistent. More urgent. Her tongue slid into his mouth, twining with his. His teeth grazed her bottom lip, and she sighed against him. Her arms wrapped around his neck, her hands sifting through his hair. When one finger nudged his horn, Cyrus growled against her mouth.

"Take me, Cyrus," she commanded. "For I am yours."

ONE
PRUE

HE GAVE up part of his soul.

For her.

Prue still couldn't comprehend it. This other witch—Jade—had tried to take it from him by force. But Cyrus had freely *given* it to Prue. She hadn't even asked for it. And he'd done it to save her.

That thought alone was enough to fuel her desire. Cyrus might claim to be a monster—and he was. He was ruthless and cruel and savage.

But he *was* capable of love. No matter what he claimed, Prue knew this to be true.

"Make love to me," Prue said, putting as much authority into her voice as she could. But he was a god, and she a mere mortal. How could *she* command him?

He drew back, his mouth quirking into that devastating smile she both loved and hated. "Yes, my lady," he growled, his sensuous tone both a suggestion and a promise.

With one quick motion, he hefted her up, her legs still wrapped around his middle, and easily carried her over to the bed. He deposited her with great care, easing her backward onto the bed so she lay sprawled before him.

Prue let her legs fall open, her skirts parting for him. A hungry look stirred in his gaze, but he slowly shook his head.

"I want to devour you first," he said in a low voice, hovering over her. "Every inch of you."

Her core throbbed at the promise in his words, and she couldn't speak. All she could do was nod, encouraging him onward. With achingly slow movements, he undid her dress. One. Button. At. A. Time.

Prue growled at his slow pace, and he smirked. He was toying with her again.

But she could play this game, too. Smiling sweetly at him, she pinched his cock through his trousers.

Cyrus let out a strangled sound somewhere between a bark and a groan. "Gods, Prue."

She batted her eyes at him, the picture of innocence.

He laughed, but the fire in his eyes told her he wasn't finished with her. And she was glad for it.

When her dress was fully unbuttoned, she shrugged out of it, discarding it on the floor. Without preamble, she tugged at his tunic, practically ripping it from him. He slid it over his head, tossing it next to her dress before hovering over her once more, his arms braced on either side of her. Prue let her fingers wander over his ink, tracing each flame, each curl of darkness etched into his skin.

"Beautiful," she whispered.

"What story do they tell this time?" Cyrus asked.

"A story of possession," Prue said. "And power to be claimed."

"That won't be the only thing I'll claim tonight," he murmured, leaning closer to kiss her again. She met his lips with fervent energy, drawing him down so his chest lay against hers. Her tongue caressed his until she wasn't sure where her mouth ended and his began.

In this moment, they were one. Their minds. Their bodies.

Their souls.

Prue tugged at his trousers, lowering them to free the hard arousal contained inside. With her legs, she kicked his trousers off the bed and examined him more fully.

Goddess, that length of his . . . Just the thought of it inside her made her throat go dry.

He often reminded her of it, but in this moment, as she appreciated every aspect of his body, it was abundantly clear: Cyrus was a god. His body seemed perfectly sculpted, the tattoos stark against his pale skin, his chest rising and falling with rapid breaths. His horns, his hair, his eyes . . . all inhuman and otherworldly, and yet . . .

He was *hers.* Flawed imperfection, raw and brutal emotion. But hers nonetheless.

"I love you, Cyrus," she whispered.

Shock flickered in his eyes, and his mouth opened slightly. For a moment, he stared at her, dumbfounded.

Shit, Prue thought. *Did I just ruin this?*

But after a moment, his expression softened, and he leaned close. "My soul is yours, Prue. All of it." His mouth was on her again, tracing the length of her throat, his tongue flicking against her skin.

Then, he had her hands pinned above her head, pressing her wrists into the mattress. She arched into him, needing him against her. With his free hand, he lifted her shift, sliding it up and up and up. His movements were slow and careful, and when he exposed the slickness between her legs, he halted. Desire blazed in his eyes, more potent than any fire, and Prue practically melted from that look.

He released her wrists and bent over, bringing his mouth to her core. The sweep of his tongue against her sex sent fire shooting through her veins. He repeated the movement, and Prue thought she might melt right then and there. She bucked and thrashed, writhing from the deft movements of his lips and tongue. He licked her, ravishing her fully, feasting on her. His tongue explored every crevice, poking and probing, gliding through her.

Stars burst in her vision, the tension in her core mounting until she wanted to scream, to claw at him, whether to urge him onward or to stop him, she didn't know. He spread her legs wider, providing better access, and his teeth grazed the most sensitive part of her.

It undid her completely. She threw her head back with a cry of delight, her body on fire, every inch of her pulsing with awareness and need. As she sank backward onto the bed, her body trembling, Cyrus continued lifting her shift, a satisfied smile on his face.

"I'm not finished with you yet, Prue," he teased.

"You'd better not be." Her voice was raspy.

He lifted the shift over her head and let it fall to the floor with the rest of their clothes. Then, just as she had, he admired every inch of her body. She resisted the urge to cover herself, not out of self-consciousness, but self-preservation. She never opened herself up to anyone. She hadn't even exposed her body to Xandros when he'd been alive.

Her instinct was to hide. To shy away. To keep her thoughts and emotions to herself.

She and Cyrus were similar that way.

So, just as he opened for her, she opened for him, relaxing against the mattress as he drank in every part of her, every freckle and blemish, every imperfection.

"I am yours, Cyrus," she vowed.

"You are mine," he echoed.

He started with her stomach, pressing feather-light

kisses along her brown skin, trailing higher and higher. He stopped at her breasts, swirling his tongue around her nipples until she arched upward with a moan. He kept one hand on her breast as he continued upward, tongue sliding along her skin. His teeth clamped down on her throat, firm and unyielding, but not painful. She leaned into his bite, demanding more. When he didn't oblige, she took hold of his cock again, knowing exactly how to drive him mad.

Indeed, he went stiff in her grip, his cock twitching.

"I can play, too," she whispered. Then, she slid under him and brought her mouth to his arousal.

"*Shit*," he choked, his hands pressing into the mattress as she took him in her mouth, deeper and deeper. "Gods above, Prue."

Satisfaction swelled in her as she roved her tongue over him, just as he'd done to her. She worshipped him with her mouth again and again. His cock pulsed inside her. He shuddered from her touch, his whole body quivering. But he was writhing against her tongue, urging her to go on.

Just before he climaxed, Prue pulled away, and he swore again.

"Thousands of years I've lived," he rasped. "And you'll be the death of me."

Prue laughed, pushing him backward onto the bed and climbing atop him. "I'll take that as a compliment." She spread her legs on either side of him, both of them gasping as his cock nudged at her entrance. "You are mine, Cyrus."

"I am yours."

She sank onto him, letting him fill her completely. She cried out, heat burning her eyes, her whole body taut with awareness. He thrust upward, harder, and she moaned, the impact jolting her very bones. She could feel his cock throbbing inside her, a firm and powerful presence that set her blood on fire. Her hands were on his chest, her fingernails digging into him as he drew back, only to plunge into her once more. Her moans intensified, tearing at her throat. His hips lifted, and her thighs tightened around him. He pushed again, deeper this time. But she wanted him. Violently. The time for being gentle was over.

She leaned closer and clasped one of his horns, her fingers pressing hard. He groaned and obeyed her unspoken demand, slamming into her again and again. The bed frame rattled against the wall. She rode him, one hand still on his chest, her gasps burning in her throat. Lights danced in her vision as she climaxed, the force of it blasting through her with the intensity of a thousand suns. He followed after, his hands tightening around her legs, his eyes closing with pleasure as he spilled into her. Ragged sounds poured from his lips, the desperate noises of a man in the throes of passion, and she relished that. *She* was the one who made this powerful god exclaim and tremble and beg for more. *She* was his undoing.

As his thrusts slowed, she cried out his name, both a plea and a promise.

I am yours. And you are mine.

GATE
CYRUS

CYRUS WOKE with Prue's naked body tucked alongside his. Her back was up against his chest. He had one arm wrapped around her, his head nestled in the crook of her neck, and her dark curls sprawled around them both.

But he didn't mind. Her hair smelled like mint. And he was beginning to learn that was just *her* scent.

He closed his eyes, pressing the barest of kisses to her shoulder.

She shifted, inhaling deeply. As she wriggled against him, he suppressed a shudder at the way his cock responded. Gods, what this woman did to him . . .

Prue must have felt his arousal because she chuckled, the sound low and raspy and *maddeningly* sexy. "Well, you're certainly awake, aren't you?"

Cyrus gathered her mass of hair and carefully draped

it over her shoulder so he could press kisses along her bare back. "Would you prefer to go back to sleep?"

She pushed against him, grinding mercilessly, and he growled in response. "What do you think?" she challenged.

In seconds, he had her flipped over, facedown on the bed, her legs spread wide as he thrust into her. She cried out, whether from surprise or delight, he couldn't tell. But he didn't care. She turned her head, burying her face into the pillows to muffle the intensity of her moans. He pulled out, only to drive himself into her further, deeper. She arched against him, her body trembling. Her hands sought him out blindly until she grasped his thigh, her fingernails digging in silent command.

He obliged. His hands clenched around her legs as his cock moved inside her, back and forth, their bodies finding a blissful rhythm.

"Cyrus," she gasped out.

The sound of her desperate sigh nearly undid him. He leaned in and swept his tongue over her shoulder, then grazed his teeth along her skin before biting down. She let out a ragged groan, tightening around him.

And then he was gone. His movements became more forceful, more urgent. He pounded into her again and again, relishing the noises he elicited from her with each thrust. When they climaxed together, she screamed into the pillow, her body writhing beneath his, her legs quivering from the intensity of it. Cyrus roared in satisfaction, eyes closing as he succumbed to the sheer thrill of it, the pleasure washing over him in brutal waves.

Gods, it was such a feeling. Such power, what she did to him. How had he not experienced this before? How had he acquired so much magic and yet never felt *this*?

When their movements slowed, Prue slid out from under him, only to turn and face him, her eyes bright and her forehead sticky with sweat. Then, she was kissing him, and he wasn't sure if it was out of gratitude or because she wasn't finished with him yet. Her mouth roved over his, tongue and teeth claiming him again and again, and for one wild minute, he felt ready to plunge into her once more.

But then she drew back, sweeping her tongue over his one last time, before climbing out of bed. Cyrus didn't bother stifling his groan of disappointment.

Prue chuckled. "Later, love. We have a gate to find, remember?"

Love. She said that word so easily. And he hadn't been able to say it in return. He tried not to dwell on that, thinking instead of the gate and how to locate it.

"Last I was here, the Book of Eyes called to me," Cyrus said thoughtfully, his mind returning to that horrid experience. "It just lay open in an alley somewhere, but I doubt it'll be in the same place." He eyed Prue as she slid into her shift. "Now that our powers have merged, perhaps we can use them to our advantage. I'll bet *you* can sense the Book of Eyes, just as I can."

Prue stilled briefly, her eyes widening with alarm. For one awful moment, Cyrus panicked. *She's changed her mind. She regrets bonding with me. She wishes last night had never happened.*

But her unease smoothed into thoughtfulness as she considered his words. "I think you may be right. I used your powers to summon a spirit, after all, and that was before we'd consummated." Her cheeks grew pink at the last word, and Cyrus almost laughed. Of all the scandalous things they'd done to each other, and she was bashful about the word *consummated*?

He couldn't blame her, though. Part of him was still shocked at what they'd done. What they'd shared.

He'd never shared that much with *anyone*, demon or no.

"I wonder if witch dust will work," Prue mused as she worked on buttoning her dress. "If I combine it with your magic, will it locate the book for us?"

"It's worth a try." Cyrus finally resigned himself to dressing as well, despite how much he yearned to drag Prue back to the bed for a few more hours.

She peered at him through her lashes as if she was thinking the same thing. Her eyes fell to his cock, her eyebrows lifting slightly.

Cyrus merely crossed his arms, not at all ashamed to

expose exactly how she aroused him so. "Care for another ride?" he offered.

Her blush deepened, and she grinned wickedly. "As tempting as your body may be, *husband*, I'm afraid I can't ignore my duty to my sister." Though her words were playful, something dark flickered in her eyes, driving all lewd thoughts from Cyrus's mind. He kept repeating *husband* to himself, still not quite believing it, but her words had a sobering effect.

She did this for Mona. Not for herself. Not for Cyrus. But to bring back her sister. Prue may have fallen in love with him—and Cyrus believed her—but in the end, her priorities were clear.

Mona came first. Above all else. And Cyrus had to respect that. Even if his priorities weren't the same.

When they were both dressed, they deposited their key at the desk downstairs, both of them hopeful they wouldn't have to stay another night—despite how much Cyrus wanted to share another sleepless evening wrapped up in Prue's body.

Gods, we are really doing this, he thought as they exited the inn and stepped out into the frigid mountain air. *Prue is going through the gate with me.* To be honest, Cyrus hadn't thought they would make it this far. He assumed either Prue would die or one of them would find a way out of the bargain.

Now that they were so close to their goal, his mind was

a storm of confusion and uncertainty. What would it be like to go to the Underworld with Prue? Would she be altered somehow? Could she even survive it? He hadn't cared before because he'd despised her when they first met; if she died, he wouldn't have batted an eye. But now, he couldn't stand the thought of losing her. What if the transition between realms killed her? What if she transformed into something immortal, something incapable of love?

Something like Cyrus?

He suppressed a shudder at the thought.

And then there was the other fear—the fear that the price for Mona's soul would be Prue's. That Prue *would* die for her sister, just as she intended.

But he couldn't bear that thought, either. He would do anything in his power to stop that from happening. He was the god of the Underworld; if anyone could keep the death magic from claiming Prue, it was him.

Cyrus shoved all these questions from his mind. They were unproductive and didn't help their search in the slightest. Regardless of how his mind spun and his very bones quivered with unease, he forced himself to focus on the task at hand.

Prue wrapped her shawl more tightly around her, her curls whipping around her face as she glanced up and down the street. "Where to first?"

Cyrus took a deep breath, quieting his raucous mind and searching inward. His black flames swelled to life in his chest, roaring with an eagerness that shocked him.

The fire burned and scorched him, almost in indignation.

His magic was angry that it had been ignored for so long.

And Cyrus was utterly baffled by this. How had he gone so long without using his magic? When he'd first been summoned by Prue, he'd been desperate for a taste of her power—and then desperate for his own power to be returned in full. But now that he'd finally gotten what he wanted, he simply . . . didn't care.

Well, that wasn't entirely true. He still needed his power, especially if he hoped to overpower Vasileios. But it just wasn't as important to him as . . . other things.

His gaze slid to Prue, who watched him expectantly. His heart warmed at the sight of her, disheveled and windswept. Even out here, her expression solemn and her hair askew, she looked breathtakingly beautiful.

His magic barked at him as if shouting for his attention, and Cyrus shut his eyes, letting his power overtake him.

Show me, he urged it. *Show me the book.*

Obediently, an image of the wretched grimoire came to his mind. It lay open, just as it had when he'd last been in Faidon. The book began to tremble, and piercing screams echoed from it.

Gods, why did the book always have to scream?

Cyrus gritted his teeth, worried he would lose hold of this vision somehow. But it only intensified, smothering him with the sounds of suffering and the smell of death on its pages . . .

Cyrus gasped, his eyes flying open. His heart thudded painfully in his chest as he regained his bearings. Prue's hand was on his arm, grounding him, anchoring him to this point, this place.

An echo of the screams still resonated in his chest, and he clung to that remnant. Beside him, Prue stiffened, her body going rigid.

"You feel that?" he breathed. When she nodded, her expression strained, he added, "Witch dust. Now."

Again, she nodded, cramming her eyes shut as she no doubt searched for her magic, just as Cyrus had. Cyrus watched her, waiting for the telltale vines to snake forward obediently. What he didn't expect was the surge of warmth burgeoning in his chest, warring with the ice-cold chill of his death magic. He sucked in a breath at the intensity of it, the two forces colliding in an explosion of power. Gods, it was staggering. If he weren't still gripping Prue's arm, he might have collapsed from the sheer brutality of it.

The snow at their feet shifted as the vines came to life, swirling around Prue in response to her magic. As if jealous, Cyrus's death magic flared, sending images of the Underworld flashing through Cyrus's mind. His throne. The rivers. The crown of bones.

He shuddered, struggling to keep himself in the present alongside Prue. She needed him. But as he tried to focus on her, his death magic dug its claws even further inside him. The fluctuation from death to earth, from dark to light, from destruction to life, made Cyrus's head spin. Growth and decay. Vines and dust. Blossoms and ash. Ivy and bone.

Cyrus's death magic was at war with his bond to Prue. He hadn't realized how incompatible they were until both fought to claim him.

Mine, his magic seemed to say, digging its claws deeper into him, cutting through flesh and bone.

But no. Cyrus didn't belong to the death magic.

He belonged to *her.*

In the midst of this turmoil, his hand sought Prue's, clenching her fingers tightly in his. They both clamped down on one another as if it was just as taxing for her as it was for him. But the sensation of her fingers curled in his warmed his body, bleeding through the chaos in his mind.

Prue, he thought. *Prue.*

His focus narrowed on her, on his bond with her, their connection and shared energy. Her magic wasn't his anchor—*she* was. She kept him grounded, linked to this realm, to this space in time.

Gradually, clarity burned through his mind, shattering the illusions of the Underworld and his death magic. He breathed deeply as if he'd been suffocating before. Something shimmered in the air in front of him, tickling his senses. He opened his eyes and found the witch dust hovering in front of them, waiting expectantly.

Prue's eyes opened, too. Just like Cyrus, she was panting, her face pale but her eyes alight with power. She exchanged a glance with him as if to say, *You felt it, too*? They both nodded to each other.

Prue waved her hand, and the witch dust spun in the air, surging forward to lead them toward the book. Without preamble, Prue and Cyrus hurried after it.

GODDESS

PRUE

ICICLES SLICED through Prue's chest, freezing her insides and chilling her bones. It was more intense than anything she'd ever felt. More intense than the normal cold presence of death magic she'd grown accustomed to.

She knew it was Cyrus's magic come to life. And she tried not to be alarmed by this.

But judging by the crease of his brow and the way his fingers twitched, as if itching to form fists at his sides, this was unusual for him.

Still, they both remained silent as they followed Prue's witch dust. The shimmering sparkles floated in the air like fireflies, leading them down a winding, narrow road that crested downhill. Several villagers called out to them, some questioning who they were and what they were doing, but Prue and Cyrus hurried past, unable to stop.

They were so close now . . . so close . . .

Cyrus suddenly stopped short, and Prue almost crashed into him. She staggered and jumped back a step. "What's wrong? What is it?"

"I . . . I just . . ." Cyrus ran a hand through his hair. "I've been here before."

Prue followed his gaze, peering around him to see what awaited them at the bottom of the hill. She squinted, trying to make out the details of what appeared to be a pile of rubble. Upon further scrutiny, she realized it was the remains of a house. The charred edges indicated it had probably burned down years ago.

Prue glanced at Cyrus, whose face had gone pale. "It would make sense," she said quietly. "If the Book of Eyes is bound to you, it would stand to reason it would choose a place you're familiar with."

Cyrus's eyes flickered with some unreadable emotion. Prue touched his arm and squeezed. "I'm here," she reminded him.

Cyrus turned to look at her, his eyes wild and frenzied as if he couldn't quite remember where he was. Or *who* he was. In that moment, he looked so lost and confused that Prue just wanted to wrap him in her arms. But she knew him, and coddling wouldn't help. Instead, she held his gaze, forcing a fierce determination she didn't quite feel. She lifted her chin, challenging him.

Remember who you are, she thought. *You are a god.*

Something flickered in his eyes, and his silver irises gleamed in recognition. He inhaled deeply, and, to Prue's surprise, he seized her and kissed her. Thoroughly. His tongue slid between her lips, his arms encircling her until their bodies seemed to meld together. She all but wilted in his arms, caught off guard and wholly claimed by his mouth.

When he released her, she gasped for breath, staring at him. Fire burned in his eyes, bringing that fearsome intensity she knew so well.

"Thank you, Prue," he murmured.

Prue could only gape at him. She tried not to see this as a goodbye kiss, but that was exactly what it felt like.

They strode down the road, hand in hand, for all the world appearing as a couple on a stroll. Cyrus's palm felt cool and clammy against her skin, and she wondered what was going through his head. Was he nervous? Or was this place bringing up unwanted memories?

Should she have any reason to be concerned?

As they approached the ruins, a low thrumming pulsed in the air, making Prue's bones quiver. She drew in a breath, determined to be strong—if not for Cyrus, then for herself—as they drew nearer. The intensity of the pulsing burned in Prue's ears, and she bit down hard to keep her teeth from chattering. Judging by Cyrus's tight grip on her fingers, he felt it, too.

Despite the quivering energy around them, Prue

focused instead on her sister. She was so close . . . So close to achieving her goal, to bringing Mona back. The thought sent a spark of hope through her heart, blotting out her fear.

She could do this. *They* could do this.

And perhaps, since Mona's body was already in the mortal realm, all Prue would have to do was find her soul and bring it back. Maybe she could achieve her goal *without* sacrificing herself.

A tendril of warmth spread through her chest as she thought of enjoying a life with Cyrus. A life with love. With her sister. Everything she desired.

They halted at where Prue assumed the entrance had once been. She recognized the crumbled remains of pillars and archways, the echoes of what had undoubtedly been an elegant edifice long ago.

Cyrus stiffened next to her, and a low growl rumbled in his throat. Alarmed, Prue's head whipped around, searching for danger. Her magic swelled in her chest, and her third eye blinked open.

Only then did she sift out the other presence. Amidst the incessant reverberation of the mighty power of the Book of Eyes, Prue sensed something . . . else. Something deadly and familiar.

"Vasileios," Cyrus bit out, his nostrils flaring.

But it wasn't just Vasileios. Layered beneath his foul death magic was a floral scent Prue knew all too well.

Mona. Or, at least, her imposter. The *thing* wearing her sister's body.

Anger surged in Prue's chest. But she was grateful for it. It burned away any trace of fear or anxiety, and she could feel that same determined fury roiling off Cyrus as well.

Wrath was their ally. And Prue clung to it.

"We're stronger than he is," Prue murmured. She wasn't sure if she was reassuring herself or Cyrus. "You and I are bonded, and he's not. Not fully." Again, she thought of that shadow parading around in Mona's skin, and a fresh wave of rage rose up inside her.

Vasileios was using Mona as a puppet. And he would pay for it.

Cyrus turned to look at her, and though the glance was brief, the scorching fire in his eyes made her own blood sing. In his eyes, the silver irises seemed to melt like molten steel, consuming her entirely.

His power and fury had once alarmed her, even intimidated her. But now, in this moment, she finally acknowledged that it drew her in, inviting her for more. She'd fought it ever since she'd met him, but after last night, she'd embraced that fury. It was hers now, too.

And a strange part of her was aroused by that fire burning in his eyes.

"Together," he vowed, his voice a low rumble that did nothing to assuage the heat flowing in Prue's veins.

"Together," she agreed.

With unified steps, they strode toward the wreckage to where Vasileios and Mona awaited them. It didn't take long to find them. After ducking under the broken archway, they found the pair standing amidst the debris, the Book of Eyes lying open at their feet. Vasileios still wore his ridiculous crown, accompanied by an elegant crimson cloak and gold-studded tunic and trousers. Besides him, the Mona imposter wore a humble but elegant emerald gown that brought out the color in her eyes. Her vacant expression and empty gaze hollowed out her features into something unrecognizable. Prue's insides coiled at the sight.

Vasileios lifted his chin, his face smug as he watched them approach. "You certainly kept us waiting."

"You really have nothing better to do than stand here in this decrepit pile of rubble and wait around for your younger brother?" Cyrus wrinkled his nose. "Truly pathetic, Vasileios."

Vasileios's eyes darkened for the briefest of seconds before his smug demeanor returned. "I'll make this simple, brother. Turn over your crown to me, and I will spare your *wife*." He practically spat the last word.

"The *wife* is more powerful than you think," Prue snapped. Just to prove the validity of her words, she summoned a kernel of Cyrus's power. Black flames welled up from the ground, interlaced with her signature vines.

Vasileios's expression slackened in shock. His eyes

grew wide as he stared at the flaming ivy rising from the ground like some monstrous demon. "Gods above," he whispered, his face going pale. "You sealed the bond."

"We did." Cyrus squeezed Prue's hand.

"So, return my sister to me, and maybe we'll spare *you*," Prue challenged, lifting her chin.

Vasileios shot a quick glance at Mona, who continued to wear a blank expression, resembling nothing more than a doll. "Cyrus, do you have any idea what you've done?" His voice had lost its taunting lilt, making him sound grave for the first time since Prue had met him.

Cyrus's eyes narrowed. "I've bonded myself to an earth witch."

"Not just any earth witch," Vasileios growled. "But the daughter of a goddess."

Time froze for a full second. Prue's heart shuddered in her chest, but she shook her head. "What the hell's he talking about?" She addressed Cyrus, but her eyes remained on Vasileios.

"I have no idea," Cyrus muttered, but his silvery eyes were shrewd and calculating, as if he was assembling the pieces of a puzzle in his mind.

"Think about it, Cyrus!" Vasileios urged. "You know she's not just an ordinary witch. She's more powerful than anything we've ever seen. How else was she able to summon you? Why else would I be so invested in apprehending her?"

"Apprehending me?" Prue shouted incredulously. "You tried to *kill* me! You sent an assassin after me!"

"You did threaten her life," Cyrus agreed. "On multiple accounts."

Vasileios groaned. "You knew I was bluffing."

"I did."

Prue shot Cyrus a sharp look. *He did?*

"So, if you don't want to kill me, then what do you want from me?" Prue asked. Alarm prickled along every nerve, sending warnings firing in her brain.

"Your blood," said Vasileios.

Prue blinked. "I beg your pardon?"

"With your blood," Vasileios said, then gestured to Mona, "and *her* blood, I can summon the goddess and finish her once and for all."

The air stilled once more. Prue cocked her head at Vasileios, thinking that he must have truly lost his mind.

"Tell me, brother," Cyrus said, his voice cool and even. "Which goddess are you referring to?"

Prue glanced at him again. His expression was carefully neutral, and it irked her that she couldn't figure out if he was masking his emotions from her or from his brother.

"Gaia, of course," Vasileios said. "The antithesis of our father. Life and death. Creation and destruction. With her end, we can ensure the well-being of our realm. The souls will have no choice but to depend on the Underworld."

Prue barked out a harsh laugh. "You think my mother is Gaia? You're insane!"

"Prue," Cyrus murmured, his voice a soft warning.

With that one simple utterance, Cyrus rendered Prue frozen and speechless. That soft admonition spoke volumes.

Cyrus believed his brother.

He believed Gaia was her mother.

And he was warning her to keep quiet before she made things worse.

Goddess, was *everyone* here insane?

But even as Prue thought the words, her memory snagged on something. The image of her mother, summoning witch fire with ease. Her flawless healing spell when Prue had broken her leg. How she performed the banishment without any difficulty at all, even though it left Prue and Beatrice breathless and exhausted. How utterly *powerful* that banishment had been, securing a barrier around the entire island. At the time, Prue hadn't questioned it; she'd only been grateful her village had been protected. But now, it seemed clear to her that Polina had power. An abundance of power. *Too much* power for one witch.

Something sharp cut into Prue's palm, and she yelped, jerking her hand away. When she inspected it, she found a dribble of blood oozing from a small slice in her hand. Shocked, she gazed up at Cyrus in accusation. His eyes were grim, his expression full of regret.

"I'm sorry," he said quietly. "But I have to know if it's the truth."

"Cyrus—" She gaped at him, stunned.

"Gaia has the power to destroy the entire Underworld with a single thought," Cyrus whispered, his voice laced with urgency. "It's my *home.*"

Betrayal coursed through her, swift and deep, as Cyrus stepped toward his brother, extending his hand. Two drops of Prue's blood glistened on his fingertips.

Prue's chest caved inward with dread and hurt. Vasileios exhaled in relief before withdrawing a handkerchief to absorb the blood. Then, he pressed a dagger into Mona's hand.

"Don't!" Prue shrieked, reaching for her sister, but it was too late.

Mona didn't even flinch as blood dribbled down her fingers. Vasileios carefully gathered the droplets into the handkerchief, mingling them with Prue's blood.

Prue couldn't breathe. All she could do was watch in horror as Vasileios muttered something in an ancient language she couldn't understand. Smoke wafted from the handkerchief, filling the air with the charred smell of death magic. Energy swirled around them, tickling Prue's senses as her third eye started to burn.

Coils of black smoke seeped from the ground, swirling into a massive whirlwind. Prue's eyes stung from the intensity of it, but she forced her eyes to remain open. She *had* to see. She *had* to . . .

From within the smoke emerged a figure. Gradually, the dark vapor dissipated, revealing a woman Prue had thought she'd known so well . . . A woman who had spent decades lying to her daughters. She looked exactly the same, save for the strange golden glow emanating from her eyes, making them look bronze instead of their usual blue.

It was Polina. Or rather, Gaia—the earth goddess.

GAIA

CYRUS

CYRUS FELT Prue's hand go slack in his grip as they both stared at the woman—the *goddess*—standing before them. Polina was the same as Cyrus remembered on that tiny island of Krenia . . . and yet she was different. There was a strange glow about her face as if she held the light of the sun within her skin. Her blue eyes were sharp like chips of glass that could cut right through him. And her curly hair whipped around her face like a fearsome mane.

Seeing Polina like this, Cyrus wondered how he hadn't known right away that Prue was the daughter of a goddess. That same fire burned in Prue's eyes. So many features were shared between the two witches, and now that it was staring him in the face, Cyrus loathed himself for not sensing it sooner.

Polina—*Gaia*—glanced around, her steely eyes scrutinizing the scene. Her gaze flicked from Cyrus to Prue, then to Vasileios and Mona, her expression revealing nothing. Cyrus held perfectly still, waiting to see what she would do; how she would react to being summoned. Would she attempt to maintain her guise as a simple coven witch? Beside him, Prue remained frozen as well, though he knew it was more from shock than anything else.

The longer the silence stretched on, the more Cyrus's dark power raged inside him, demanding to be unleashed. He had never experienced such raw, untethered chaos from his magic before. Usually he could leash it, keeping it contained, but the more it thrashed, the more his vision blurred, threatening to go dark completely. He could only attribute it to the presence of a goddess before him, though a small part of him knew this couldn't be the reason his magic was misbehaving; after all, he had been in Polina's presence before and his magic hadn't reacted this way.

Then again, he hadn't fully bonded with Prue at that point. Perhaps this was a reaction to *her* magic.

At long last, Gaia lifted her chin, her eyes flashing. "Which one of you summoned me?" Her voice was commanding and regal. Cyrus remembered that about her; how she emanated such power and authority.

"Mama?" Prue breathed in a broken voice, her eyes moist and full of shock and betrayal. Cyrus's chest twisted at the sight, knowing he'd played his part in that betrayal. Even if he hadn't actively opposed her, he'd seen the look of hurt on her face when he'd sided with Vasileios.

Gaia turned her steady gaze to Prue, her expression still cold and impassive. "I'm sorry, daughter."

Prue stiffened at her mother's words, as if the apology was as good as a confession. In a swift movement, Prue dropped Cyrus's hand, but only so she could step closer to her mother. "Is this true, Mama? Are you—are you *Gaia*?"

Gaia continued to stare blankly at her daughter. "I am."

Prue shuddered, then balled her hands into fists. In that moment, Cyrus knew that Prue had embraced her anger. It melted away her shock, transforming her into the fiery and defiant witch he knew so well.

"How. Dare. You." Each word was a hiss. An accusation. Power thrummed in the air from Prue's words as if she had cast a powerful spell.

Gaia only blinked, seemingly unaffected by Prue's rage.

"More lies?" Prue shouted, spreading her arms. "Should I really be surprised at this point? I guess I should ask who my father is—he wasn't just some nameless soldier you met in passing, was he? Was he a god, too?" She laughed without humor. "All this time! Goddess, *all this time,* and you've been Gaia? You could've done *so much more* for our coven, for Krenia—

for *Mona*!" Prue's fury exploded in a palpable wave that sent shivers down Cyrus's body. "Mona died, and you did *nothing*!" Her voice ended in a scream that echoed and reverberated against Cyrus's bones. Vines crawled out of the ground, mingling with thorns and brambles that clawed forward, eager to attack.

For the briefest of moments, Gaia's eyes filled with sorrow. "I couldn't change anything. Your sister's fate was sealed long ago."

"What the hell does that mean?"

"It means my powers are bound, Prudence. I've been imprisoned in this realm, in this form." Gaia gestured to her own body.

"Am I supposed to feel *sorry* for you?" Prue spat, her arms trembling. "Poor Gaia, trapped in a mortal body, cursed to raise twin daughters and lie to them their entire lives, cursed to live among a coven of witches who love and adore her. Yes, you've truly *suffered*, haven't you, Mother?"

Gaia's eyes darkened for a moment. "You know nothing, Prudence."

"You're right! I know nothing, thanks to you. And you know what? I don't care! I don't care who imprisoned you or why. I don't care who my real father is. I don't care about your past or your powers or any of it. All I care about is the fact that *you* let Mona die. That alone proves to me you never loved us at all." Prue's voice became level and eerily calm, but Cyrus knew better. This was simply the calm before the storm. "You can rot in Hell for all I care."

Cyrus sucked in a breath. In the distance, thunder rumbled, and the clouds in the sky darkened. A storm was coming indeed.

Uncertain, Cyrus glanced around and found Vasileios watching the two witches argue with a broad smile on his face. A hungry gleam glinted in his eyes.

Oh, gods. That couldn't be good. Cyrus had no doubt his brother could feel the energy rippling in the air, the threat of a battle to come.

Vasileios was hoping Prue would destroy Gaia on her own. And with Prue's fury, she just might.

Cyrus stepped forward and took Prue's hand in his. Her fingers were still curled into a tight fist that wouldn't relax, and her skin felt hot and sweaty.

"Prue," Cyrus muttered in warning.

"Don't," she bit out, not once breaking eye contact with Gaia.

"*Prue*," Cyrus said more insistently.

"What?" she snarled, finally whirling to look at him. Her lavender eyes were wild and slightly crazed, her face blotchy and flushed. She looked unhinged.

Cyrus held her gaze, refusing to back down. In a low, steady voice, he said, "She's a goddess. Don't do something you'll regret."

"Oh, so now you're going to lecture me about reining in your powers? About schooling your emotions? Isn't that rich." She scoffed, sounding nothing like herself. This woman before him was a stranger, something mangled by anger and betrayal.

He could recognize that all too well. He had to bring her back before she was lost completely.

Though every instinct of his warned him to stay back, to protect himself from the incoming storm, he drew closer, placing his hands on both her shoulders and forcing her to look into his eyes.

"You are mine and I am yours," he whispered, his thumbs tracing circles on her shoulders. "If you wish to murder this goddess in front of us—if that's *truly* what you desire—then I will stand by your side and help you butcher her into a thousand pieces." He paused as a frightening luster filled her eyes at his violent promise. "But I need you to be certain. Please, Prue. I cannot lose you." His hands moved from her shoulders to the back of her neck before his fingers tangled in her hair. She closed her eyes, her eyebrows knitting together in part arousal, part confusion as his hands framed her head, tilting her back so her face lined up with his, her nose brushing against his cheek.

"My wife," Cyrus murmured. "My heart. My soul. I am yours to command. I am *here*. Stay with me, darling."

Prue's eyes opened, and heat burned in her gaze, fueling the fire churning in his belly. "I am yours and you are mine," she whispered in agreement.

Relief flooded Cyrus's chest as he nodded encouragingly.

After a long exhale, Prue's body deflated, her shoulders drooping. Slowly, she turned away from Cyrus to face Gaia once more, but her body was more relaxed. The thorns and vines receded back into the earth.

Gaia watched their interaction with interest, and for one insane moment, Cyrus could've sworn she'd seemed *disappointed.* As if she'd *wanted* Prue to attack.

What was this goddess playing at?

"The Triple Goddess," Prue said quietly, her gaze fixed on Gaia. "Is it you?"

Gaia nodded. "Part of my curse is that I cannot use my powers for myself. But I can bestow them on others. The Crone and the Maiden. You and Mona. Sybil." Brief regret stirred in Gaia's eyes, and Cyrus wondered how much of it was real. This life, this farce Gaia maintained —how much of it had been an act?

Prue huffed another cold laugh, but it sounded more tired than before. "Sybil? Does she even know?"

"She has long since suspected something is different about me. But she has never asked outright. She trusts me to confide in her in my own time."

Prue was shaking her head. "Then, she's a fool."

"Perhaps."

"What happens if Prue goes to the Underworld?" Cyrus asked suddenly. The question had been prickling in his mind ever since Gaia's identity had been revealed.

If Prue was the daughter of the Earth Goddess, would this affect her transition to the realm of the Underworld? A Goddess of earth and life descending into death and decay . . .

Gaia's icy gaze shifted to him, and he held it, refusing to waver or falter under her powerful glare. "Son of Aidoneus," she hissed. "You dare address me?"

"He is my *husband,*" Prue snapped. "He can do as he pleases."

Satisfaction and pride swelled in Cyrus's chest. "Answer me," Cyrus pleaded. "Prue and I are bound to return to my realm. I must know she's safe."

Gaia offered a cruel, mocking laugh. "No witch is safe with you, Osiris. Your power consumes everything —and everyone—in its path."

Her words rippled over Cyrus's skin like a whispering breeze, bringing his cold magic rising up in response. He pushed it back down, but it kept writhing, kept screaming . . . He felt like he was trying to keep a dam from bursting using nothing more than his hands.

It was useless. He was only prolonging the inevitable.

"Don't try to dissuade me from doing this, Mother," Prue said. "I'm going to the Underworld, and I'm bringing Mona back."

Cyrus's gaze flicked to Mona, still standing there with a vacant expression. Then, Cyrus's insides went cold with dread.

Vasileios was no longer next to Mona.

Dammit, Cyrus thought, glancing around in a panic, realizing his brother had used their arguing as a distraction. But where was he?

Suddenly, Gaia's back arched, and she cried out, her body going stiff. Behind her, a long vine had embedded itself into her back. It withdrew, revealing a sharp, spear-like appendage with the goddess's blood on it.

Vasileios lurked behind Gaia, his hands sweeping through the air. With a jolt, Cyrus realized the vines followed his movement. Vasileios was wielding Mona's magic.

"No!" Prue shrieked, reaching for her mother.

But Cyrus was faster. He lunged forward, shooting black flames as he went. His unholy fire lashed at the vines, burning them to a crisp. Cyrus leapt, catching Gaia just before she collapsed, her back oozing blood.

Power thrummed in the air. The dark clouds swirled overhead, cloaking them in shadow. Thunder rumbled, and Cyrus's dark magic burst to life, finally breaking free of its restraints. With a groan, he hunched over, barely holding on to Gaia's limp form as jets of black magic erupted from his chest. Pain sliced into him as the icy coldness seeped into his bones, claiming him.

"No," he gasped, his vision going dark.

"I've got her." Prue appeared by his side. "Cyrus, you have to—" She broke off with a scream that pierced through the fog of Cyrus's vision. In a flash, he could see again, and found Prue clutching at her chest as blood quickly soaked her dress.

Then, he saw it. A blade had been thrust into her from behind, slicing straight through her body. Impaling her completely.

"*Prue*!" Cyrus bellowed.

Prue fell to her knees, her face bone-white. Behind her, Vasileios withdrew the bloody sword, a triumphant smirk on his face.

"You knew this could never happen, Cyrus," Vasileios said. "You cannot be with her. If she goes to the Underworld, her magic could destroy the entire realm!"

But Cyrus wasn't listening. His fury took over. His magic had already been freed, and it needed a target.

Now, it had one.

With an almighty roar, Cyrus sent his black flames directly into his brother's chest. Within him, his magic exploded with triumph, untethered and unrestrained. The rush of power coursing through him was startling and all-consuming. He thought he'd known power before; he thought he'd experienced it all. But the burst of death magic gushing freely showed him just how much he'd been holding back. It flowed and flowed like an endless waterfall, the flames shooting forward until they completely devoured Vasileios's body. The fire climbed up his shoulders and neck before they smothered his face. Vasileios's screams echoed around them, but Cyrus pushed onward. More. His magic hungered for *more.*

Laughter echoed inside him, and he couldn't tell if it was from his own mouth or from his magic. Deep down, a small part of him registered alarm and panic at the sentience within his magic, that it could laugh, that it could feel triumph and victory . . . But the power had consumed him, too, and he was beyond feeling. Beyond caring.

"Cyrus," a weak voice rasped.

The tiny sound split through the haze of Cyrus's vengeful assault like a beam of light spearing through the darkness. He'd been shrouded in death magic, seeing nothing but shadows and fire . . . but that voice had startled him, jerking him free, providing a shard of clarity that he clung to. Somehow, amidst the thunder and Vasileios's shrieks, amidst the chaos of his own magic, Cyrus heard Prue's whisper with perfect clarity. He faltered, glancing down to find her sprawled on the ground, one hand covering the wound in her chest. Her entire torso was stained crimson with her blood.

"Cyrus," she said again, before her eyes closed and her head lolled back onto the concrete.

DESTROY

PRUE

"PRUE," said a voice.

But Prue was so exhausted. All she wanted was to remain in this dark bliss, this cloud of nothingness. She was adrift at sea, a body floating among the waves. No troubles. No pain.

"Prue!" The voice was unrelenting.

Prue felt her eyebrows knit together in annoyance. Goddess, couldn't she just be left alone? For what felt like the first time in her life, she was blissfully *free*. And she wanted to remain here forever.

"I'm fading, Prue. He's killing me."

The words jolted her. Prue's eyes snapped open, but all she saw was an empty, black void. "Mona?" She'd been certain it had been her sister.

"I'm here," said Mona.

"Why can't I see you?"

"Because I'm . . . almost gone."

"What?" Prue's voice was panicked. "Mona, no—you can't!"

"Vasileios is using my magic. He's draining me completely. If he keeps this up, I will be erased from existence. You must stop him, Prue."

"How? How is he using your magic if he isn't fully bonded to you yet?"

"I told you, a remnant of my magic lingers with my body. That's what he's using. If he depletes my body entirely of magic, the separation from my soul will be complete. That magic is the only thing holding these two pieces of myself together. Please, Prue. I need you."

Panic twisted Prue's heart. "I—I can't *do* anything! I don't even know where I am!"

"You're dying. But you have more power than you know."

Prue's blood went cold. *Dying.* No . . .

"You're the daughter of a *goddess*, Prue," Mona went on. "You are unstoppable. Don't let some pitiful mortal wound be the end of you. You are so much more than that."

Prue wanted to shake her head, to cry and scream all at once, but she still couldn't see. She didn't even know if she *had* a body right now. She simply . . . existed. "I—I can't. Mona, our mother—Everything she did—"

"I know." Mona's voice was full of regret. "But there will be time to process it. Time to sort through it all. For right now, I need you to dig into that well of power. Find the same strength you used to summon Cyrus. To find *me*. You can do this, Prue."

Prue inhaled deeply, her chest rising. With each breath, the dark fog clouding her vision receded, little by little. Mona's presence drifted away, but not before Prue heard her final words:

"I believe in you."

Then, Prue's eyes flew open, and pain burned between her breasts. She choked on blood, gasping for air.

Vasileios had stabbed her. But he'd narrowly missed her heart. She was bleeding out, and she *would* die if she didn't do something. Quickly.

Heal, she thought, struggling to form a coherent thought among the anguished haze of her mind. *I must heal myself.*

Goddess, she couldn't move. She tried to sit up, but all she felt was utter pain. She cried out, but it was nothing more than a gurgle against the blood rising up her throat.

"I'm here," said a familiar voice. The warmth of that voice seeped through her, melting away her pain.

Cyrus. Prue wanted to close her eyes in relief, but she feared if she did, she wouldn't be able to open them.

Gentle hands grasped her, helping her upright. Prue leaned against Cyrus, allowing him to steady her.

"Let me heal you," Cyrus said.

"No," Prue said sharply, surprised by the firmness of her voice. She would *not* let Cyrus give up part of his soul. Not again. "I just . . . your blood."

Cyrus didn't protest. He grabbed a jagged rock at their feet and pressed it into his finger until a bead of blood appeared.

"Press it . . . to my chest," Prue ordered.

Cyrus obeyed, bringing his finger to the raging wound in her chest. She closed her eyes, feeling the heat of their mingled blood, and murmured, "*Integro.*"

Her skin warmed, and a prickle of awareness shot through her, opening her third eye. Her body lurched from the motion, exacerbating her wound, making her cry out. Cyrus's grip tightened around her, grounding her against the storm around them.

Cyrus sucked in a breath, and Prue knew her magic was drawing from his strength. But she couldn't even apologize. Her mouth clamped down, her teeth gritted to keep from screaming as fire scorched every part of her. Cyrus's arms grew tense, his fingers digging into her from the strain of it.

Then, gradually, the pain faded, leaving behind a stretch of heat in its wake—as if Prue and Cyrus's magic had melted her wound, sealing it over her skin. Prue gasped out, breathing in, relishing the untethered flow of air in her lungs. She stood, no longer relying on Cyrus, and gingerly patted her chest where her injury had been.

Nothing. No pain. Her dress was still soaked in blood, but she was completely healed.

Smiling, she turned to Cyrus, but his face was ashen. His eyes, normally a vibrant silver, had dulled to a muddy gray. He slumped over, and this time it was Prue's turn to support his weight.

"Cyrus?" she asked.

"I'm fine," he mumbled. "Just . . . give me a moment. See to your mother . . . and your sister."

Prue nodded, remembering the crisis at hand. She carefully set him on the ground, propping him up against a nearby hunk of concrete, before looking around to inspect the scene. In the sky, a storm raged. Thunder cracked and rain began to drizzle from the clouds. Wind whipped at Prue's hair, and she smelled the pungent tang of magic in the air. In the distance, the wispy forms of ghosts drew nearer, lured by the magic and power saturating the air. It wouldn't be long before they arrived and possessed them all.

A few feet away rested a figure, his face charred and blackened beyond recognition. But she could tell it was Vasileios. His chest still rose and fell with his labored breaths, indicating he still lived.

It took all of Prue's restraint not to slice his throat open. But he was a god, and she was almost certain cutting his throat wouldn't kill him. Besides, she had to find her mother and Mona. They were more important.

Prue's eyes roved over the wreckage, the jagged slabs

of concrete, the cracks and vines and coiling brambles . . .

Prue's heart lurched in her chest when she recognized her sister, lying motionless on her mother's lap. Gaia's face was white, her eyes drawn and haggard as she held her daughter. At first glance, it seemed that Gaia was simply clutching her daughter in an embrace. But as Prue scrutinized them, she realized Gaia's eyes were closed, her hand pressed against Mona's throat as she uttered a spell.

A snarl built its way up Prue's throat as she lunged forward. "Get away from her!"

Gaia's eyes snapped open and fixed on Prue. "She is already dead."

"I said *get away from her*!" Prue screamed. The ground rumbled, and fissures split the earth. Alarm flashed across Gaia's features as she scanned the rubble. The cracks deepened, widening as Prue's vines climbed out, snaking toward Gaia.

"Prudence," Gaia warned.

But Prue's anger only intensified. "Release her," she growled, "or I'll strangle you."

"I am your *mother*," Gaia hissed.

"You are no one. You are just a monster leeching the life out of my sister."

"This isn't her, Prudence. You know that."

"She needs her body. I didn't come all this way just to watch some pathetic, self-centered goddess stand in my way."

Gaia's lips thinned as she stared at Prue. But the goddess must have seen the fury burning in Prue's face because, ever so slowly, she shifted, laying Mona's body on the concrete before rising to her feet.

"You're making a mistake," Gaia said softly. "If you reunite Mona's soul and body, it will undo her sacrifice."

"I don't care," Prue said at once. "I will offer up myself in exchange."

"It doesn't work that way."

"And why not?" Prue shouted. "Why do you and the other gods get to make the rules? Why are *you* the ones who get to decide?" Her voice rose with each word, and the ground quaked again. Prue's vines had transformed into thick, slimy ropes of a barbed plant she'd never seen before. But some innate instinct told her this plant was venomous. Indeed, as it slid closer to Gaia, the Earth Goddess jerked backward in alarm.

"Prudence—"

Prue sent her magic forward, and the thick vines wrapped around Gaia's feet, rooting her to the ground.

"You can't kill me," Gaia said, her voice becoming shriller. "I *created* this realm. If you kill me—"

"I know," Prue spat. Her anger was a part of her now, fused into every facet of her body. She clung to it, because her fury made her powerful. All she wanted to do was destroy her mother.

But she couldn't. The goddess had indeed created

this realm. Even Prue wasn't foolish enough to tamper with that magic.

"I can, however, prevent you from interfering again," Prue said with a smirk. Her ivy shot forward, curling around Gaia's throat and mouth. Gaia uttered a choked sound before her voice was cut off, her lips and chin covered completely. In mere seconds, Prue's vines had tied her up more efficiently than any ropes or bindings could have. Gaia wriggled her body, but to no avail. She was trapped.

A howl pierced the air, and Prue looked up. The ghosts drifted closer, mingling with the rain pelting from the clouds. Their moans intensified as if the presence of such powerful magic made them hungry and desperate.

Free Mona, Prue told herself. *Then get Cyrus to the Underworld. This has taken long enough.*

The spirits needed to be returned home.

Prue approached Mona's limp form and checked for a pulse. *Thank the Goddess.* She was still alive. With a deep breath, Prue drew on Cyrus's magic. The cold chill of it bit into her, cutting into her bones.

"Goddess above, grant me power," Prue said. Her third eye was already alert and ready, her body flowing openly with unrestrained power. "I invoke the death magic of Osiris, god of the Underworld, to summon Pomona Donati."

Despite the cool rain sliding along her skin, Prue's skin prickled with awareness, raising small bumps on her arms. The wind intensified, howling louder than the approaching spirits. Prue's chest swelled with power, the ice of Cyrus's magic nearly suffocating her. She bit down, hard, to keep from crying out, to keep from succumbing to the pain.

A translucent form appeared before her, barely visible in the rain.

"Mona?" Prue breathed, daring to hope.

"I . . . can't . . ." Mona's voice was faint.

"Your body is here, Mona!" Prue shouted, gesturing to her sister's imposter. "Take it!"

"Spell, Prue," Mona said, her voice fading. "Cast the spell!"

Shit. What was the spell? Of course Mona would know it; she knew everything. But Prue found herself guessing most of the time—hence how she ended up accidentally married to the god of the dead.

"Trust yourself," Mona said, her voice gaining strength. "Trust your magic."

"Right," Prue whispered. She crouched to the ground, her hands hovering over her sister's body. Mona's skin was cool to the touch, and Prue wondered how weak the body was. How long did she have left to live? Would Mona merely die as soon as her body and soul were reunited?

Prue shoved the thoughts from her mind and closed her eyes. "*Integro*," she murmured, pressing her hands against Mona's chest.

Mona's eyes flew open, but Prue instinctively knew it wasn't really her sister—just the imposter. The shell of a person Vasileios had been parading around. The girl only blinked blandly at Prue, her face expressionless.

Prue called on Cyrus's death magic once more, resisting the urge to cringe away from that deadly cold poison that swept through her. "Pomona Donati," she said, her voice firm and commanding. "I summon your spirit to reunite here with your body. Be one and live." Her magic swelled, growing more and more, until Prue felt like her body couldn't contain it anymore. She thought the spell was done, but something inside her told her there was one last step.

Prue lifted a hand to her mouth, biting down hard until she tasted blood. Then, she brought the blood to the imposter's chest. "*Renovo*!" she cried, just as an almighty *boom* shook the earth. Lightning flashed, illuminating the sky, and a clap of thunder rattled Prue's bones.

Nothing happened. Prue sat there, drenched from the rain and still covered in blood, cradling her sister's body. The foreigner inside Mona only stared vacantly, unmoving and emotionless.

"Come on!" Prue growled. Every part of her ached, throbbing from the intensity of the magic around her. She was spent. The adrenaline from the fight had vanished, and now she was ready to collapse and sob in frustration. This had to work. It *had* to.

From the corner of her eye, Prue caught movement. Her gaze snapped to the Book of Eyes, its pages whipping in the wind as it somehow magically stayed dry amidst the storm. Prue's heart lurched as she remembered what Cyrus had said aboard the ship taking them to Voula City.

All the souls that are lost, that are possessed or obliterated . . . What if the book absorbs them? What if those souls fuel the magic in the book?

"Goddess above," Prue whispered, her blood chilling with realization. "Her soul is trapped inside the book!"

She lunged for it, fighting off the urge to shudder away from it, to remain as far from that cursed grimoire as possible. She slammed her bloodied hand onto its pages, and her whole body lurched as if the book was trying to suck her in, too. Gritting her teeth, Prue crammed her eyes shut, wrenching herself and her magic away from the book's influence. In her mind, she could hear the screams of the souls trapped within.

But she only needed one.

Pomona Donati, she thought, too afraid to use her own voice for fear it would break her concentration. *I summon thee.* She focused on Mona's face, her brightened expression when she discovered something new about her magic, the high-pitched laugh that echoed in the air when she couldn't control her giggles . . .

Next to her, Mona inhaled a deep, shuddering gasp. A wispy white form hovered over her before sinking lower and lower, vanishing entirely into the girl's body. Light ignited in Mona's sea-foam eyes, her face gaining color and her mouth hanging open in shock.

"Prue?" she whispered, glancing around in confusion.

Prue's face crumpled, and she pulled her sister into a tight embrace, weeping into her shoulder. Mona softly patted her back, pressing her face into Prue's chest.

"It's all right, Prue," Mona said. "I'm here. I'm alive."

CONSUMED
CYRUS

SOMETHING WAS WRONG. Cyrus could feel it. The coldness had completely taken over his body, numbing him as if he were dying of frostbite.

Surely, Prue's healing spell couldn't have drained him *that* much . . .

But no, this was something more. Something else. He'd sensed it since that morning, when he'd summoned his magic for the first time since bonding with Prue.

For several minutes, he lay there against the rocks and debris, unable to move, unable to muster any strength at all. Perhaps he would just die here, a feeble death.

But then he caught sight of something shifting in the rubble. Gaia, perhaps? No, he'd heard Prue shouting at her, had heard the goddess's silence indicating Prue had bested her. Not that Cyrus was surprised.

No, this was someone else. *Something* else.

Distantly, he heard Prue sobbing. He had to move. To get up. To do *something.*

Gritting his teeth so hard his head throbbed, Cyrus pushed off the rocks, the sharp edges cutting into his palms. But the pain brought a burst of clarity to his mind, and he clung to it, relishing the metallic scent of his blood. His senses sharper, he staggered to his feet, then went perfectly still.

It was Vasileios, wriggling along the ground like a serpent, drawing closer and closer to Prue and—

Gods above. It was *Mona.* Even Cyrus could tell she was different, no longer wearing that hollow and empty expression. Her eyes were vibrant, and they crinkled in the same way Prue's did when she smiled. Her mouth curved into a delighted smile as she held her sister's hands. They only saw each other. They did not see the oldest prince of Hell drawing closer to them.

Cyrus wanted to shout, but cold fatigue had him frozen in place. He was too tired to even shiver.

Vasileios was only a few steps away from them now. In the darkness, the gleam of a dagger glinted against a flash of lightning. Vasileios would stab one of the twins—or both of them—if Cyrus didn't interfere.

Death magic, come to my aid, he pleaded. *One last time. I swear it.*

The darkness in him seemed to laugh at his request.

But before Cyrus could sink into despair, the black fire swirled inside him, roaring to life.

It hadn't been a laugh of mockery, but a laugh of triumph. His magic had been biding its time, waiting for Cyrus to open himself up to it.

You are mine, his magic said in a low hiss.

And in this moment, he didn't care. He would do anything to save Prue, even if it meant allowing the death magic to take over completely.

Flames shot from his fingertips, erupting in the air. The smell of death and blood filled Cyrus's nose, and he inhaled. The power—gods, the *power*. It felt alluring and invigorating. How had he gone so long without it?

"Going somewhere?" Cyrus asked in a low voice.

Vasileios stopped moving. With a raspy groan, he slowly turned to glance over his shoulder.

Cyrus grinned at him, delighting in the blackened skin of his brother's face. All he could make out were a few patches of pale skin and those silvery eyes glaring at him.

"She'll be the death of you," Vasileios croaked.

Cyrus's smile didn't falter. Because right then and there, he knew Vasileios was defeated. And his brother knew it, too. It was why he didn't issue idle threats or promises or angry insults. Vasileios knew Cyrus was about to obliterate him.

And his pitiful attempt to drive a wedge between Prue and Cyrus was laughable. This once mighty heir to the throne of the Underworld was nothing now. Absolutely nothing.

"But *I* will be the death of you," Cyrus vowed. "Goodbye, brother."

Cyrus unleashed his flames on Vasileios, who screamed and writhed in agony as the unholy fire consumed him. Cyrus pushed and pushed, relinquishing control to his magic, letting it take over. On and on the fire burned until Vasileios's skin melted off his bones, until nothing remained but a smoking husk.

But Cyrus couldn't stop. A shrill scream surrounded him, making his ears throb. Soon his fire was everywhere, darkening his eyesight until Cyrus wondered if the fire was burning up his own body as well.

He tried to rein it in, but it was no use. The fire took and took, sinking its claws into Cyrus's mind until it had consumed him entirely.

Then, Cyrus realized what had happened. He was a fool for letting his guard down.

He had fallen prey to the manipulations of his death magic.

It had him in its grasp.

And it wouldn't let go.

His magic *was* alive. It was its own entity, real and powerful. It was angry at Cyrus for ignoring it, for abandoning it in favor of Prue.

He should've seen the signs. The way his magic warred with his newly sealed bond with Prue. The way it raged and thrashed about, desperate to break free, desperate to keep Cyrus all to itself once more.

Ordinarily, the idea of his magic being jealous was laughable. But this was no laughing matter. Because now, thanks to Cyrus's weakness, the magic had a leash around *him*. Their roles were reversed, and Cyrus was a prisoner now, bound to the whims of his death magic.

The screaming intensified until Cyrus realized it was coming from his own mouth. Then, everything went dark.

UNDERWORLD

PRUE

PRUE FINALLY DREW AWAY from Mona to find Cyrus finishing off his brother. He seemed to be laughing with delight as his magic suffocated Vasileios, burning him up completely.

Prue forced herself to watch, shoving down the revulsion at the sight of Cyrus so eager to destroy.

He is a monster, she reminded herself. *But so am I. He is mine and I am his.*

"Is that . . . your husband?" Mona asked uncertainly.

Prue bit back a smile. "Yes. He isn't always like this, I promise."

Mona huffed a weak laugh.

At long last, Cyrus's flames receded into his hands. Panting, he wiped sweat from his brow and brushed the hair out of his face before fixing his gaze on Prue. Prue's heart lurched at the strangeness of his eyes, no longer glistening silvery orbs. They were that same dull gray, the color of muddy water.

Perhaps he was merely weak from exertion. She was certain once he recovered, his eyes would return to normal.

Even so, she couldn't quiet the strange restlessness churning in her stomach, the prompting that something was wrong.

"He won't be bothering us anymore." Cyrus's eerie gaze shifted to Mona. "And with him dead, he no longer has any claim to your powers."

Mona exhaled in relief, and Prue squeezed her hand.

"Shall I end Gaia as well?" Cyrus offered, glancing at the goddess still trapped by Prue's vines.

"No," Prue said quickly. "Leave her. She'll find her own way out."

Cyrus frowned but made no objection. Prue glanced at Mona, who stared at their mother with a grim expression that Prue couldn't decipher. Above them, the storm raged and the spirits howled.

"The book," Prue said, turning to Cyrus. "Where is it? We need to finish this."

Cyrus's eyes glinted almost hungrily, and Prue didn't like the way her skin felt clammy under his gaze.

Wrong, wrong, wrong.

"Yes," he said. "We do. This way." He jerked his head, indicating Prue should follow him.

Before she could, Mona gripped her arm. "Prue—"

"I *have* to go," Prue said. "I'm bound to uphold this bargain with him. I sealed it with my blood."

"You *can't*." Mona's voice broke on the last word.

But a strange calmness settled over Prue. Mona was here. She was *alive*. Everything else could work itself out.

Before finding the gate, a small part of Prue had hoped it wouldn't end this way. That the Underworld would simply offer up Mona's soul freely and allow Prue to live her life.

But it wasn't that simple. The Book of Eyes called to Prue, beckoning her. That dark magic would not relent.

Not without a fight.

Prue offered her sister a smile. "This was the plan all along."

Mona shook her head, her eyes filling with tears. "Prue, *please*."

"I will do what I can to come back to you," Prue promised. "Our mother is a goddess; if there's a way for me to use that power to come back, I'll find it. But . . . if I can't, swear to me you'll live your life. That you'll be *happy*."

Tears streamed down Mona's face. "Don't do this! I'm begging you."

Prue's heart twisted at the way her sister's voice broke, at the devastated look in her eyes. But the deal had already been made. And it was time for Prue to uphold her end.

She touched Mona's cheek, wiping away a tear. "I love you."

Mona's shoulders shook as she sobbed, still shaking her head.

Prue rose to her feet, trying to ignore the way her own eyes burned. *It's worth it,* she told herself. *Even if I have to part from her again, at least this time she's alive.*

And Prue would be with Cyrus. The burst of warmth in her chest at the thought was surprising. But there it was.

Hope. Relief.

Love.

Prue loved him. And if she couldn't survive this, at least she would be with him. He was the god of the dead. Even if she died, she would still find a way to be with him.

Was that enough, though? Could Prue be happy with only Cyrus . . . but not her sister?

Was there truly no way to have both?

Just finish the mission, Prue thought. *Finish it, and you can worry about all this later.*

Because if she didn't cross over to the Underworld right now, she would be tempted to stay here with Mona and damn the consequences. It *had* to happen now.

The ghosts still hovered above them, circling like vultures. At any second, one might dive down and latch onto one of them, possessing their bodies entirely.

Yes. It had to happen now. The spirits had been here long enough.

Swallowing the lump of emotion in her throat, Prue took a deep breath and followed Cyrus deeper into the rubble. Even through the storm, she could sense the power rumbling from the Book of Eyes. Somehow, it had dodged the destruction of everything that had transpired. Despite the rain, the pages remained completely dry. But Prue shouldn't have been surprised. This book could never be destroyed, and it appeared of its own volition.

It really did have a mind of its own. And the thought made Prue shudder.

Cyrus stood next to the book, gazing down at it with a cold smile. For a moment, Prue just watched him, wracking her brain to discern what about him was different. Right here and now, he seemed like a stranger to her. None of that taunting gleam in his eyes, the smirk he reserved for her, the heated look they shared . . .

It's fine, Prue told herself, though she didn't believe it. *It must be the lingering magic or the closeness of the gate that's affecting him. That's all.*

Cyrus extended a hand to her, and Prue took it, trying to ignore the strange chill that swept over her at his touch. This was nothing like the scorching fire she felt when they touched the night before. No, this felt like the touch of death itself.

"*Open*," Cyrus hissed, his voice like a trickle of sand amidst the crackling thunder.

The book opened on its own, the pages flipping in the wind. Light burned from within, intensifying until Prue had to cram her eyes shut against the force of it.

Then, the book began screaming. Prue gritted her teeth, loathing the sound with every fiber of her being. Why in the Goddess's name did it always have to scream?

The howling spirits joined in, creating a cacophony of anguished cries that chilled Prue to the bone. A tickle of awareness brushed along her skin, and she knew the spirits were being pulled back into the book. She kept her eyes shut tight, resisting the urge to watch. She didn't need to see this. Just *feeling* it made her stomach churn.

The air around her spun with a sickening intensity that made her want to vomit. When the wind settled, Prue finally opened her eyes. The light from within the book faded, as did the screaming. Cyrus's grip on her hand tightened, and, without warning, he tugged her forward until they fell.

But they didn't meet the ground. Instead, they fell *through* the book as if it were, indeed, a portal. Darkness surrounded Prue. She tried screaming, but no sound escaped her. Instead, she focused on the feel of Cyrus's cold hand in hers, even if it made her skin crawl with apprehension. The world spun, and Prue's stomach dropped. Nausea roiled inside her, threatening to rise up, but she bit down and swallowed hard, forcing herself to relax, to let the darkness take her.

At long last, Prue's feet met solid ground, and she gasped out, finding her breath at last. Her heart hammered in her chest as she took in her surroundings.

She stood in a dark, damp cave. Rocky walls enclosed around them, and a glistening silver river snaked through the ground, providing a faint light for them to see by. Her breath caught in her throat as she gazed at the wispy souls floating along the river. Goddess, they were magnificent . . . and also frightening at the same time. They were pearly and striking, just like the ghosts in the mortal realm. But these weren't shaped like figures; they resembled swirling orbs, almost like stars in the night sky.

They were beautiful. Breathtaking, even. Prue was almost tempted to draw nearer and touch one, just to see if it felt as silky and smooth as it looked.

Only then did she realize Cyrus was no longer beside her. Prue straightened, scanning the cave. Alarm filled her chest, screaming at her that something was wrong.

"Cyrus?" she called, her voice bouncing off the cave walls. She whirled, only to find herself utterly and completely alone. "*Cyrus*!"

In a flash, he was there, a malicious smile spreading across his face. Prue's blood ran cold as she stared into his eyes.

They were all black.

"Hello, darling," he murmured, but it wasn't his voice at all. It was something else entirely.

Prue tried summoning her magic, but nothing happened. She searched inside herself, only to find a cold and empty void of nothingness.

No, she thought in horror.

"Apologies, dearest," Cyrus said. "But I had to take your magic. You see, just as *you* had control over *my* powers in your realm . . . now *I* have control over yours." His teeth flashed as his smile widened. "And now, you are my prisoner."

EPILOGUE

MONA

LONG AFTER THE Book of Eyes had swallowed Prue and Cyrus, Mona remained among the wreckage, frozen and numb from the events and revelations she'd endured.

The blinding white glow had vanished, along with the otherworldly wind sweeping around them. The storm dissipated, though the dark clouds still lingered, the only evidence of the powerful magic that had been there moments ago. Mona's eyes still stung from the dust particles flying into her eyes. She glanced upward, blinking rapidly as she scanned the skies for the pearly forms of ghosts.

But they were gone.

She loosed a breath of relief. She'd feared that upon her return, her sacrifice had been nullified—that the spirits would reappear again as if the blood debt hadn't been paid.

Mona shifted, tightening her bodice around her chest. Her clothes were sticky with blood and dirt. Her skin felt too tight around her body, as if when her soul had returned, it hadn't quite *fit* the way it should have. In addition, there were thoughts and memories in her mind that did not belong to her. It was unsettling, this feeling of sharing a consciousness with someone she didn't know. Who had Vasileios put inside her body all this time? Mona shuddered at the thought. She wasn't sure she wanted to know.

Then there was her mother—or rather, the goddess Gaia.

The *Triple Goddess.*

Mona still couldn't believe it. There had been moments during her studies throughout the years when her brows would scrunch together as she remembered something her mother had done that didn't seem quite right, especially for a witch of her age. But now that she knew, it made perfect sense. Of course Gaia would seclude herself on a remote island, far from prying eyes. Of course she would serve as the Mother of the coven—with all her magic, it was the best excuse for where her power came from.

And *of course* she would seek to produce twins in order to harness the Gemini magic—the power of Janus's two faces manifesting into twin witches.

But in order to conceive twins, she needed to find a male whose family genealogy boasted of a long line of twins, just to be safe. Mona's throat knotted with unease as she mentally sifted through the gods she'd read about, along with their family histories.

She had a few theories about who her father might be. But she didn't want to dwell on that now. She *couldn't.* Her sister had just followed the devil himself down into the Underworld, and she had to find a way to get her back.

With a deep breath, Mona stalked right past her mother, still tied up among the rubble. She felt Gaia's probing eyes on her as she strode onward, chin jutted out and head held high.

You are strong, she reminded herself. *You are not a coward.*

Prue had told her that once. Despite how Mona's limbs seized up in the face of fear, she clung to those words. *You are not a coward.*

So she shoved her emotions down deep, burying her love for her mother, the betrayal of being lied to and deceived all these years. Mona pushed these thoughts away, though her eyes burned and her throat knotted. Her lips trembled, and for one moment, she thought she might succumb to the grief and trauma of it all. She thought she might just break down and sob until she had nothing left.

But no. She was strong. She had to be. With Prue

gone, there was no one else left to carry on. No one except Mona.

She reached the charred outline on the concrete that marked where the Book of Eyes had lain mere moments ago. Now, the cursed book had probably reappeared in a different hiding spot, waiting to be sought out once more.

But every grimoire left a trace of magic in its wake. And Mona could use that. She leaned closer to the rubble, inhaling deeply.

"Sage," she muttered, identifying the scent. She waved her hand, and a plant sprouted from between the cracks of the concrete. She plucked a sprig of sage from the plant and crushed it over the outline of the book. The sharp scent filled the air, mingling with ash and death magic. Then, she dug her fingernail into her palm until she drew blood.

A muffled shout made Mona jump, and she whirled to find Gaia struggling urgently against the vines, her eyes wide and pleading. As if she knew what Mona was about to do.

One of the vines snapped. Mona was running out of time.

"I summon thee, Prince of Hell and guardian of my spirit," she said in a rush, slicing deeper into her wound until a droplet of blood poured onto the ground. Pain burned in her palm, but she clung to it; the harsh sensation cut through her fear and grief. The drop of blood sizzled when it met the ground, and then a plume of smoke drifted from the book's outline.

At first, nothing happened. Behind her, Gaia continued thrashing, and another vine snapped. Mona's heart beat faster. *Come on, come on. Answer me!* She tried not to focus on how nervous she was about speaking to him once more. *This is for Prue,* she reminded herself. *Not for your girlish whims.*

After a few seconds, a voice echoed in her mind, deep and soothing. "Mona? Is that you?"

Mona closed her eyes, relishing the sound of that voice. Goddess, she had missed him.

But that didn't matter. Not right now. Prue was more important. And Mona had to reach out to the one person who could help her.

Gaia stopped writhing, going utterly still. Mona wasn't sure if it was in defeat or if the presence of another god had silenced her.

Clearing her throat, Mona whispered, "Evander, I need your help."

THE JOURNEY CONTINUES...

AN IVY & BONE NOVEL

LEARN MORE AT

rlperez.com/thorn-and-ash

NOTE TO THE READER

Thank you so much for reading! I greatly appreciate you taking the time.

If you would be so kind, please leave a review to let others know what you thought of the book!

ACKNOWLEDGMENTS

Being an indie author is no picnic, and I certainly couldn't have done it without the help and support of others.

Jo, Jenni, Day, and Sharlene, my alpha readers.

Belle, Paul, Sara, Tori, and Melissa, my beta readers.

My Tuesday Tribe, for the laughter and venting and never-ending support.

My amazing ARC team and your enthusiasm and excitement, for your eagerness to read in advance and your thoughtful reviews.

Joss, my colleague and friend, opening doors and opportunities that allow me to shine and grow. I couldn't have done this without you, friend.

Shannon and Kaitlin, my cheerleaders from the start. Thanks for always rooting for me, even when my stories were nothing more than ideas.

My wonderful readers. Thank you for taking a chance on a tiny, insignificant indie author. Thank you for picking up my books and risking it. You have made my dreams come true.

Alex, Colin, and Ellie. Thanks for being patient and supportive, even on my dark days.

ABOUT THE AUTHOR

R.L. Perez is an author, wife, mother, reader, writer, and teacher. She lives in Florida with her husband and two children. On a regular basis, she can usually be found napping, reading, feverishly writing, revising, or watching an abundance of Netflix. More than anything, she loves spending time with her family. Her greatest joys are her two kids, nature, literature, and chocolate.

Subscribe to her newsletter for new releases, promotions, giveaways, and book recommendations! Get a FREE eBook when you sign up at subscribe.rlperez.com.

ALSO BY R.L. PEREZ

Timecaster Chronicles

Twisted by Time

Devoured by Darkness

Bound by Blood

Nightcaster Chronicles

The Cursed Witch

The Fallen Demon

The Lost Phoenix

Bloodcaster Chronicles

The Demon's Kiss

The Angel's Vow

The Reaper's Call

Jayne Thorne, CIA Librarian (with Joss Walker)

The Eighth Road

Master of Shadows

The Keeper of Flames